THE LIGHT OF MIERA:

A Guard's Request

BOOK TWO

Written By Ash Hester

Edited By Amy Wilson

Cover Art By ArtWomble

Published By Treat Your Geek

Print ISBN: 978-1-7385534-5-7

Ebook ISBN: 978-1-7385534-4-0

A Guard's Request

Copyright © Ash Hester 2025

1st Edition

Content Warnings:

While the utmost care has been taken when dealing with darker storylines, we appreciate some readers would prefer to be warned of triggering content and adult themes. Those already present in the whole series include MC death, magical manipulation, drug misuse, child endangerment, reference to miscarriage and stillbirth, mild graphical description of gore, reference to SA/R, mental health themes including anxiety, depression and addiction.

This book continues these themes with heavy reference to medicinal drug misuse and addiction starting Part 1 Chapter 6, and tortuous experiments in Part 6.

For Papa Mash

"If we're going to be damned,

let's be damned for what we really are."

- Captain Picard

INTRODUCTION

Dear Reader,

So here you are, about to read the second novel of the Light of Miera series. A thrilling and emotional adventure awaits you (I'm not kidding about the emotional) but if you have not read A Guard's Refrain first, then I implore you to do so. It is a vital piece of the journey that you should undergo before taking on book two.

I became aware of who Ash was when she reached out to offer me a place in her community group on Discord, Treat Your Geek. Although, reach may not be the word to describe it actually; she inserted the link into a Twitch chat, coupled with verbal demand of my presence! We clicked fast and I became a settled member, over time becoming an internal cog of the TYG content machine.

It didn't take long within our many conversations to discover she was an author – and a talented one at that. We would often talk in depth about her books, discussing characters, plots and worlds. I found it fascinating and would already have a favourite character. (It's Callius).

Having a keen interest and background in the therapeutic field, I enjoyed pulling apart the characters and observing their behaviours, backgrounds and lore. It was no surprise upon reading that Ash had jam-packed these characters with so much personality. She really understands the behaviours that would follow the situations she puts her characters in and sets the reader into the mindset of each character in each moment, delivering emotional highs and devastating lows.

What's the secret to this?

These characters are more than mere imagination come to life. Ash has scattered parts of herself in her book, like a slightly unhinged treasure hunt. Every character holds a part of the life she has experienced, or part of her current being. A piece of soul in every one. She bares all of herself to her unsuspecting readers, springing life into the world unfolding around us. You only have to look at our leading ladies to understand this.

Ash is truly selfless. She opened up TYG as a community and has become a safe haven for the geeks, the gamers, or even the lonely. She goes through hard times, more than any one person deserves, and she still holds out her hand to pull someone back onto their feet.

Ash does not give up. She strives for what she believes in, and these novels have been a necessary passion project, I am honoured to have witnessed grow into completion.

Enjoy your travel readers, adventure awaits.

Tan00ks

THE JOURNEY SO FAR...

Alamantra's Guardian has been watching over their planet for thousands of years, but is now on trial for breaking their oaths. But what did they do?

Witches began poisoning the Manastream, corrupting the mana held within the bodies of those living on the planet's surface. This sickness presented as a black rash that blistered and sapped the energy of those afflicted. High Priestess Elsafrey tried everything she could to heal the sickness, but there is only one way to cure it.

Auldafrey, the first of the Frey, called Reyla and Tharin to his shrine and told them of the Hand of Miera, a powerful artefact that could reverse the damage caused by the sickness. However, in order to obtain this relic, they must first pass the trials of the Ten Ancestors. And so, they began their quest, with Reyla leaving her dear princess home and alone.

Meanwhile, negotiations between Dura and Sudra broke down when King Drazah challenged Emperor Gabris to a duel. Having claimed his prize, the Emperor looks towards a new future as a twist of fate draws him ever closer to Sudra's Demon Queen.

The Light of Miera

A Guard's Request

Book 2

A Guard's Request

BENEATH THE SURFACE

11 MONTHS BMF

* * *

I obeyed my oaths and watched,

helpless as corruption prospered

and innocence perished.

I hoped in time the Gods

would hear my pleas.

But with eight trials still to go,

I feared time was not on Alamantra's side.

* * *

CHAPTER ONE

It was mid-morning.

The Manastream twinkled through a cloudless sky as two figures clad in green travel cloaks left the safety of the forests, reaching the end of the Freya road. A wide bridge spanned the river Leste before them, connecting Freya to Sheya.

Reyla Fenwilt's feet slowed as she neared the border. The rubber of her leaf-leather boots crunched over the broken stone. Salted air breezed from the coast through her chestnut mane causing it to bluster about her face as a grim ire pressed upon her green features – this was not a place she had ever hoped to return to.

The river Leste divided the continent cutting east from the Lenara Ocean to the centre of Halda, often growing to over three hundred metres wide, with treacherous falls and rapids. There were few places for anyone to cross safely, and only two bridges passing between Freya and Sheya; this one, the Pruval, being the westernmost.

Until a few years earlier, this area had been filled with guards, the bridges barricaded on either side and tensions high as the two great nations teetered on the edge of war.

However, once the war had ended, both sides had agreed to withdraw, leaving behind an eerie silence. Sentry towers lay in ruins among the remains of toppled barricades and abandoned structures. Scorch and sword marks scarred the landscape – as nothing dared to grow in the harrowed grounds of a battle not quite won.

Reyla allowed Tharin to get ahead of her and peered over the side of the bridge. She usually found peace in water but was unsurprised to find it lacking that day. Neither Frey had been overly talkative in the days since leaving the capital. The loss of their queen had hit them both like an arrow to the heart, but as they continued north, their grief subsided, overshadowed by the importance of the task ahead of them.

In every town they passed, and every villager they met, they saw the sickness everywhere — and it showed no signs of stopping. The villages further afield only showed early symptoms of the spreading corruption, but it was clear the drain was already affecting the morale of the citizens. And indeed, the ones chosen to save them.

Reyla closed her hazel eyes, listening to the river as it thrashed over the rapids below. The hissing spray brought back memories of Reyla's one and only venture into Sheya. She reached for the ancient wound upon her shoulder, rubbing it absent-mindedly, and tried not to dwell on the past any longer than was necessary.

"Hey, Reyla," Tharin called out from behind her. "Come check this out."

Still rubbing her shoulder, Reyla joined Tharin in the middle of the Pruval. Large cheek dimples appeared beneath the perennial blue of Tharin's shining eyes. He waved his arm back and forth in the air with much amusement.

"You've got to see this," he encouraged.

"See what?"

"Well, I was just wondering how long we had to go, when my ring started tingling," he explained, his cheek dimples deepening even further with every second.

"So?"

"So, just try it," he insisted, moving his arm left and right. His fringe gained air as his head followed the movement, whipping from side to side like a cat watching birds.

Reyla held out her arm with the same muted enthusiasm she imagined doting parents held when entertaining their child's latest whim. The silver ring on her finger shone in the sunlight as Reyla waved her hand back and forth, but nothing happened. Her brow furrowed with the suspicion that Tharin was playing a trick on her. She flicked her eyes back to his.

"I don't feel anything."

"Not there, here!" He took her hand this time, guiding it a little further north. "Try it now. Think of the shrine."

Reyla followed his instructions lazily but started as

static bounced from the points of her ears to the tips of her toes. As she looked to her ring for guidance and thought of the shrine they sought, the static drew into focus and a gentle pull tugged on her finger. Reyla then waved her hand back south along the bridge where the pull of the ring stopped abruptly, only to come back as she moved north once more.

Reyla snorted. "I guess this is where the border really is."

"I wonder if it's the same all along the Leste? Could save a whole lot of bother if we could map it all out for sure," Tharin suggested.

"Hmm, maybe..."

It was certainly something to consider, but Reyla doubted it would make much difference in the long run. Most of the trouble between Freya and Sheya was over the borders, but it was hardly the sole cause of the conflicts. As the Shey specialised in water artes, they claimed the River Leste was theirs and wanted to maintain control over the bridges and surrounding seas. The Frey had similar interests, although Reyla was never sure why the Frey cared so much about the river; she wasn't entirely convinced King Galafrey knew why either.

"One quest at a time," she added, her brow popping in jest. "We've got enough work to do already."

"Let's just hope the shrine's nowhere too sacred," moaned Tharin. He brushed a hand through his hair, his fringe falling perfectly back into place. "There's no chance we'll get in anywhere sacred."

Reyla agreed.

Like the Frey, the Shey were highly religious, but, while the Frey worshipped the Life Tree and the cycle of nature, the Shey worshipped water. Tensions had certainly reduced between the two kingdoms since the war ended, although Reyla still suspected few Shey would welcome them with open arms, which could prove problematic.

"We'll fell that tree when we come to it," Reyla assured him, looking once more to her ring for guidance.

Tharin agreed. "A bit late to be worrying now I guess." He shrugged.

"Shoot for gold," Reyla cheered, a term used among Frey soldiers whenever they played Groppin; one of their favourite games.

"Yeah. Shoot for gold."

* * *

Things were easier after that – at least on the surface.

Tharin had never been to Sheya before and was like a wide-eyed child as he discovered everything for the first time. Reyla indulged his curiosity, his mood seemingly infectious as she shared her vast knowledge of the world.

He decided that Sheya was much like Freya only wetter. The thick foliage was often divided by brooks, rivers and streams, leaving more breaks in the canopy and the soil perpetually damp. A cornucopia of vibrant papyrus and reeds covered the surrounding verges. Purple lotus flowers rested upon a bed of browning lily pads in crystal waters, running west towards the ocean. And the animals... Incredible creatures he had never even heard of were just flying, climbing and zooming all around him, and Tharin was determined to learn them all. Except perhaps the spiders – he never seemed to get on well with spiders.

Despite his upbringing, Tharin wasn't particularly academic and had spent the majority of his tuition time sneaking into Low Town to see Dalliah. He continued asking Reyla questions about the plants and animals native to Sheya until there was nothing left for him to discover. However, his curiosity would soon get the better of him as the pair set up camp by a stream.

A large willow tree hung over them as they laid out their bedrolls and arranged a campfire, their new fire artes making the process much smoother.

"You were there when it happened, right?" Tharin dared to ask as they finished dinner.

The question didn't seem to register with Reyla, and she continued staring into the fire, watching nothing in particular as water boiled in a tin above. She rested her elbows on her knees as she hunched forward, zoning out as she had more frequently since leaving Freya.

Tharin wondered if she was worried about someone back home.

"Reyla!" He startled her this time.

"What?" she snapped in his general direction, squinting as her eyes readjusted to the muted light.

"You were there when the negotiations went sour, right?"

"Yeah." She laughed awkwardly, shifting her weight to the left and away from her shoulder. "It was my first trip out with the king's battalion."

Tharin reflexively mimicked her laugh – he hated it when he did it. "That's a tough deal."

"At least I came back." Reyla sighed and shook her head as her eyes returned to the fire between them.

There were many things Reyla didn't talk about; the war was one of them. Truthfully, Tharin wasn't sure what prompted him to ask that evening. Many had asked over the years and received little in return, so he was happy to leave it at that. However, for whatever reason, on this occasion, Reyla decided to share.

"I can't even tell you how it all started." She paused, casting a glance over her shoulder as if sharing some dark secret. "I'd fought in loads of skirmishes on the border in the years since training, but I was still a rookie and kept outside the palace while negotiations went on."

Reyla's eyes flickered with concentration as if trying to remember some significant detail which may hold a clue to what actually happened.

"Then Commander Flaxel comes rushing out of the palace with his sword drawn. Screaming at us to take arms.

"There was no thinking involved. We all just did as we were told. Swinging at anyone who got in our way, until we collected Galafrey and made our escape. We returned to the horses, only to find them slain and our supplies alight." Her voice ran low, burdened. "Galafrey was injured, but Flaxel was masterful in organising what remained of our battalion—leading the retreat—but by the time we left the city limits, we were only twelve.

"We were days from the border. No horses. No supplies. And the Shey Army hot on our tails."

Tharin's boots pressed into the soil as he leaned forward. The wind hushed then whispered. Crickets hummed with a growing accord, their rising vibrato calling for Reyla to continue.

"Through rivers and swamps, night and day, we pressed on. With no food or rest, the days merged into one another. Until eventually finding the River Leste, except…" Reyla released an exhausted groan as she relived the disappointment. "We misjudged the angle and came out a mile east of the Pruval. As close as we were to the border, we had no idea whether anyone even knew what had happened; no one was coming to save us. No one even knew we were there. We were *all* alone."

The fire cast deep shadows over Reyla's face as it shuddered against the wind.

"Our plan was to wait 'til morning and make a run for the Pruval, but the Shey found us before we'd even had the chance to figure out the details. We sent up several flares hoping help would come, but we were prepared for the worst."

Tharin already knew how the story ended, and his heart raced in anticipation. The weight of Reyla's words imprinted on his very being, resonating with the younger, bright-eyed Tharin who had joined the army after hearing a fifth-hand account of this very story.

"I found out later it was Gurrien who spotted the flares," she added, to the amusement of both of them – Gurrien was prone to telling the tale to ladies in the tavern. "He raised the alarm, but by that point, the Shey were already upon us."

Reyla removed the tin from above the fire, placing it on a flat stone. She dropped tea leaves into the boiling water and left them to stew. Tharin watched, his breath held, afraid to do anything to deter Reyla from continuing her tale.

"Positioned in the rocks, with the river at our backs, we created a bottleneck, slowing their progression. But they kept coming and coming...

"They got in a few lucky shots, breaking our defences

as our numbers dwindled. Flaxel was one of the last to fall." Reyla's hand pressed to her chest in memory of her mentor. "I saw him take on six Shey single-handed, but it wasn't long before there was only me and Galafrey left standing.

"Then out of nowhere comes this kid," Reyla growled, shaking her head. "A kid, no older than me – a soldier just like me. Running right towards Galafrey…

"I deflected the sword but as I cut him down, I slipped. And this sword comes down with a smack." Reyla clapped her hand in unison. "Right into my shoulder. There was nothing I could do. I dropped to the floor, sword still firmly in my shoulder, as Galafrey squared off against the coming troops…"

Tharin listened so intently he didn't realise he was leaning further and further forward towards the fire. Sweat beaded his brow, but he remained fully captivated by the rare first-hand account of Reyla's heroism. His heart swelled with pride. Few had ever heard the account directly from the king's saviour herself.

"Then what happened?" he asked without meaning to.

Reyla straightened, looked at the starry night sky, and released a long sigh.

"I don't know for sure," she admitted, decanting their tea into travel mugs and passing him one. "I passed out before the cavalry arrived. Woke up in the hospital weeks later and spent the rest of the war in recovery."

Reyla went quiet, the fire glittering in her hazel eyes as she smiled knowingly to herself.

"What're you smiling about?" asked Tharin, blowing on his tea.

"Nothing..." she mumbled and wiped her smile away.

Tharin couldn't help but become jealous of how effortlessly cool Reyla was – although she would never think so, which only added to her mystique. Her thick chestnut mane was overgrown and reaching towards her shoulders, making her seem all the more roguish. At some point soon, he knew that Reyla would tie her hair back into a ponytail before taking her knife to it – as he had seen her do many times before. Just one of her many habits which Tharin found admirable.

"What about you? You just missed it right?"

"I signed up the second the war started... The *second*," he stressed, suddenly embarrassed at how inexperienced he was compared to his comrade. "My dad was strongly against it, but I was determined and did it anyway."

Truth be told, Tharin didn't have much of a story to tell – at least not in the ways he felt mattered most – but he made do with telling the stories of others.

"Training was such a wake-up call," he confessed. "On my first day, I realised how spoilt and sheltered I'd been – and quickly. But, I worked hard, graduated from boot camp..." His voice cracked, the tone dropping with his shoulders. "And then my dad uses his power to get me a place on the Princess' Guard..."

"That sucks."

Reyla picked at her fingers, unsure what to say.

She felt his pain.

Shame, devastation, guilt.

It was a surprisingly common feeling amongst those who were already cemented in the inner palace guard. They were needed in Ceynas and those sent to the front lines were either inexperienced or unimportant. Reyla, it turned out, was both.

She returned her attention to the fire, listening to the crackle of twigs and kindling as she sipped her tea. A gentle breeze sighed through the landscape as she searched deep for some way to console her friend, but remained unsuccessful.

"Hey, Reyla?" asked Tharin, a tremor in his voice which clenched her chest. "What's it like?"

Although perfectly certain she knew what he was asking, Reyla needed to hear him say the words. She had to be sure.

Her eyes remained locked on to the fire as Tharin stammered and strained. He struggled to the point that Reyla worried how he'd react when faced with the real thing. No small part of her hoped Tharin would change his mind as he sucked in air, ready to try again.

"...What's it like... to kill someone?"

Her stomach dropped. *He had to say it.*

Reyla maintained her composure as a shiver of panic ran down her spine. She turned to the fire, looking for answers, but it offered her little support.

Reyla had little family of her own but considered Tharin a brother – albeit a spoilt and naive one. He was so innocent. So pure. Her instincts told her to protect him, yet, if they were to be successful in their mission, she could no longer shield Tharin from the horrors of the world; no matter how difficult that may be.

"It's hard at first," she managed, before swallowing the lump in her throat. "But then it gets easier."

Tharin just stared at her blankly. His green skin paled as he cradled his cup with his mouth ajar, waiting for her to continue.

"I guess at the end of the day, you gotta do what you gotta do. You know?" she added, hoping her sagely tone was enough to lend her true wisdom. This wasn't something covered in basic training. "You do what's right."

"But, how do you know what you're doing is right?" he asked with wide perennial-blue eyes.

"Well, that's the problem with war, isn't it?" Reyla replied, having wondered the same many times before finally reaching her conclusion. "When everyone's just doing their duty, everyone thinks they're right. At the end of the day, we're all just following orders. Anything other than that's above our pay grade, right?"

She flashed Tharin a wry smile, but he didn't seem convinced.

Reyla sighed and reached into her pack. She pulled out a green apple and tossed it to Tharin, then went back to collect one for herself. She drew her knife from her belt and proceeded to cut it into slices.

"Back when everything broke out," she started between apple pieces. "There was a Shey girl caught up in the mess. The swords came out and she just cowered behind a pillar as the fighting moved toward her."

"What's a kid got to do with anything?"

"Nothing. I mean – she didn't do anything; she was so innocent. I couldn't just leave her there to die," Reyla explained. "So, I scooped her up sharpish, stashing her behind some furniture before joining the retreat." She stopped to take a bite of her apple, but it seemed Tharin was having a hard time keeping up. "My point is, I had a choice. *We* have a choice. And I chose to save that girl. I chose to save a life rather than take it."

"And that helps?"

Reyla both envied and pitied his innocence. It made her eyes sting. She didn't have the heart to explain it to him. She couldn't.

"It makes it easier," she replied quietly.

Tharin didn't seem comforted by her answer and fell

unusually quiet as he considered her response.

Reyla never doubted in Tharin's ability, but the difference between their military careers and lived experience was hard to deny. Was their encounter with the Duran Tharin's first real confrontation away from the security of the training yards? Had he taken on their journey knowing he would likely have to take a life? Or had it only just dawned on him?

A heaviness filled Reyla's heart. She wouldn't put it past him. Tharin may not have been the brightest of Frey, but he was a good Frey. *One of the best.*

"I wonder what she's doing now," he finally mused, having given her words much thought. "At least then we might have one ally in Shey."

"I'm sure she doesn't even remember." Reyla chuckled and doused the fire with what remained of her tea. "Now get some rest, we've still a long way to go before reaching Alensya…"

* * *

CHAPTER TWO

Across the continent in Sudra, the armed forces of the Duran Empire prepared for another night in the desert.

Troops gathered around growing fires and passed rations between them. White tents with red roofs signalled where their captains rested and crimson banners waved their golden suns in the slight breeze.

Freed from the constraints of his former position, Amynus Tamun was largely ignored by those in command and left to do as he pleased whenever they made camp. He stole food from the officers' tent before returning to his own.

Amynus boasted the keen body of a Sudran champion in the making, but had yet to achieve the greatness of his expectations – self-imposed or otherwise. He dressed in a loose tunic which tied at the waist and skimmed his knees, exposing the hard muscles of his legs. His azure eyes and slate-coloured skin gleamed in the orange sun, fresh with youth and ignorance, but his tail wrapped around his middle like a safety harness and his shoulders remained squarely below his jaw at all times.

The Duran-made tent was hardly the most luxurious of

accommodations, and he had been left to share with his younger brother, but at least he got a bed and a roof over his head. No doubt the emperor considered it some act of kindness to win his mother's graces, which he supposed must be working as she'd hardly paid Amynus any attention since leaving Halda. Not that he was complaining.

His mouth still filled with pork, he chewed the last morsels and pushed through the door.

Amynus recoiled upon finding a young Sudran woman waiting for him. She swirled around to meet him, her tail doing figure of eights behind her.

"What're you doing here?"

"How rude." She pouted, her hands behind her back as she fluttered thick eyelashes over covetous ochre eyes. "How's about, 'Thank you for making my bed, Feliss?' You know it's not my job to do it."

"What do you want, Feliss?"

She whipped her hair over her shoulders, a faded black which was cut too similar to his mother's style for Amynus' liking. "Malaki is with your mother, so I thought I'd come to see if you want any company."

"What? So you can run off and tell Aeryn?" he barbed.

"Are you still mad about that?" She scoffed and rolled her eyes. "That was years ago. Oh, come on. Everyone knows how much time you spend in The Narrows. Surely you're missing it by now."

"I'd rather sleep with a scorpion."

"You're so mean." She crossed to him and ran her hands into the collar of his tunic. "A girl has to feed y'know?"

"Then go feed with the rest of them. I don't see the rest of Mother's staff in here. Who are they feeding on?"

"We've all been snacking on the Sudra in the Second, but it's hardly substantial enough." Her hands grew warm as she activated her artes. "Come on. Would it be so bad?"

Amynus pushed her away and growled. "Don't bother. I can smell you from here. Go charm some other poor sap."

Feliss bared her fangs, her tail taut as if ready to pounce.

He huffed and waved her off like the pest she was. "Whatever. I'm outta here."

* * *

Amynus escaped his tent and turned for the Second Division's camp to the north.

It was much cooler this close to the Duran border and the waning sun cast long shadows over the camp. His toes brushed against the grass through his sandals, the sensation bizarre. The landscape to the east was dappled in orange and brown but still glowed with vibrant reds and exuberant greens that were so foreign to the former Sudran Prince.

He found Sabutok and a handful of Sudran troops gathered around a roaring fire. Each sported the crimson cloak of the empire, but many still wore their tattered, old armours from the Sudran army. They were sand-beaten and tired from weeks of travel and sleeping on bedrolls in the sand. Sabutok even had sand pressed into the scar on his forehead, but Amynus wasn't about to tell him so.

"Coming to slum it with the rest of us, I see," Sabutok teased, patting the crate so that Amynus sat beside him. "What's the point in having a fancy tent if you're going to spend all your time with us?"

"I still have to share with my brother. Besides, the harpies are circling, it's safer here."

Sabutok chortled, flashing the teeth between his oversized fangs. "Ah, to be young and in demand. What a burden."

Amynus smirked and allowed Sabutok a few additional jibes for the amusement of those around them. He probably would have accepted the invitation if anyone but Feliss had offered. Saffia perhaps. Not that he had seen Saffia since they'd departed from Halda. He wondered why she hadn't called on him. Had he not been substantial enough for her last time? Did he do something wrong?

A pang of jealousy ran through his stomach. His azure

eyes arrowed, notched as if ready to shoot as he scanned the men surrounding him. *Which of them did she choose over me?*

Amynus dug his nails into the wooden crate, his nostrils flaring. He didn't like that she made him think that way. Jealousy was as beneath him as the soldiers yielding to the empire's leash, and he would not allow himself to feel it any moment longer for some wench on his mother's staff.

"What's going on with yer mother's staff anyway?" asked Sabutok. "Summat's not right."

"Huh, you noticed it too? Something definitely happened. They stopped us for a full day to interview everyone."

Sabutok squinted his eye, his scar stretching over his brow. He opened his mouth to respond but held his thought as Commander Danrock Hurlts called the men to attention.

"Gather round. Listen up," he called over the ruckus of the camp.

Hurlts was a fair commander. The battle-hardened Dura was pushing forty but still kept his hair short along the sides giving him a rust-coloured Mohawk. He had more notches missing from his skin than a training post, but a greater muscle mass than any, save perhaps the emperor himself. This gained him some favour among the Sudra, but they were still wary of Duran customs and kept him at arm's length.

"Orders from above are to split you Sudra between the forts and capital postings," Hurlts announced to many murmurs. "Those in the Sixth Division are coming with me and the Second to Puwhar – we'll be breaking north in the morning. Fifth will be joining us as far as Sebaldis before turning east to Estra. The Fourth are going with the Third Division aimed south, and everyone else is to stay with the First, and will be spread between Bauros Fort and the capital."

"Which are you in?"

"Seventh." Sabutok grinned as a breath escaped Amynus' lips. "Looks like you'll be stuck with me a while longer."

He was glad, but wouldn't say it aloud. With everything changing, Sabutok was his one last connection to his father and the life he had thought he was going to have. He wasn't ready to give that up just yet.

Sabutok sat back as Hurlts finished his briefing and went to inform the rest of the men scattered around the camp.

"So, who's been sniffing around?" he asked.

"Feliss."

"Yer better off staying away from that one," said Sabutok. He clicked his tongue. "Summat about her doesn't sit right with me."

Amynus straightened but pushed no further. Sabutok was a decent judge of character and trusted more than most. He would even go as far as to think there was no one on Alamantra he trusted more, but had no one else to compare against and wasn't ready to confront how this made him feel.

"C'mon, best make our rounds," said Sabutok, clapping his knees as he rose to his feet. "We've got a lot of men to see off before tomorrow."

* * *

CHAPTER THREE

For thirty days after the attack on their palace, the Kingdom of Freya came to a standstill. A veil of darkness seemed to settle over the forests like a fog that moved through notices and thrived on gossip as those left behind tried to adjust to life without their queen and high priestess.

During this time, King Galafrey seldom left his office and only Captain Valren dared enter. His mother, Yarafrey, reprised her previous role as high priestess and kept the temple running smoothly, allowing Arafrey to tend to Elsafrey's body for the duration of Passing.

For thirty days Arafrey tended her mother's body with duty and with care. She watched over their flock in her mother's stead as thousands of Frey amassed at the palace in mourning. She shared in their stories and settled their fears. She held their hands and shouldered their pain. Through heartache and grief, Arafrey remained the light her people required her to be, and they returned to their lives unburdened, oblivious to her pain.

Princess Arafrey entered the throne hall on the morning of the thirtieth day, an air of trepidation seeping through the cracks in her facade. The porcelain green of her skin was greyed from stress and fatigue, and the once vibrant emerald green of her eyes shone like unpolished coal.

The heavy layers of Arafrey's ceremonial robes dragged upon the polished wooden floor as she approached the dais. The ornate thrones had been removed and replaced with an altar holding the glass coffin where her mother lay. Flowers and tributes, left by hundreds of Frey who had come to pay their respects, surrounded the altar and spilt along the outskirts of the hall.

Candlelight flickered over Arafrey's face as she approached the coffin. Her mother's face remained pleasant even in death as Arafrey ran her hands over the glass and summoned mana to her palm.

It was a long-standing tradition among the Frey to use their artes to reduce the rate of decay after death, allowing their loved ones to remain whole for the duration of Passing. This could be done for short periods, but after thirty days the effects became less potent, at which point the Frey returned their loved ones to the soil. However, a kingdom-wide alert had been issued warning citizens not to use their artes unless absolutely necessary, as a sickness now spread through the Manastream, and anyone using their artes held the risk of contracting it.

Arafrey activated her artes and pressed her hands to the glass to begin the process. The sickness could claim her if it wished, she had passed the point of caring for herself some time ago, but she would see her mother to a peaceful end – it was her duty, after all.

Arafrey stepped back as the men of the Queen's Guard collected wordlessly around the glass coffin. They lifted it onto their shoulders and marched as one, following Arafrey as she turned to the door.

It wasn't tradition – although Arafrey felt perhaps it should be – but Elsafrey's guards had retained their Queen's Guard uniforms and had remained by her side since Passing began. Many of them felt guilty they had not been able to protect their queen, others were angry that they hadn't done more, and the rest were torn between the two feelings – but each of them missed Elsafrey dearly, and none had recovered from her loss.

Both King Galafrey and Yarafrey were waiting in the foyer as Arafrey left the hall, each dressed in white robes of their own.

Arafrey had never seen her father look so ghastly, his eyes ringed with black and sunken into his skull. His cheekbones seemed to protrude more than normal, and his long oaken hair lay streaked with grey. She struggled to imagine her father being capable of any kind of emotion, but it made her uncomfortable to see him so dishevelled.

In contrast, Yarafrey appeared almost radiant. She wore her white hair in a tight vertical roll with a single silver streak running from above her temple. She had adorned herself in jewellery made with white pearls and shining diamonds about her breast and lifted her nose into the air as if smelling something rotten.

"I suppose we should get on with this," said Yarafrey, seemingly having more important things to do that day.

Arafrey despised her grandmother and inched ever closer to telling her as much. Although it would no doubt bring Arafrey great joy to see her grandmother squirm, she wasn't about to allow Yarafrey the satisfaction of making her mother's funeral about her as well.

Her father appeared not to notice and looked to the skies as he left the palace. "This weather is certainly fitting. I hope it doesn't rain."

Dark clouds gathered overhead as Arafrey descended the stone stairs to the courtyard. Every member of the palace guard and staff huddled onto the gravel and spilled into the gardens. They all looked so lost and helpless; their green skin greyed like wilting flowers. Arafrey's heart would have broken for them if it were not already in tatters.

She crossed the courtyard to the gates with her father and grandmother beside her. The men of the Queen's Guard carried Elsafrey behind them as their procession began down the road. Those who came to pay their respects followed her coffin and together they marched through the harrowed city to the Crossroad Pavilion and south to the cemetery.

Normally, their high priestess would be taken to the catacombs and buried along with their ancestors, as was tradition, however, Galafrey had decided upon something much more suited to Elsafrey.

Arafrey held on to her tears as they marched to the beat of deep drums. Each beat echoed around the forest as citizens lined the forest paths, their faces streaked with tears. It was when she reached the giant stone Urobus bears twinning the cemetery gates that Arafrey's tears finally fell.

A stone statue in her mother's likeness presided over an open grave in the very centre of the cemetery. The statue was spectacular in craft and design with smooth surfaces and intricate details. There wasn't a hair out of place and even the stone smile upon her face radiated with a warmth and kindness Arafrey could never hope to imitate.

She wavered, desperate to hold her composure as the men lowered the casket onto the supports set over the grave. The men stepped back and held to attention, awaiting instruction.

The procession now filled the cemetery and overflowed into the streets and around the cemetery walls. Hundreds, if not thousands of Frey watched as Arafrey and her father stepped forward and turned to face them, ready to begin Elsafrey's last rites.

With the statue behind him, King Galafrey's eyes seemed to search the skies, the trees, the ground and anything else but the people before him. His jaw clenched so tightly it raised the muscles in his neck and pulled his chin down as he settled on watching the patch of grass right before his feet.

"Today we..." His monotone voice cracked and faded

into whispers. "Today… Today we say goodbye to a… To an…" He tried again, but tears welled and drowned his efforts.

Arafrey faltered as he lost his strength. Her chest tightened and trembled her breath, but she felt no weakness, this was something else. Something deep within her soul. Something powerful and decisive that guided her forward. She reached out.

"It's okay," Arafrey assured him, placing a gentle hand on his arm. She waited for his eyes to find hers and smiled. "I've got this."

The feeling spread through her body and burned in the pit of her stomach as Arafrey stepped forward. It calmed her nerves and set aside her emotions. It stripped her of anything she had been and anything she had ever hoped to become and left behind only the princess she was born and raised to be.

The princess she had no choice but to be.

The high priestess she never wanted to be.

All eyes on her, Arafrey placed her hands together in prayer and slowly inhaled.

"Upon his death bed, Auldafrey turned to his kin and said: Do not mourn my passing. For when I am dead, my spirit will live on in the Manastream."

Arafrey knew the scriptures well and needed no book as she recited their words to the silent crowd. With each new verse, her facade stretched and strengthened. She detached from her words with every syllable, her voice relinquishing its tune to become a steady monotone.

"When I die, my body will return to the earth and nourish those who come after me. I will watch over you from the Manastream in the skies, from the deepest roots of the Life Tree and through the smallest of brooks. I will be with you always."

Arafrey caught her breath, the words sticking in her throat. She had always expected it would be her job to perform her mother's last rites but never imagined that it would be so soon.

She wasn't ready. It wasn't fair.

"I know many of you are angry, and believe me, I feel it too, but that isn't what my mother would want." Arafrey's fingers balled into fists as she clung to her strengthened facade. "Remember my mother, not for the way that she died, but for the way that she lived. Remember the values by which she lived her life and live your life, not for vengeance but love and compassion."

Arafrey motioned to the Queen's Guard to begin lowering the casket.

"As she returns to the Manastream, may we continue to grow from the lessons she gave us…

"And let us pray she finds peace."

* * *

CHAPTER FOUR

"Hold up," instructed Reyla as they crested the hill.

A vast lake glistened before them, the surface dyed orange with a mid-morning sky so crisp and clear they could see the mystic blue tendrils of the Manastream skirting the atmosphere. The path ahead was framed by the yellows and browns of autumn leaves as it ran down to the water's edge, greeting an elegant gatehouse of aquamarine stone.

Reyla came to a stop beside Tharin, taking in the sights as their eyes were drawn from the gate along wide spans of sleek stone that formed the bridge that stretched across the water towards the Sheya capital of Alensya.

The circular city lay in the very centre of a grand lake; a cyan jewel of twinkling rivulets and canals among buildings of turquoise stone and grey-tiled roofs. It appeared to float on the water's surface, connected to the land only by the single bridge – an alien sight to the two weary travellers. And yet, for Reyla, all too familiar at the same time.

"The shrine must be this way," urged Tharin. The Manastream converged overhead, but each of the Frey checked the pull of their rings to be sure. "They're not all going to be out in the sticks like Igniros."

"Just pull your hood up," grumbled Reyla as she did the same. "Let's try not to draw any attention. The last thing we want is to start any trouble."

The sun warmed the skies as they crossed the stone bridge, spying a vast array of fishing boats, ships and galleons docked along the city's circumference. Although they were inland some distance, the rivers flowing from the lake ran west to the ocean, salting the air and attracting all manner of gulls, geese and herons to their skies as the clear waters below brimmed with fish and invertebrates.

It was all very picturesque and those around her were enjoying the fine atmosphere quite pleasantly. Tharin was captivated and his mouth held ajar as he peered over the side of the bridge. Reyla, however, couldn't shift the sense of impending doom – with the increasing pull of her ring only adding to her burden.

The lake bridge was met by a road leading into the centre of the city. Shey Guards were posted on either side, their positions indicated by the navy-scaled armour of the Sheya Army. They shuffled their steel-tipped spears, each making sure to eye the two Frey thoroughly in warning as they passed.

The Frey and Shey were similar in stature, except where the Frey were green with pointed ears, the Shey were shades of blue with ears like rounded butterfly wings. Many Shey civilians they passed on the outer rings wore their hair in braids, a sure sign of their working class. They were likely merchants or fishermen and wore light-flowing garbs in shades of green and turquoise. These often covered tight waterproof base layers of varying designs so they could enter the water as often as they liked.

Reyla kept her hood close and head low as they weaved through the busy streets. No one acknowledged them besides the guards, but still her discomfort increased as the pull of their rings guided them north-west towards the centre of the city, where the palace lay.

The city itself was created from nine concentric halos circling the palace, each separated by waterways opening out onto the lake below. Shey used their artes to control water and push supply-burdened gondolas through the waterways and shallower channels cut into each halo, allowing the flow of goods between the ports and inner districts. Bridges were built in abundance, allowing the two Frey safe passage as they continued along the path from the bridge.

The buildings grew progressively taller and more official-looking as the two Frey continued inwards. More guards were patrolling the inner rings, and the civilians here wore tighter-fitting garbs with their hair often loose and trailing down their backs.

Reyla found it amusing how similar these Shey were to the nobles back in Ceynas. It was strange such similar kingdoms were unable to get along, although she couldn't deny that it was likely their joined interests in aristocracy and bigotry where they'd find common ground.

Bells chimed in the distance announcing midday as they reached the sixth halo inwards, the streets now littered with armoured guards on patrol. Reyla's ring tugged ever stronger, guiding them straight towards the palace. Anxiety circled her bowels and bubbled through her stomach – the palace was the last place she wanted to go.

"We should take this ring around," she suggested, hastily eyeing the glass roof of the crescent palace in the distance. "We don't want to enter the palace without reason."

"But the rings-"

"Just humour me, I'd rather not face the palace guard unless we have to," said Reyla, securing her hood as she led them north.

Leaving the main road, they followed the sixth halo around to the north-west of the city. Reyla's eyes darted to the skyline with militant regularity, painfully aware of the palace they now circled.

The buildings on this particular halo appeared to be residential. Turquoise terraced houses framed their path, their designs uniform, except where the colour of the doors and windows changed. Shey children ran past, their artes activated as they chased a water-filled ball along the paved path of cream bricks running between the houses. Metal lampposts decorated the walkway, each holding hanging baskets of pink and purple flowers with ivy-like tendrils reaching toward the ground.

Once they had circled the halo and put the palace firmly behind them, Reyla checked her ring once more. Relief washed over her as it pulled her forward, away from the palace, towards the outer halos. She quietly informed Tharin of her discovery.

"Guess it's a good job we didn't go marching into the palace." He chuckled and they worked their way back to the outer rings.

They crossed between halos and followed the paths and bridges around and back again as they homed in on their target. Until finally, their rings guided them to an unassuming building on the third halo inwards. They paused, the pulse on their fingers now strong and consistent, spurring them on.

Reyla stepped back, admiring the same turquoise stone as the rest of the city, bemused. Their destination stood out little among the buildings of the third halo and drew no attention from the Shey passing on the street. Standing only one storey tall, the stained-glass windows spanned much of its height. From the tiled roof grew a single spire, which held a silver bell – presumably the one they had heard earlier. And, much to their surprise, it was entirely unguarded.

"Seems this is the place. Should we do this thing?" Reyla nodded to Tharin as she started their routine.

"Yeah." He puffed his chest as he drew a deep breath, returning her gaze with a dimpled grin. "Let's."

Reyla pushed on the thick oak door. They entered quietly, each pulling their hoods back in respect.

Inside, a sleek dark-tiled floor ran below eight rows of polished wooden pews framing a small aisle. Reyla wasn't especially well versed in Shey religion but there was a cold seriousness in the air that reminded her of several temples back home and she quickly concluded they had arrived in a temple of some kind. It didn't look like there were any patient rooms, however, and Reyla wondered where the Shey housed their medics.

Her gaze was drawn along the aisle to the front where a large statue of a woman resided in a pool of water. The feature shone, backlit by a blue and green stained-glass window, casting a spectacular glow over the temple.

The feature itself was carved from Lapis Aquae, a special stone native to Sheya which surrounded itself with a water-like substance giving off the image of fluidity. Beads of glass and precious stones decorated the weaves of the woman's locked hair. Her hands were held wide, reaching up over the pews, and her face was beautiful. The eyes twinkled with hope and acceptance, captivating Reyla and holding her attention. She thought for a moment she caught the features moving her way, but was unable to catch it again.

"Can I help you?"

Reyla started as a young Shey woman appeared in her periphery, but managed to keep her expressions polite.

"Welcome. My name is Wilona." She smiled, beckoning them in. The woman wore a loose white dress that hung over her thin shoulders down to her ankles and the arm holes stretched down to her hips, revealing a navy bodysuit below as she bowed. "I tend the temple here."

She had a sky-blue complexion and eyes a deep royal blue. White freckles scattered across her cheeks and over the bridge of her nose which waved and wrinkled as she spoke. Reyla guessed she was barely twenty, but the young woman held herself with wisdom, her seaweed-green hair laying in large loose plaits over either shoulder like a thick stole.

Wilona put her hands together, touching her fingertips to her delicate wrists to create a circle, a welcoming gesture among the Shey. Reyla did likewise and stomped on Tharin's foot when she noticed he had not done the same.

"We're on a pilgrimage from Freya and were looking for somewhere to pray," offered Tharin while flashing his cheek dimples.

"Our God may not be the same but we're hoping yours would maybe take a message," added Reyla with a reluctant smile. This caused Wilona to blush, but neither Frey understood why, and they chose to ignore it.

"I'm sure Lady Roshia won't mind," Wilona replied as she gestured to the podium. She indicated for them to follow her down the aisle towards the statue. "Lady Roshia, the mother of my people, stands over our congregation, her hands reaching out as she showers her followers with love. They say she was buried beneath the fountain here and that praying to her will bring you great fortune."

Wilona stopped by one of the pews, motioning with her hand to suggest they take a seat. "If you require anything, please ask."

Reyla and Tharin thanked her and dropped their packs to the floor as they settled into the pews. Dipping their heads, they held their hands together in prayer.

Doing her best not to alert Wilona, Reyla checked every inch of the temple. Her trained eyes scanned to the front and sides. She took in the designs of the stained glass and the pattern framing the windows, following the stone walls up into the wooden rafters where a large hatch was set in the roof – no doubt leading to the spire. There were many patterns and motifs for her to discover, however, there was no sign of the tear-drop winged butterfly emblem they sought anywhere.

Reyla turned to Tharin and received an unhappy glance.

"I don't see anything," he whispered.

"Me either. We have to move around and take a better look, but we don't want to draw any attention..."

"No, but–"

"Is everything all right?" came Wilona's voice.

Reyla panicked and her eyes darted to Tharin's, holding a silent conversation.

'Maybe we should ask her.' Tharin shrugged.

Reyla wrinkled her brow. *'Can we really trust her?'*

Each squinted their eyes at the other.

'What else can we do?' Tharin huffed.

Reyla shirked her lips in agreement and sighed. She returned her attention to Wilona.

"We're looking for a symbol," she offered casually. "Looks kinda like a butterfly but with teardrop wings."

"There's a dot, then a diamond underneath it," added Tharin, outlining the symbol with his finger in the air.

"You should have asked me sooner." Wilona giggled, a smile widening on her teal lips. "I worship in this temple daily and I know the emblem you speak of well."

Wilona walked over to the statue and knelt in prayer. Reyla lifted from the pew, excitement bubbling in her stomach, as Wilona activated her artes and a blue hue emanated from her hands. The surface of the Lapis Aquae statue glowed in response, a soft light quietly blinking in the breast of Lady Roshia. The light grew brighter as a familiar emblem began to appear, shining on the surface – only, this one had three teardrops to its wings.

"What are you doing?" Wilona protested as Reyla and

Tharin pushed past her, climbing up onto the fountain to place their hands over the emblem. The statue rocked the instant Reyla's hand touched the cool Lapis Aquae.

Reyla leapt back, Tharin and Wilona beside her as the water in the base of the statue began to wave and drain away. She steadied herself as the temple shook and a long still mechanism found the effort to clunk into action. The pool creaked as the Lapis Aquae base opened up, and the water rushed down. The water swirled and drained from the pool, leaving behind a spiralled staircase of the same stone which descended into the lake below the city.

"How?" Wilona whipped her head around with a pointed glare. "How did you know that was here?"

"Long story." Reyla pulled her shield off her pack, intending that would be the end of it.

"I have time."

"We don't," Reyla returned, her eyes on Tharin as he tightened his armour. "You ready?"

"Almost." He stretched his arms out behind him.

"If you want to go down there, you're taking me with you," Wilona huffed, her chin rising to assert her limited authority.

"No." Reyla wasn't interested in getting anyone involved unless they had to. "We don't know what's down there, it could be dangerous."

That much was true. So far, they had yet to face any

actual trial and, other than the fact the Shey used water artes, they had few clues. It may even prove useful for them to have someone with Shey artes with them, but Reyla wasn't sure how they were supposed to explain away anything they were to find without sharing their knowledge of witches, poisons and gods. Besides, she had no idea who Wilona was; she could be a witch for all Reyla knew.

"This is my temple, I go where you go," Wilona demanded, her plaits bouncing as her foot stomped in a way Reyla knew only spoilt nobles of Freya to do.

"Fine. Just stay behind me," Reyla instructed, her face stern as she tried not to make any further comparisons with her princess back home. "But at the first sign of trouble, you're to turn tail and don't look back. Do you understand?"

Wilona returned a firm nod, her seaweed brows scrunched with determination, but Reyla just sighed, resigned to the possibility their trial may be much harder with a third body to protect. She climbed into the empty pool and peered down into the staircase.

"Looks like there's some light down there. Not much though."

Reyla turned back to offer Wilona a hand, but Wilona hesitated, her fingers held out towards Reyla as if scared. She squinted her eyes, unsure why the woman didn't just take her hand. Was Wilona unwilling to take Reyla's hand because she was a stranger? Or was it because her skin was green? Not that Reyla was all that fond of Shey or even Pudra for that matter, but she would never be rude on account of it.

"Whatever." Reyla grumbled with a furious promise to herself not to bother next time as she turned down the spiralled staircase.

The surrounding walls were made of the same stone as the sculpture. Reyla ran her hands over, or rather through, the surface of the stone. It was cool and smooth with a rippling density to it, fluid but dry. Like water, the Lapis Aquae absorbed light shining down on the surface of the lake above, casting the distorted shapes of orange and silver fish skirting the outer walls of the staircase as they continued their descent, the lake-bed growing closer.

"How come no one ever knew this was here?" asked Tharin, his voice echoing off the wet stone.

"The city is built upon pillars of Lapis Aquae," Wilona explained. "Although, I never imagined one would conceal a staircase."

"Doesn't anyone swim into them?"

"Only if they're not looking where they swim." Wilona chuckled, although neither Frey was confident they'd be able to tell the difference themselves.

The staircase opened out into a small, flooded chamber of Lapis Aquae creating a dome like an inverted fishbowl. Stone columns carved with strange runes that hummed with the soft undulating light of mana supported the translucent roof. An umber glow came from the sun far above, the beam broken by water and the shadows of passing fish.

"These runes look like the ones from the Nasai-ten. Relics from the language the First Ones used." Reyla's boots filled with water as she moved around the column to take a closer look. She only knew of the runes through her time studying with the princess, but the language was long lost and not even the most dedicated experts knew what they meant for certain. "I don't recognise any of them."

"I think this one represents water or life," said Wilona, pointing to another column.

"Those words are not meant for you, children of Alamantra. The words of the Gods are no longer meant for the ears of mortals." The voice echoed around the chamber.

A thick mist gathered over the water's surface. Swirling deliberately, it combined above the water, growing steadily thicker until the features of a being started to emerge.

Locked hair formed first, sprouting from translucent butterfly-winged-ears, and loose strands dropped to frame a face as a sharp jaw set into place. The spirit of Lady Roshia D'Sheya, first of the Shey, hovered before them. She looked just like her sculpture. Flowing robes hugged in at her waist but the skirts fanned behind her, tussling in a non-existent breeze. Except, the artist had not quite captured her eyes. Although she was only a spirit, Roshia's eyes shone as bright as sapphires – both beautiful and haunting at the same time.

"Welcome," said the spirit, her voice musical and soft. "You come seeking my blessing in the Trial of the Ten."

Reyla and Tharin gave gentle bows in response, but Wilona dropped to her knees, water crashing around her as she held her hands in prayer.

"How can it be that I am in the presence of our Lady Roshia?"

"I was not expecting a guest," Roshia chided, her eyes on Wilona. "It is of little consequence, however, and, seeing as our princess has waited so long to meet you, I suppose I can make an exception."

"You're the princess?" gasped Tharin, his face confused, but Wilona went quiet, her face turning all the more beetroot by the second. "Why'd you want to meet us?"

"I... Um..." Wilona mumbled and shrunk closer to the water.

"You can tell us later." Reyla looked up to the spirit. "We have a trial to complete."

Roshia released a haughty laugh, her hand to her chest as she threw her head back and flashed pearly white teeth. "Right down to business, I see. Very well, children of Freya. You have made it this far, but I'm afraid this is where your journey ends."

Roshia's voice ripened with sinister undertones which chilled the chamber.

"This entire room is made of Lapis Aquae. The water hides the surface, making it the perfect home for my pet.

"Are you ready, children?"

Roshia lifted her hands into the air with a soft yet menacing laugh. The water's surface shivered and a low grumble rose from deep within the ground. The sound echoed through the chamber, growing louder as the water below Roshia bubbled and spat. Anticipation consumed the challengers as a dark shadow formed within the Lapis. The shadow expanded and burst through the surface. Each shielded their faces as water rained down upon them.

Reyla's stomach dropped as her eyes beheld a large serpent-like monster. Its thick length curled around itself and into the Lapis Aquae as if it were water.

Reyla could only think to compare the creature to a flightless wyvern as its thick body coiled forebodingly, the turquoise scales armouring its body, changing hue in the dappled light. A sharp snout ran over the serpent's brow into pointed black horns which curled over a mass of kelp-like matted hair. The serpent snorted as it stared them down. Its fish-like tail flicked eagerly as Roshia hovered beside its head with a mischievous grin on her face.

"Do you like him? He is magnificent, isn't he?" asked Roshia, clapping her hands as she bobbed up and down in mid-air, seemingly happy with herself. "Najra, I call him.

He was a gift from the Manastream and came to me as the tiniest of tadpoles one day while I was swimming. Over time he grew into the incredible creature you see before you." She rubbed the mighty serpent's chin lovingly. "When I died, I was buried here within the Lapis Aquae, and he chose to join me in my solitude while I awaited your arrival.

"Najra has been sleeping for a very long time, waiting for champions worthy of challenging him." Roshia returned her attention to the two Frey, shadows forming upon her face as her mouth formed a thin line. "I hope you do not disappoint."

Najra roared in agreement, causing the water to shudder and ripple around the liquid chamber. Reyla gritted her teeth, and the two Frey drew their swords and shields. Wilona gasped and cowered behind Reyla.

"Defeat Najra and I'll give you my blessing. Fail, and you all become his lunch. Simple." Roshia shrugged.

The spirit didn't wait for their reply. Instead, she cackled, prompting Najra to storm forward.

Reyla retreated, her arm stretched wide to catch Wilona, pushing her away from the serpent's attack. The princess stumbled backwards and crashed into the rising water.

"Return to the stairs," Reyla ordered, tossing the surprised princess a glance before returning her attention to Tharin and the fast-approaching serpent.

Tharin was quick to respond. He lunged forward, shield first, to meet the serpent's face, and rammed its snout. Najra snorted as it ricocheted off the wooden surface. With Najra recoiling, Tharin swung his sword against the serpent's length, but the blade sparked and bounded off the turquoise scale. Tharin landed in the pool, ducking just in time to avoid Najra's tail-fin as it whipped past and into the Lapis Aquae below.

"My sword hardly touched it!" he exclaimed, bracing himself against turbulent water. He looked down as if to notice the water now lapping at his knees. "Is this getting deeper?"

Reyla agreed with his suspicions but held her words as she awaited Najra's return. She wasn't sure how the serpent tracked its prey and didn't wish to give away her position so readily, especially not with the water slowing her down.

Reyla's toes already ached from the cold water. Their uniform was water-proofed but only to a point and she was drenched. Her gear gained weight, and her base layers clung to her skin as the wool and leaf-leather soaked up water, restricting her movement. She shifted her weight and braced herself.

The serpent reared to the ceiling, towering overhead. The water churned, a self-motivating wave that slowed their pace. Roshia hovered beside him, her fists clenched and pulled up into her chest, watching intently as Najra narrowed its yellow eyes before diving forward.

"Together," Reyla called to Tharin, casting off her shield and tossing her sword to her left hand. Right-handed as she was, her left arm was the stronger of the two and Reyla needed all her strength if she had any hopes of penetrating Najra's armoured scales.

In unison the two Frey ran towards the serpent's head. Tharin went right, and Reyla left. Swords held in their respective hands, they closed in, swinging upon Najra's neck.

Their blades landed with masterful precision, crossing like scissors, landing mere inches apart. The blow forced the serpent to recoil, throwing its head back as it cried out in pain. Najra plummeted into the water, waves swallowing it whole before disappearing into the Lapis Aquae.

Still underwater, Najra circled, casting a ripple along the surface of the pool. Reyla traced the pattern, her heart racing as she and Tharin prepared for Najra's next assault.

The serpent burst from the water towards Reyla, snapping its jaws with malicious intent as she spun out of the way. She gritted her teeth as scale armour grazed her shoulder and tore her tunic before returning to the Lapis Aquae.

This time, Najra didn't wait before returning, taking Tharin by surprise. Reyla turned as Najra reappeared in a burst of water, snapping jaws down upon Tharin's shield arm. Tharin dropped his sword, his legs flailing as it pulled him into the air.

Reyla charged through the water, but the waves pushed her back as she fought her way forward. Tharin cried in anguish. He blindly pummelled against the beast's face, each effort growing gradually slower as pain and panic flooded his senses.

Reyla drew her sword, spinning as she ripped it across the serpent's soft underbelly. Her blade slicked with blood as the single sweeping movement sliced Najra's scales.

Najra roared, whipping its head around, its teeth still firmly clamped around Tharin's arm. Reyla retreated, helpless as Tharin flailed above her. Then, *a lucky punch.* Tharin used the momentum to smash his hand into the soft flesh of Najra's yellow eye, causing it to release him into the pool, before disappearing below the surface once more.

Tharin discarded the remnants of his shield, blood trickling down his left arm as he willed all the mana in his body to collect in his right palm. His skin beaded with water as he urged a flame into being. A warm glow spread over his palm, causing steam to wisp through his fingers as the smallest spark burst forth. Fire collected in his palm, swirling into a fist-sized ball. He flexed his fingers around the flame to hold it still.

Reyla had yet to relinquish her sword, and urgency prickled her senses as the serpent circled. She tightened her grip around the hilt, shuffling her feet to maintain balance as the ripples grew larger, directed at her. The water's surface darkened as Najra rose. It burst from the water, jaws open wide. Reyla deftly rolled from its trajectory and the jaws clapped shut on the space she had just filled.

Tharin didn't hesitate. He threw his fireball towards the serpent's head with a strong-over-arm throw. The fire crashed into the beast's head causing it to bellow with frustration, but the flames merely brushed over the shining scales, coming to rest in its seaweed mane. Any remaining embers were quickly extinguished as the serpent dived below the floor once more, smoke and steam rising from the water as the fire extinguished.

"I have an idea," called Reyla as she directed their next assault, but the serpent was already returning.

Reyla drew upon her mana core and summoned fire as if she had been doing it her whole life. She and Tharin then cast their fire into the pool, all the while darting around the room, agitating the water as Najra continued his assault. And, as fire landed upon the water's surface, steam rose; the water's temperature with it.

Red and orange lights twinkled around the chamber as Reyla and Tharin activated their artes and cast their fire. Soon enough the whole chamber steamed like a sauna. The air grew thicker by the second and the water bubbled, but still, the Frey continued.

The draw from Reyla's mana core slowed as she began to tire. She fought against it, her fingers straining as she struggled to hold the mana in her palm. The water sloshed manically along the side of the room making it harder to traverse. Even with the power of her blessings, each fireball sapped at her mana reserves and the well was finite. Her muscles ached from exhaustion, sweat adding to her already weighty gear as steam filled the chamber. They had to finish this before they gave themselves manaburn or died from exhaustion.

Reyla could still follow Tharin dashing between the columns, flashes of fire tracing his movement. Wilona pushed against the Lapis Aquae wall, where she fought to keep upright in the raging waves, but it was getting difficult for Reyla to track her movement. She could only hope and pray it would be the same for Najra.

The serpent burst from the water. This time it aimed straight towards Reyla, steam rising from its scaled snout as its jaws clamped down onto thin air. However, instead of diving, this time the creature remained. It whipped its head around, snapping wildly to the left and right, catching nothing but air. Its nostrils flared in hopes of catching her scent.

It couldn't see her.

Najra released a snort of disappointment, steam swirling away from its icy breath as it swept around the chamber. Spinning in the water, it returned to its assault. Sharp and fast. It chomped blindly into the spray.

Reyla retreated, rolling and jumping to avoid the attacks. Najra roared, its patience short as its blood boiled. It was then that Najra saw him.

Reyla caught her breath as Tharin held still, frozen in

fear as Najra locked in on its target. It sped forward, mouth wide open, teeth sharp and ready to close shut around the Frey's torso. Najra was almost upon him when Tharin's face changed from that of gut-wrenching horror to a smirk.

Reyla rushed in, tackling her comrade. She knocked Tharin off his feet and carried him to safety. The pair crashed into the water as the serpent snapped its jaws, just missing them. The momentum from its speeding body carried it forward crashing into the stone column Tharin had been concealing.

Roshia gasped as her precious serpent followed through, hurtling into the column with incredible force. The stone shattered, debris crumbling on top of Najra as its body went limp and slipped down into the Lapis Aquae floor. The ceiling cracked, allowing water to trickle in. Reyla braced herself, half expecting it to fall.

"Will... Will he be okay?" Wilona whispered, concerned even as she clung to the wall.

Neither Frey answered as the steam cleared. Their faces grim, their bodies tired, they turned to the floating spirit. They stood silent, panting, drenched in water and sweat. The serpent's eyes closed tight, showing no signs of life as the floor swallowed Najra's head and the water level receded.

"Congratulations. You have passed my trial and proven yourself worthy of my blessing. I'm so very proud of you, children of Freya. Although, I had little doubt." Roshia grinned as she turned to Reyla. "After all, I saw you fighting once before, Reyla, warrior of the Leste."

Reyla returned Roshia's gaze, wondering if the spirit had truly seen all she had done in the war or just the events on this side of the river. The spirit's eyes glittered like the Manastream, her smile passing onto Reyla as an air of incredible pride came over her.

"Now then," said Lady Roshia, beaming towards them as she threw her arms out, just like her statue. "You're here for a blessing, are you not?"

An invisible font of pure warm mana hit Reyla, flowing through her body and wrapping around every fibre of her being on its way to her ring finger. The silver band shivered as the metal warped and gained a third twist. Reyla straightened with newfound vigilance as the blessing took hold and her mana capacity surged, unlocking the power within.

"My descendants are at one with water. Like them, you too now possess the power to control water," Roshia told them. "Now, take your new powers to Ruglor and may you find what you seek. But beware, children of Freya. Power is as much a curse as it is a blessing. Relish the artes we bestowed upon you, but your power is a gift not all are prepared to wield. Make sure you use it well."

Lady Roshia faded away, leaving the air thick with foreboding as the two Frey waded through the water to collect their gear. Each quiet with contemplation, they ascended the stairs to the temple above, the spirit's final words echoing around them like a bad omen.

'Use it well.'

* * *

Reyla stretched her shoulder as the trio emerged from the shrine. Their clothes dripped onto the tiled temple floor as they climbed from the pool.

Still processing the events of that day, Reyla inspected her arm. Her sleeve was torn and her skin grazed, but nothing serious. She summoned mana to her hand, hoping to activate her artes, but was too drained to focus and gave up quickly.

Tharin also sat down to inspect his arm more closely. It oozed fresh blood where Najra's teeth had penetrated the skin, but it was merely a flesh wound in the face of Frey artes. He ran his artes over the gouges, quickly knitting the skin together to stop the bleeding, leaving a clean patch of fresh pale-green skin in its place. Reyla begrudged him momentarily. *He was always better at healing.*

"I have so many questions," stated Wilona.

"As do I, Princess," replied Reyla, her disapproving tone plunging them into silence.

A metallic clunk broke the tension as the shrine entrance closed of its own accord and the pool refilled.

"I'm sorry. I didn't mean to deceive you," Wilona pleaded, her hands pressed to her chest. "Please, allow me to make it up to you. You're wet and have travelled so far. Come, stay in the palace. Rest up and dry your clothes before continuing your journey. It's the least I can do."

Reyla hesitated. She was less than thrilled with the prospect of returning to the Sheya palace. Her shoulder ached at the mere thought of facing Shey guards. However, Tharin looked at her with the wide eyes of a begging dog and Wilona appeared no better.

"We really should get going," Reyla insisted. "Besides, wouldn't your father take issue with having two Frey in the palace?"

"He's visiting my uncle in Cauldis with my brother," Wilona replied. "They won't be back for at least a week or two, depending on how sick he is."

"Oh come on, Reyla. It's been weeks since we've had a roof over our heads and I'm soaked through," Tharin complained, his clothes squelching as he lifted his pack onto his shoulders. "What's one night?"

Reyla rolled her eyes, quick to concede.

"One night," she agreed. Collecting her pack onto her own soggy shoulders, Reyla followed Tharin and Wilona to the exit, the two Frey leaving a trail of sodden footprints in their wake.

* * *

CHAPTER FIVE

Princess Arafrey awoke that morning with a headache. Be it from stress or fatigue, she wasn't sure, but it was persistent and had stretched her patience long before breakfast was even finished. She would have given anything for the chance to return to her bed, but rest was not a luxury Arafrey could afford in such turbulent times.

"Hurry up, Ara," stressed Yarafrey. She had spent the night at the palace and had arrived in Arafrey's bedroom early enough to encourage her pain. "We should have arranged a carriage. You don't want to be late to your own coronation."

Yarafrey grated on Arafrey at the best of times, but the longer she spent with her grandmother, the more her head hurt. They rushed along the forest paths without stopping and took the back ways through the residential district to avoid the market – or perhaps just to avoid people in general, as Arafrey very much suspected was the case.

"Chin up, dear, and do smile. You look like a slapped toad," Yarafrey chided through a tight smile as they entered the temple. She stomped towards the courtyard doors as if she owned the place. "Just like Elsa to leave us to break centuries-old traditions. The least you can do is look like you're happy to be here."

"Yes, Grandmother," Arafrey parroted, forcing her face into action.

Taking the position of high priestess was a great honour, but it also added significant pressures on her marital status, given she would normally have to wait until she was married to do so. This put Arafrey in an extremely unpleasant position. Accepting the crown felt like a giant leap towards becoming queen and getting married, neither of which Arafrey was interested in doing. With no other relatives to take her place, however, Arafrey's abdication and lack of an heir would more than likely push Freya into a civil war between the high lords. She couldn't even begin to imagine how many innocent civilians would get caught in the crossfire or how it could shape Freya in the long run.

"It will do." Yarafrey's brow wrinkled into a different kind of frown as she fixed Arafrey's collar and straightened the emerald stole over her shoulders. "Not much we can do now."

Arafrey held her tongue and followed her grandmother. Two guards pushed upon the double doors, allowing them to pass into the courtyard.

The Life Tree stretched far above them, its bark glowing with the mystic-blue hue of the Manastream. Its roots flowed seamlessly around the courtyard into the walls of the temple and cotton sheets were strung in the air over the pews to shelter them. A pool of water gathered at the very base of the Life Tree. It glittered with mana and cast blue lights over the front of the courtyard, like a spotlight setting the stage for Arafrey.

She shrunk in on herself and kept her eyes ahead.

Her audience waited expectantly. Hundreds of smiling faces turned and watched as she shuffled towards the manapool. Her cream robes bunched over Arafrey's feet as she inched forward and pretended to be elegant. A cool breeze kept the cotton sheeting above them moving in an endless wave, accompanied by an ever-present rustling as the breeze continued through the crisp autumn leaves.

Arafrey reached the manapool with her grandmother and they turned to face the busy courtyard together.

A quiet came over the excited crowd and Arafrey looked up and saw her people for the first time. There were so many of them. Had they all come for her?

The pews were filled with prominent members of Frey nobility, with her father, King Galafrey, sitting in the front pew, solemnly waiting for the ceremony to begin. Less important Frey were permitted to fill what space they could, with Bodair standing proud at the very front of them all. Instinctively, Arafrey scanned the guards for a face she knew wouldn't be there, but instead spotted the members of the Queen's Guard who had finally removed their colours.

Arafrey's heart clutched her breath and whirled around her chest.

Until that moment, her mother's passing had all felt much like a bad dream. Arafrey had carried on with her duties as if her mother were only on holiday, but things were starting to get real, real fast and it terrified her.

Her heart tried to jump from her mouth as she looked over her people. Was she ready to lead them? She had been preparing for this moment her whole life. Everything she was taught and trained to do had been done in preparation for the day she would have to take over her mother's duties. Now the time was upon her, she felt like a deer confronting a tiger, and the deer said – *Run*.

"Make sure you project your voice," Yarafrey sniped under her breath. "Let's hope you do a better job than your mother."

Arafrey suspected there would be more snide comments about Elsafrey to come, so tuned out her grandmother's words as she led the coronation. She clung to her smile as she pretended to listen. She steadied her breaths and strengthened her core, taking in her last moments of freedom until it was time to accept her fate.

"Please kneel," Yarafrey instructed.

With a deep breath, Arafrey took a knee before Yarafrey. An aide Arafrey was unfamiliar with approached with the silver crown her mother once wore, upon a red satin cushion. Yarafrey's claw-like fingers coiled around the silver as she removed the crown and held it above Arafrey's head like a guillotine.

"Arafrey, Princess of Freya," Yarafrey called, but only loud enough so those she cared about in the front rows could really hear her. "You kneel before me today intent on taking your birthright. As acting High Priestess of Freya, it is my great pleasure to lead you in taking your vows."

Arafrey's headache continued its assault and stretched behind her eyes. Her brain pulsated against her skull. It was as if hot pokers were being pushed into her temples. If only she had walked to the temple alone that morning. She would have used her artes to soothe her headache had Yarafrey not awoken her. So, Arafrey blamed her grandmother for her suffering, warranted or not.

"Repeat after me," Yarafrey projected to the temple. "I accept this crown, and the responsibilities adhered to it."

Arafrey repeated the words without sentiment. She had practised the ceremony many times before but never had the words left such a bitter taste in her mouth.

"I swear to heal and protect, teach and learn…"

Arafrey considered at that moment just standing and leaving the temple. She imagined walking away and giving up her title as she had often dreamt, but even that felt like a hollow ambition without Reyla standing beside her. Reyla…

It's time we grow up…

Arafrey had no desire to grow up or give in to conventions, but circumstances were not on her side. Had fewer of her relatives died in the war, perhaps things would have been different. Perhaps, in another life, Arafrey could have lived the life she wanted, become the Frey she wanted, and loved the Frey she wanted, but alas that was not the case. There was no one.

As she finished reciting the last few lines of the sermon, Arafrey's eyes came to rest on the silver crown still hovering ominously in the hands of her least favourite grandparent.

"And with this crown, I dub thee, Arafrey, Princess and High Priestess of Freya."

Yarafrey clamped the crown around Arafrey's head, the silver weighing her down as she rose to face her ecstatic people. Cheers and applause filled the fevered courtyard. Arafrey waved in response, a smile painted upon her facade as she remembered her final words with Reyla.

Make sure we have a kingdom to return to…

It had seemed like such a simple request when asked – and in truth perhaps it had been – only Arafrey hadn't seen it at the time. Were they the true terms of their bargain?

Their love for the sake of their kingdom?

Their pain for the chance of hope and peace?

Arafrey judged herself cruelly for thinking the cost too great. But what if it was enough? What if…?

The guilt only irritated her headache further. It was not

the role she wanted, but if this was to be her life, then she would do her best for her people. She would do her job well. She would be their light and make them proud. Make Reyla proud.

Until the time Reyla and Tharin returned to their kingdom, Arafrey could not allow herself to rest or resent. Her pride. Her emotions. Her wants and dreams. They were all nothing to her now. All that remained was her duty, and she vowed to herself that she would do it well.

Besides... She had a promise to keep.

* * *

CHAPTER SIX

It was late afternoon by the time Reyla and Tharin arrived at the palace with Princess Wilona.

Set in the very centre of Alensya, the Sheya palace was built in the shape of a crescent moon. The turquoise stone curled around a sleek circular courtyard, which connected to the main road that ran to the bridge they had entered on. Water ran around the outskirts, causing it to feel like a small island, and raised flower beds with purple flowers fenced them in. The island had two short drawbridges, one leading to the innermost city halo, and the other to the palace itself.

Tharin remained quiet as he tried to take in everything at once.

Built over several floors, the tiled roofs of the palace radiated from a large dome of glass, indicating the arboretum throne hall he had heard so much about. The reclining sun reflected off the polished surface as they crossed the courtyard, and by the door where two armoured guards who were held to attention. They wore scaled navy-blue armour and grim expressions, but each bowed their heads and smiled to Wilona as she approached. Their sentiments didn't stretch to Tharin, however, and they returned daggers as he politely inclined his head and passed into the palace.

The entrance opened out into a large hall featuring two curved staircases that led up to the second floor. Glistening tiles swept along the floor through framed archways and along corridors.

A Shey man in an unusually tailored grey suit hurried towards them. "Princess, you're back early," he fussed. "And you have… erm…"

"Guests, Fitchely. They're called guests," Wilona insisted, her tone heightened with snobbish authority. "You'll give them a room each and bring a fresh set of clothes to their rooms."

"Ah- um- Yes, Princess," he replied, bowing his head.

"And I'll need fresh clothes myself. I smell like a bottom feeder." Wilona's nose wrinkled as she picked at her clothing. "Also, tell Chef I'm hungry. Have dinner prepared for us in the arboretum when we're dressed."

"Of course." Fitchely bowed again. "If our honoured guests would like to follow me to the guest rooms." He motioned to the staircase before crossing the tiled floor and beginning his ascent. Tharin waited for Reyla to go first, then fell in close behind.

He was thrilled to be staying in the Sheya palace. Accustomed to the finer things in life, Tharin had little interest in camping or scruffy inns. The palace was much more to his liking with its polished floors, sweeping halls and nary a cobweb in sight.

Fitchely guided them through the second floor, showing Tharin to a room on the outside of the palace before taking Reyla to another. The outer wall of Tharin's room was curved, the glass windows overlooking the city. Besides a rather comfortable-looking bed, there was a chair, a mirror and a set of drawers. Water constantly trickled through a sink-like feature and there was an unlit fireplace, but the turquoise stone made it all feel terribly cold.

Tharin activated his artes and summoned fire to his palm. He tossed it into the fireplace as if skipping stones, causing the logs to kindle. Tharin removed his soaked clothes and laid them in front of the fire as he rubbed his extremities in hopes of warming up, eventually resorting to pulling a sheet from the bed while he waited.

He wondered if the Shey were less susceptible to cold than the Frey, seeing as they used water artes. Or perhaps if they were cold-blooded as most reptiles were. Tharin's suspicions only continued to rise when he received his Shey attire.

He was given a pair of large, off-white harem trousers rimmed with royal blue along the waistband and legs. These stopped about halfway up his calf – for some reason he could not explain – and left his ankles bare. Instead of a shirt, he was given a wide satin sash of royal blue, which hung off his left shoulder and was embroidered with a golden wave pattern. There were no socks either, but he didn't want to appear rude so opted not to take a spare pair from his pack.

By Frey standards, he was practically naked, but Tharin admired his toned body in the strange clothes. Although he was unaccustomed to wearing such revealing attire, Tharin was hardly ashamed of his appearance and flexed his arms in the mirror with a grin. He ran his hands through his caramel-coloured hair, quickly brushing his fringe into its parting before turning towards the door.

His shoes drying by the now crackling fire, Tharin continued down the corridor, his feet clapping against the cool tile.

* * *

Tharin was the first to arrive in the arboretum.

It was over three storeys tall, and the domed roof was crafted from triangular panes of glass that caused the temperature to rise. The sound of water trickled through marble stone features and flower beds, dividing the arboretum like rivers through a forest. The floor's shining tiles ran towards the outer wall to a wide clearing where a row of four royal chairs dominated a wide dais.

Tharin turned as the pat of footsteps upon tile announced Reyla's entry. Her shoulders were hunched up to her ears and her arms pulled tight into her chest as she shuffled over to greet him. A sleeveless gown of crinkled cerulean fabric trailed behind her – which only worked to exaggerate her uncomfortable stance. A satin belt cinched her waist in a highly feminine, un-Reyla-like way. Even her hair had been brushed back, yet the untameable lengths still flicked wildly like brown wisps of fire.

Tharin smirked.

"Just don't," Reyla warned him in stern yet whispered tones. "They wanted to put me in a corset."

"It's not so bad," he admitted rubbing his palm over his bare chest. "Bit chilly though."

"How's your kit?" Reyla asked, clearly wishing for him to move on. "Mine's soaked through, but nothing's damaged."

Tharin's gear was in a similar state, and he was telling Reyla as much when Wilona joined them. She guided them to a table among the trees and flowerbeds where they sat and awaited dinner.

"I hope you're hungry," said Wilona, grinning as Fitchely poured tea into their cups. "I had Chef pull out all the stops. Although, I can never remember, do Frey eat fish?"

"Not usually," replied Tharin. "'Nothing that's got eyes' is the general rule. Though there was this crazy old Frey on the shores who ate loads of muscles and turned into a giant sea urchin."

"That's just an old wives' tale," scoffed Reyla.

"Nu-huh, I swear I saw him myself as a lad," Tharin protested. "We went to the coast on holiday. I was watching the fireworks when all of a sudden, I saw this mighty mound of seaweed coming up out of the water. It waved in the air." He threw his hands up and flailed them around in example. "And then it ripped a mighty roar. So, I legged it all the way home, my heart in my mouth, and I never looked back."

Reyla and Wilona laughed.

"That doesn't make it real," teased Reyla.

"Perhaps it was a walrus or a whale who had lost his way?" suggested Wilona.

The three were just discussing mermaids, comparing folk tales and legends, when dinner arrived. An entourage of Sheya servers brought out glorious platters of fresh vegetables steamed with bowls of bamboo shoots and rice.

Tharin's mouth watered. Much like the Frey, those in Sheya didn't eat a lot of meat, although in their case, it was more of a preference than a belief. The Shey generally preferred eating fresh fish they had caught themselves – and raising livestock is difficult in wetlands. Tharin wasn't interested in trying fish in the slightest – their vegetables though – Tharin had only ever heard stories of bamboo shoots and sea lettuce before, and he piled them onto his plate.

"Roshia said you were taking the Trial of the Ten

Ancestors. Is that true?" Wilona asked suddenly, her tone concerned.

Tharin's eyes darted to Reyla as he panicked and remembered their orders to tell no one of their journey. He held onto his tongue and hoped Reyla had a suitable answer as his mind ejected all other thoughts.

"It is," Reyla replied, effortlessly disguising her intentions behind a blank expression.

Tharin burned with envy. It was all he could do to mimic Reyla's stone face. His insides trembling, his breath held as he waited for Wilona to respond.

"There's a story passed down by my people, which speaks of ten trials set out by the Gods of Creation. They say that in times of great upheaval, the spirits may call upon worthy champions to cast out the darkness," Wilona explained, the timbre of her voice giving nothing away. "Pray tell, would this have anything to do with the blight that poisons my people?"

Both Frey started. Their eyes dropped quickly away, silently indicating the affirmative.

"I see..."

Wilona pursed her lips in concentration and ran a painted nail around the edge of a discarded spoon. She looked upon them as if reading their souls, the air around her so serious that Tharin couldn't decide if Wilona thought their presence was a good thing or not. *Did that make him a champion of the gods?* He had to restrain himself from asking any questions, but it was difficult to ignore the implications: the sickness was in Sheya.

"And how do you plan to reach Ruglor?" Wilona asked, but neither Frey had ever been further than Alensya and had no idea. Although, Tharin supposed they were probably going to walk. "In that case, may I suggest taking a boat as far as Tepps, near the eastern border? If you'll allow me, I can arrange your safe passage and have you there within a matter of days."

"We'd appreciate that," said Reyla. "As you can imagine, we are rather pressed for time."

Tharin squinted his eyes and tried to follow the conversation. He wasn't entirely sure what they were admitting to, but Wilona seemed to be appeased by their exchange. They also hadn't shared anything they weren't supposed to, so he wasn't about to argue.

Wilona wiped her mouth and set her cutlery aside. "I've not travelled to Agrana myself, but there's a path running through the south and into the foothills of Ruglor from Tepps. The Rugla raised a path through the marshes for trading, it will take you over the river Ballish, but please, I implore you, do not leave this path under any circumstances."

"Why not?" asked Tharin.

An intense graveness took hold of Wilona's features which sent a shiver down Tharin's spine. "Whispers of missing travellers have even reached my ears. Please do be careful."

"Thank you," replied Reyla, with a tight smile. "We'll remain vigilant."

Wilona returned the smile, but Tharin knew better than to trust this particular smile, making note of Reyla's careful word choice. After all, both Frey knew, they had little control over the location of the Agrana shrine.

* * *

Reyla returned to her room to find a filled free-standing porcelain bathtub sitting before the fire. She sighed, elated.

It had been so long since she had taken a bath. The palace barracks held only showers and she was always sure to spend as little time in them as possible. But a bath, to herself, in a private room. It was like a dream come true.

She undressed and welcomed the bath's warm embrace without questioning how or why it was there.

There was no soap, but the water was aromatic, and oils slicked her olivine skin. Her muscles rejoiced as she sank along the porcelain, the rising steam scented with patchouli, rose and lavender.

Reyla's grimace cut through the steam. *Of course it was lavender.*

Already weary from travelling, Reyla's body hummed

from the additional strain caused by their battle against Najra. Bruises formed around her knees from rolling over the stone. Her shoulder pinched with each deep breath and her hips ached, but it was nothing she couldn't deal with herself – at least not now she had the third blessing.

Reyla reached for her ankles and activated her artes. Mana pushed from her core and along her arms to her hands, where the palms glowed white. She held it there and pushed her fingers into the joints and along the tops of her feet, her toes cracking as they stretched. The bitter sting of her cold Frey artes against her tender ankle joints was softened by the heat of the water.

'*Three down, only seven more to go...*' she thought, her mind wandering as she worked her way up her calf muscles – but the lavender steam drew her home.

It was as if Princess Arafrey were there with her. Reyla could still smell the fresh lavender fragrance upon her hair. The thought of the silken sheen of waving lengths slipping through her fingers lingered, her touch still vivid as she reached her knees. The pressure behind her kneecaps eased as Reyla massaged the surrounding muscles, each breath drawing on her memories as her hands continued along her thigh.

Her mind's eye perfectly traced the shape of Arafrey's body as her fingers began to trace her own. She lost herself to the indulgence and pictured once more the softness of Arafrey's pale skin as Reyla's hands slipped along her back, brushing her neck as she reached into her long green hair. Reyla would then pull Arafrey close and–

What was that?

Reyla stopped, her breath held as she surveyed the room around her.

She grumbled and threw her arms over the side of the tub. Reyla was certain she had heard something move, but now she had stopped she was sure it was probably just the bathwater. Even so, she had lost her train of thought and wasn't sure she had the energy to start over. Besides, thinking of Arafrey like that was only a hop, skip and jump away from wanting to go back. Which was no longer an option. If ever there were a more hopeless Frey on the planet, Reyla had yet to meet them.

Reyla's head dropped back against the porcelain. *What an aptly disappointing end to her relaxation time.*

"Don't stop on my account," an ethereal voice echoed around her.

Reyla braced herself on the sides of the bath, frantically searching for the source of the voice.

Where was it coming from?

She scanned the room again, the beat of her heart rising rapidly as blood rushed through her body. Her limbs were primed for any sudden action, but there was nothing there.

Reyla lifted her body from the tub, and was preparing to exit, when the water around her moved. The water swirled with speed and purpose, rising above her naked body and pushing her back down. It bubbled and waved, and features appeared as the water gained shapes and took the form of a person – no – it was Wilona!

The water settled around them and Wilona, or rather the top half of her body, formed from the bathwater. She wrapped her hands around Reyla's face and brought her eyes to meet Reyla's.

"What the–? Wilona, what are you doing here?"

"I shouldn't be surprised you noticed me," Wilona whispered, seeming to ignore Reyla's shock and horror as she brushed the hair from her face. Wilona's head tipped to the side. "You really are magnificent."

Reyla's cheeks burned. She knew of the Shey ability to turn their bodies into water but had never seen it in person and thought it a legend. Still, that didn't stop her spirit from leaving her body as she tried to decide what was happening. *Wasn't she just-?*

"When I first saw you, I knew." Wilona's breath was cool as she breathed. "But then Roshia confirmed my suspicions. How miraculous it is that we are reunited again."

Reyla gaped. *What was Wilona talking about?*

Although her entrance was alarming, Wilona looked at Reyla with warmth, admiration even. Her skin flowed seamlessly from the bathwater. Only the translucent shape of her body was visible up to her neck, where she became more solid. The water moved with her as Wilona leant forward and brought her face in closer to Reyla's, her eyes wide and gazing with wonder.

"Look, Princess, I appreciate *whatever* this is, but–"

Wilona placed a watery finger on Reyla's lips.

"I remember you from the last time you came here. When the fighting broke out. You saved me back then…"

Reyla could almost hear her jaw drop into the bathwater as she realised what Wilona was talking about. But how could she have known it was the same girl? Would it have made any difference if she had?

"I didn't know who you were, but every night I could see your face when I closed my eyes. It made me feel safe, thinking of you. All this time. I've wanted to meet you again ever since." Wilona's cheeks blushed despite her translucent state. "Then you came back. I just knew it was destiny."

"D-Destiny?" Reyla stuttered, suddenly praying for the ground to swallow her whole. "Princess I–"

Reyla hesitated and resisted the urge to scramble away naked and avoid the conversation altogether. Wilona's eyes twinkled as she waited for a response. She truly believed what she was saying, but Reyla was the last person to be handing out any kind of advice. How could she?

Reyla didn't have the heart to tell Wilona that she hadn't remembered her at all. Until that moment, she'd had no idea who she had saved all those years ago. Possible heart attack aside, it was kind of endearing to be remembered so fondly and maybe only a little creepy. Okay a lot, but it seemed Wilona's heart was in the right place, even if it was liquid and translucent in that moment.

Reyla took a deep breath and tried to forget the fact she was still naked. "Princess, I am truly flattered but, even if I didn't think it would start a war, I couldn't. I…"

She trailed off, searching for a reason, although her heart trembled with a pang of guilt as she realised it. Nothing was holding her back. The only thing stopping her was her love for a princess – just not this one.

Reyla stared blankly, then sighed deeply.

"I've no real reason why," she admitted, her eyes stinging. Wilona pulled back, upset, but Reyla continued before she could find the words to argue. "I long for someone I cannot be with. And you? You chase after a daydream I have no hope of ever living up to…" She half snorted. "I guess we're both hopeless"

Wilona looked away, disappointed. Her body still melted away from the neck down, vanishing into the bathwater as she wavered.

"I think maybe destiny brought us together so we could both move on," Reyla insisted, but her heart ached as she heard the words leave her mouth.

Although she was the one who had broken things off with Arafrey, there was always a hope one day things would work out for them. But as she said the words, Reyla knew them to be true.

"Sometimes- Sometimes we have to let go of the past so we can face the future," she asserted, almost convincing herself.

"Can we face it tomorrow?"

"I wish we could." Reyla forced a smile, but it was an awkward effort.

"Hmph." Wilona pouted and rested her head on Reyla's shoulder. "If this is all destiny can afford me, then I shall treasure this time we had together."

Wilona sniffed into Reyla's shoulder. She clearly wasn't accustomed to being told no.

* * *

CHAPTER SEVEN

The makeshift furniture creaked as Emperor Callius Gabris sat back in anticipation. He watched as Hellard, his distant cousin and squire, tested their food and wine.

The Duran Emperor was a man of exaggerated height and proportions whose natural presence dominated any space he happened to be in. Dura were generally peachy in complexion but Callius boasted a bronzed sheen that complimented the cream tunic currently straining over his pectorals. His hair was a fawn-brown which he kept short to accommodate his helm, with sideburns that ran into the stubble of his beard.

Hellard swallowed, his face pale as he awaited his fate.

"This is ridiculous," Nymati fumed, her tail lashing out to the side of her.

Nymati lounged over a pile of cushions across from the emperor. She wore some Sudran attire which amounted to little more than a tube of dark fabric which ran from her breast to her thighs. The tight fabric appeared to defy gravity by willpower alone as it hugged every curve and swerve of the Demon Queen's figure. The fashion was not something Callius was familiar with; he wasn't complaining though.

"Our food will be cold by the time any poison takes effect. Get out of here. Shoo." She waved at Hellard to dismiss him.

Callius lifted his chin to the petrified squire. "Go on."

Hellard nearly ran from their tent and the door whipped against the fabric as it fell shut behind him.

"Would you rather we get poisoned again?" Callius asked in a strained whisper. They didn't wish anyone to know someone had managed to sneak by their security. "What else can I do? We have no lead or suspect."

Nymati scoffed and flicked long raven hair back over her shoulder. "It's a miracle we survived the first time."

"Then what would you have me do? We've interviewed everyone we can. The perpetrator could be long gone by now."

"No, they will still be here," Nymati hissed, the ruby of her eyes glowing blood-red from her fury. "This was personal. They will have waited to see what happened. It was someone close to us. Someone who expected they knew us enough to ensure we drank their poison and carried out their schemes."

"It still makes no sense to me. What poison causes such effects?"

"I doubt that was their intent," Nymati replied, venom practically foaming on her lips.

Callius liked this side of her. If the stories were to be believed, Nymati should have terrified him, and perhaps she did, but the grieving widow couldn't hold a candle to this calculated tenacious beauty.

"They intended for me to kill you. Likely hoping I'd be tried and executed for my crimes." Nymati growled as she reached for her wine. "Such cowardice. Whoever it was will pay for their insult."

Callius allowed Nymati's temper to simmer and tried not to smile as he thought back to the night they had been poisoned.

If they had wished for her to kill him, then what really happened that night? He only remembered waking up the next morning naked and blood-soaked with Nymati beside him. Everything else was a blur.

Callius was just working up the courage to ask his follow-up questions when Commander Raltz burst into the tent.

"Eminence, urgent word from Halda." He thrust out his arm, a scroll sealed with red wax and ribbon in his hand.

Callius snatched it from Raltz and cracked the seal, but straightened upon reading the notice.

"What's the matter?" asked Nymati.

Raltz went to leave but Callius lifted his hand, stopping him. "Stay. You'll want to hear this," he warned, clearing his throat. "Our spies report the assassination of High

Priestess Elsafrey of Freya. Sources say the assailant was Dura and was slain before being interrogated. Rumours circulate, blaming the empire but no official statement has been issued by the crown."

Nymati gasped. "And are you to blame?"

"Of course not." Callius frowned, a little hurt she thought so lowly of him. "Why kill their queen? It makes no logical sense. I thought Galafrey runs their army."

"Indeed," Raltz agreed, the wrinkles between his eyebrows deepening.

Callius groaned. "Well, there goes any hopes we had of peaceful negotiations with Freya and Pudron. Write back to Tidus. Tell him to mount our defences and prepare for retaliation, but keep it close to the Ballish to avoid further provoking the Frey."

"You think they will retaliate?" asked Nymati, tensing as if already prepared for battle.

Callius paused to think about it, then shook his head. "Regardless, Freya was the most practical target to annex next. We were going to march on them eventually, but we should leave it for them to make the first move until we are ready."

"Understood." Raltz saluted, promptly leaving.

Callius dropped back into the furniture with a sigh.

"You don't think they tried to poison us in retaliation, do you?" Nymati mused.

His eyes dropped to his untouched meal as he mentally calculated the time it took for news to travel. "The timeline's too short. Even poison requires planning, and they'd still have to get here with it. Unless you know some way to cross kingdoms I haven't heard about."

"If only." Nymati smirked momentarily before her face turned serious again. "So then, we're back to our staff."

Callius sucked his teeth. It wasn't anyone on his staff, but there was no use arguing the point. Nymati was paranoid, shaken. No doubt the ineffable Demon Queen was merely unaccustomed to having her defences broken, but he could not run an Empire through caution. He could only hope that, with time, she would recover. She was surely resilient enough.

"You know…" Nymati started, a sinister smile appearing on her ebony lips. "The Shey may be more amicable if they think you ordered a hit on Galafrey."

Callius squinted his eyes. "But I didn't."

"They don't need to know that." Nymati shrugged.

"You surprise me still." He chortled to disguise his concern. "I pray we never find ourselves on opposing sides. I fear I would be no match."

"My Dear Emperor…" She paused, batting her eyelashes with a fang-filled grin. "You wouldn't stand a chance."

* * *

CHAPTER EIGHT

Arafrey sighed as she closed the office door behind her. She pressed her fingers against her temples, her eyes dropping shut.

The pain from her headaches was distracting and ever-present. It had not stopped since her coronation. The temptation to use her artes grew with each pulse of her pounding head. She assumed the headaches were simply due to grief and stress, but seeing as neither was going anywhere any time soon, she decided it was time to seek a solution.

Arafrey opened her eyes, grateful for the small windows and soft light.

The office had remained unchanged since her mother's passing. Arafrey had been putting off sorting through Elsafrey's possessions, leaving the wooden counters and workbench littered with books, tools and ingredients her mother had been working with. She had cleared the rectangular desk at one point, but the polished surface was no longer visible under the mounds of notices and papers she had collected since her coronation.

Arafrey sought the medicine cabinet; a wooden frame

that nearly reached the ceiling with glass panels set into the doors. She pulled on the brass handles, easing the doors open to look inside. As she ran a slender finger across the wooden shelves, Arafrey read the labels of the many pots and vials. She found what she was looking for on the middle shelf: a small bottle with a dropper in the lid. The silver liquid inside swirled as she pulled it from the cabinet and checked the label.

Savulin Tonic.

It was a creation of her grandfather on her mother's side. A painkiller of considerable strength that was often used on the battlefield – and even more so now, as the sickness spread to affect more souls every day. It revolutionised the way Frey treated pain they could not heal with artes and solidified his place in history books. The irony was not lost on her that it was the same tonic that gained her grandfather his status, which had ultimately led to her conception, position and increasingly present headache.

Arafrey loosened the lid, lifted the dropper over her open mouth, and released two drops to rest on her tongue. It tasted so bitter, and her face soured as she returned the tonic to the shelf. She then closed the doors, resting her head where they met as she waited for her pain to subside.

With her eyes to her feet, Arafrey caught sight of something in her periphery. It was tucked in by the base of the cabinet. A square package which had no business being on the floor.

Her curiosity piqued, Arafrey collected it and turned to the desk. Placing the package on the surface, she dropped into the desk chair.

The package itself was unassuming. There was no name, just the address of the temple. It was about a foot square and rather heavy, wrapped tight with thick brown paper and tied with a string.

Did the person who sent the package intend for it to be delivered to her mother or was it just for the temple? Either way, she determined that the best way to find out was to open it.

She pulled the string and unwrapped the brown paper to find a plain wooden box. The box lid had a brass latch and two hinges, but no lock. Arafrey lifted the latch and opened the lid to find four books stored neatly inside. They were old, thick leaf-leather bindings with rough yellowed pages, and the strong scent of something familiar Arafrey couldn't place, which filled the room as she took them each out in turn.

The first book was a lot thinner than the others. Its cover was ivy green and dog-eared, and the pages were mismatched and carelessly pinned to the bindings, so that they stuck out at strange intervals. A cursory glance revealed dates and musings with scrawled, cursive handwriting, suggesting it was a journal, although there was no name of the author. Arafrey set it to one side for later reading.

The remaining three books were of similar thickness,

and each had a red cover. One appeared to be a comprehensive guide to healing artes; much of it was common knowledge but there were some interesting chapters explaining in great detail how it all worked. The second was a book on the artes used throughout Alamantra. Although this book was a little more generalised, it had a chapter comparing the various nations and noting the similarities in their process. However, it was the last book, 'The History of Dark Artes', which really caught Arafrey's attention.

She flipped through the pages with gusto, in hopes of finding anything similar to the sickness within their bindings. Knowing all Reyla had told her, it was easy for Arafrey to figure out what her mother would want with this particular volume or why someone would send it to her. It was an interesting read, but focused more on theory and history than actual practices and much was left to speculation.

Bells chimed out through the city, telling Arafrey it was now three in the afternoon and she had been reading for several hours.

Arafrey dropped the book, releasing a heavy sigh. She may have no hopes of finding a treatment for the sickness, but at least her headache had subsided and she had learnt much about dark artes that she hadn't known before.

Normal artes used the mana held within an individual's body and converted it into an external reaction, but they had limitations decided by birth and latent ability. Dark artes removed these limitations, instead invoking words of power to direct their desires. These words were derived from the language of the First Ones, the language of the Gods, and were forbidden for the corruption they caused within their users.

Arafrey pushed against the back of her chair. She had known dark artes were terrible but had never realised quite how dangerous they were. Dark artes had long fallen into obscurity in Freya, and were only ever mentioned in scary stories or rumours from Old Wood Prison. She found it incredibly worrisome to know there were people with such capabilities out there, somewhere in Alamantra.

Mulling over the many things she had read, Arafrey idly flicked the pages. The book fell open on a section about mana burn, a side effect of overusing your artes, which burned the user's skin.

Arafrey's nose wrinkled. She had given herself mana burn only once before. She had been young, but it had caused such a lasting impression that she was sure not to do it ever again. There was no cure for mana burn. Much like a normal burn or a smaller flesh wound, it would just need time to heal – but if you used any artes on it your whole body would burn as if it were on fire, and there were few remedies for soothing it.

A spark of inspiration wrapped around Arafrey's brain and she grinned. She returned to her books with renewed vigour in search of her prize.

This was it.

She could feel it.

* * *

It had gone six when Arafrey finally settled on her next course of action.

If a person could develop burns from their artes, then why not dark artes? The marks left by the sickness were merely a reaction to dark mana and responded poorly to artes, so, in theory, they were no different to mana burns. But this left Arafrey with a problem: there was no known treatment for mana burns by dark artes.

Arafrey returned to the medicine cabinet, quickly searching the contents for the soothing balm most commonly used for mana burns, but was unsuccessful. She was, however, able to find the base ingredients, including the main activator: a rarer ingredient, the nectar of a hushin flower.

With her bottles in hand, Arafrey sized up the workbench. There were many books and discarded pages scattered over the surface. Some half-realised concoctions still lay in the mortar bowl – the pestle nowhere to be seen – and an open ink-pot had been left so long it was completely dried up. Arafrey swept it all aside with one arm and retrieved a clean pestle and mortar from the shelves below.

She was in a rush of emotions and nervous energy as

she devised two batches of soothing balm.

For the first batch, she used the same formula as the original balm for mana burn. She mixed the materials into the mortar and blended the nectar and herbs to create a thick, creamy paste. It was a long shot – she knew that – but still, she had to try.

When making the second batch, Arafrey decided to try something different. She held her hand against the glass bottle and activated her artes, causing her palm to glow around the nectar as she pictured the molecules tightening. The yellow nectar inside agitated and reduced, the colour turning a deep orange. Although using artes ran the risk of infection, Arafrey hoped that concentrating the hushin nectar would provide her with a stronger balm and a stronger defence against the sickness. They would have to decide if the benefits were worth the risk before creating larger quantities, but she was confident in her hypothesis. She just had to put it to the test.

By the time Arafrey had finished her preparations, many of the medics had gone home, and Sister Francis was awake to take on the night shift. The courtyard was empty, apart from the two guards stationed by the entrance. They saluted as Arafrey passed and she continued quietly through the wooden corridor to the ward for long-term patients.

The door was left ajar, and she pushed it gently as she stepped into the temple ward. There were eight beds, each separated by a cloth divider, which was drawn to allow the patients privacy while they slept.

Arafrey allowed them their rest and padded across to the bed closest to the window where Nasir rested against a mound of pillows. He was looking out through the open curtain to the moon as she approached, a single candle burning on the table beside him.

Nasir strained as he rose to greet her, wincing through each breath as he sat up in the bed. He had been bedridden since the outbreak, but kept his cheery disposition despite the lack of relief they were able to offer.

"Good evening," said Nasir softly. "A little late to be doing your rounds isn't it, Princess?"

Arafrey liked that he still called her Princess. "I know it's late, but I hope you'll forgive me when I tell you why."

Arafrey forced a smile in an attempt at reassurance, but she wasn't sure where to look when talking to him and felt awkward.

Only a few fingers of pale green skin remained on Nasir's face as blackened blisters covered his cheeks and flashes of white ran through his ginger hair. His torso looked as if he had been doused with ink as the dark burns of the mana sickness streaked their way around his body.

"How are you feeling?" asked Arafrey, placing a hand against his forehead to check his temperature. It wasn't as high as it had been before.

"I'll live." Nasir smiled, the motion causing his burns to

crease. "Or not. Perhaps I will be the first to die of this sickness. Then I would be remembered in the history books as the man who died first of the scourge. And you would get to tell my tale! We will both be famous."

Arafrey chuckled. "It would be my honour to tell your tale, but I have no intentions of letting you become the first victim of this sickness any time soon," she told him. "I do, however, have a favour to ask of you."

"For you, Princess? Anything." He held his hand to his chest, leaning forward as if to bow. "I am your humble, yet useless, servant. Any way I can, I will be happy to lend my assistance."

She explained her theory to Nasir and showed him the pastes she had made.

He shrugged. "It's worth a shot, right?"

"Indeed, I believe it is. Please may I have your arm?"

Nasir presented his arm. It shook from the strain causing her to take his hand in hers as she pulled back the sleeve of his gown. The skin blistered over his hands and forearms and stank from the many open, oozing wounds they were unable to keep clean. This was where she placed the pastes, on his right arm in two strips, two fingers wide and about two fingers apart.

"If you have any negative reactions, please tell one of the medics right away. I shall be back to check on you in the morning."

* * *

As promised, Arafrey returned to the temple the next morning to find Nasir sitting up in his bed. He grinned, his arm held out proudly as she approached.

"Look," he cheered, pointing to his arm. "A scab!"

In any other time and place, perhaps the statement would have held less weight, but for Arafrey it was everything. She was ecstatic. "That is incredible news."

Arafrey moved in to inspect Nasir's arm more closely. The black marks showed no signs of expansion, as they did in other parts of his body, and scabs now formed over the open wounds – which was positive since they had been unable to use artes on those afflicted, and the risk of infection was high. However, it appeared the concentrated nectar yielded more positive results. The scab was solid and fully formed – there was no denying the difference between the two.

"How're you feeling?"

"Good, a lot of the stinging is gone," he replied. "I even managed to get some shut-eye."

"I'm glad." Arafrey smiled and the tension in her shoulders dropped a degree closer to normal. She reapplied the paste and thanked Nasir deeply.

It was still too early to get excited, but she was hopeful.

If the soothing balm proved effective, they would need to produce it in large quantities. Unfortunately, hushin nectar was difficult to come by, and she only had enough for a few more samples.

"You have done your kin a great service." Arafrey beamed as she cupped her hands around Nasir's. "But now I'm afraid the real work begins."

Arafrey returned to her feet with newfound strength.

Her skills with plant artes were lacking compared to others, and she would need a specialist to concentrate the nectar, but for now, she would do. The process reduced the volume, but in theory, it would mean a little would go a long way – which would be helpful considering the rarity of hushin nectar. It would require time and testing to get the blend just right, but she was determined to do it.

'Now for the real work to begin.'

* * *

CHAPTER NINE

Princess Wilona insisted on accompanying Reyla and Tharin to the docks the morning after her failed gesture.

Wilona remained quiet, walking as close to Reyla as possible without tripping her up, hoping their hands would brush past each other if only for the briefest moment. She watched with desperation as the hardened Frey scanned everything from the buildings and benches to the Shey guards and citizens they passed, all the while managing to avoid the ever-wanting glance of the princess.

She bubbled with fury and rejection. She could see that Reyla was ever alert and mindful of her companion, yet made sure not to pay too much attention to Wilona herself. It was surely done on purpose, of that Wilona was certain. The princess balled her fists. She had dreamt of her hero for so very long, and she was not willing to let go of her dreams so easily.

She had been too forward. Reyla was shy, a romantic. Wilona saw that now. She had scared Reyla away, but she could fix it. *She had to.*

Wilona guided them from the palace along the main road to the northeastern area of the Deuxel – the second ring inward – as it was filled with merchants and shops for the Frey to resupply. She took them the long way around and showed them every shop in the market, hoping to find some way to make amends in their extended journey, but it was hopeless. Reyla didn't see her.

It was still early morning as they closed in on the docks. Shey lifted all manner of crates and wares onto the waiting ships while others queued for departure.

"It's been a true pleasure meeting you both properly." Wilona's heart shook despite the smile plastered across her face. "I wish you well in your journey and hope we can help each other in the future."

"Thanks, Princess. We had a great time." Tharin grinned and shovelled snacks into his pack. "We'll let Princess Arafrey know you helped us out for sure."

Reyla returned a nod in agreement but was still careful not to catch Wilona's eye directly. It sapped at Wilona's strength as her heart stopped and slowly sank deeper into her chest. How was she supposed to fix things when Reyla wouldn't even look at her?

Wilona sucked in air as she fumbled through her pocket. The cool metal of a silver pendant lent her strength as she marched the few steps over to Reyla and grabbed her hand. She thrust the necklace into Reyla's palm and clasped her fingers closed around it.

"I want you to take this," Wilona announced as evenly as possible while her pulse ran like rapids through her eardrums. "I want to apologise – well, thank you. Yes, thank you for – um – for last night."

Tharin's ears twitched towards them, but he said nothing.

"This amulet has the ability to find water, even in the harshest desert. Your journey is an arduous one..." Wilona squeezed Reyla's fingers around the pendant and, finally, their eyes met. "May it save you, as you saved me all those years ago."

"Thank you, Princess, but don't worry, we'll be fine."

Wilona's knees went weak as Reyla flashed a reassuring smile, but it was short-lived as she removed her hand to wrap the chain around her neck.

"Take care, Princess. May our next meeting be less exciting." Reyla bowed and Tharin joined her.

Wilona held her hands together and bowed similarly – deciding the bow was a Frey custom and wishing to be polite. "You too and may the Gods bring you fortune."

Reyla and Tharin waved as they boarded the boat and went to find seats among the other passengers.

Wilona remained on the pier as their ship pulled away from the harbour. Flurries of anguish and excitement swirled amongst the hurt and confusion hailed by her formative years as she clung to the minuscule chance that Reyla could one day come to see things the way she did. It was fate, after all, that brought them together – and the

Gods themselves had played a hand in their reunion. What could that be other than destiny? And nothing, not quests nor distance nor lost loves could come between destiny.

Wilona followed as their boat faded into the horizon, her heart fluttering as her hands pressed to her chest.

'I'll let you save Alamantra for now, Reyla,' she thought to the world. *'One day you'll realise no one will ever love you the way I do... Then you'll come back to me.*

'Just like this time...

It's our destiny...'

* * *

The two Frey had long left Alensya and were resting against the stern of the ship when Tharin finally asked:

"So then, what happened *'last night'*?" His voice and eyebrows were raised accusingly.

"You wouldn't believe me if I told you." Reyla laughed and brushed a hand through her chestnut mane to rub the back of her head. The look on her face was not one Tharin was sure he had ever seen before and he was unsure just what it meant. Was it embarrassment or perhaps pride? It only made him more curious.

"Come on, you can't say that," he pleaded. "I'd tell you, you know I would."

Reyla chuckled. "Oh! You would, would you?"

"You know I would."

"Treshin Day," Reyla accused.

"Treshin Day? Treshin Day! You always bring up Treshin Day." Tharin's arms waved with his exasperation. "I told you, I swear, I didn't mean to. It was an accident."

"An accident? You stabbed me!"

"I didn't do it on purpose."

"You took your sword out of its sheath and stabbed me. How is that an accident?"

"I wasn't aiming for you. Look, I'm sorry. I really am. Hand on heart," he replied doing so.

"Fine, I believe you." Reyla scoffed and rolled her eyes. She was likely hoping that would be the end of it, but the question bubbled in the back of Tharin's throat like a sherbet candy.

Tharin only managed to remain quiet a minute longer before he asked, "Are you going to tell me then?"

Knowing they had a long trek before them and little to distract Tharin from pestering her, Reyla was quick to yield. She grumbled, "She came to visit me is all. Turns out she was the girl I saved all those years ago."

"Really? How about that?" Tharin grinned. "Small world isn't it?"

"Could do with being smaller if you ask me. It's going

to take us weeks to cross Agrana to Ruglor…"

* * *

CHAPTER TEN

Arafrey rushed to the local apothecary. It was normally a ten-minute walk, but she managed it in six.

Excitement bubbled in her stomach. After thorough testing, she now had a treatment to ease the symptoms of the sickness. Each step brought her closer to fulfilling her promise to Reyla and living up to her mother's reputation. There was only one problem.

"I'm sorry, Priestess." The apothecary wheezed. He was an old Frey with greying caterpillar eyebrows. "Most of the ingredients you require are common use and easy to bulk order, but hushin nectar…"

"I realise it's an arduous task that I'm setting you, but this is of the highest importance," Arafrey insisted.

"Normally I'd be able to send my son out to try to find some, but the woods are getting dangerous at night, and I fear for his safety," the apothecary replied, his wide body shifting behind the counter. "There's been something off with the woods since this sickness came in. Animals being aggressive and the like."

"Could you show my men where to collect it? I can send someone in your place," offered Arafrey, her headache returning as hope slipped through her fingers.

"They'd need the skill to harvest the nectar. If you pull the plant, it dies and the nectar along with it," the apothecary warned. "Ye could try breeding your own, but it'd take a while to grow 'em to buds. They don't flower over winter either."

"What if we offer you protection?" Arafrey countered sharply, her temple suddenly throbbing. "An armed escort?"

"I'm just a frail old man–"

"Then send someone in your place," Arafrey burst out, her urgency in the matter indisputable. "We require that nectar!"

The old Frey stammered a few syllables of protest but dropped his head in compliance. His brow creased as he yielded to her will. It wasn't her proudest moment, but it got the job done.

"My son is capable. But it's dangerous the closer you get to Old Wood. Would you promise his safety?"

"I will assign the finest men we have to offer," Arafrey promised. "No harm shall come to your son."

The apothecary sheepishly agreed. He quietly collected the ingredients he could and placed them on the counter.

"And some Savulin Tonic," Arafrey added, knowing there was little left in the cabinet. "Send the bill to the temple."

"I'm sure I don't need to tell you to be careful with that stuff," warned the apothecary, placing the supplies into a burlap sack.

"It's not for me," she lied, collecting the sack and holding it close. "I'll have guards meet your son here in the morning. Thank you."

* * *

Arafrey returned to the temple where she stowed the supplies, quickly pocketing the Savulin Tonic for later consumption. She checked in with the medics on duty and tended a few patients before returning to the palace.

The sun was setting by the time she entered the timber palace, and the air was so tense it caused the oak walls to creak uncomfortably. The guards had remained on high alert since her mother's passing and were stationed in pairs from the entrance to the throne hall.

Arafrey crossed to her father's office, her escorts parting to take positions by the entrance without orders. She knocked on the door firmly and drew a deep breath as she awaited a response. There was no way for her to avoid involving her father and Captain Valren any longer. She needed to share her findings with them, and although she loved each of them dearly, they didn't always see eye-to-eye.

Arafrey hoped her father was in a better mood than he

had been the last time they had spoken. She wasn't sure she had the strength to fight with him today. Not that she remembered when she had last spoken to him…

"Come in," came the monotone of her father's voice, prompting her to open the door.

Arafrey entered the office to find her father sitting behind his desk. Standing beside him, as always, was Captain Valren – a greyed horse-faced Frey – which she found quite fortunate for a change.

"Ah, Ara."

"Father. Captain." She greeted them with a tight smile. "I've augmented a soothing balm to create a treatment for the burns caused by the sickness."

"That is good news," said Galafrey, although his voice didn't reflect the sentiment. The rings around his eyes were somehow darker than before and his robes seemed to hang from his shoulders like a coat rack.

"It is. Unfortunately, the serum requires concentrated hushin nectar, which is difficult to come by and requires synthesis." Arafrey clasped her hands tightly together. "The apothecary expressed concerns over collecting nectar with the rise in wild animal activity, so I'd like to assign two guards to his service to ensure his return. If possible, I'd like them to bring back seeds or plants to breed from. I was thinking Mika and Gurrien should do him well."

Arafrey knew of them from the Queen's Guard and they seemed reasonable enough given their limited interactions. Reyla always spoke fondly of them, so Arafrey was sure they were up to the task. She squeezed her fingers in anticipation of their response.

Galafrey looked to Valren.

Valren's head tilted to the side as his brow raised. "We can easily spare them. They have yet to be reassigned."

"Very well, have them gear up," said Galafrey, scribbling the order with a quill before passing it to Valren. "Anything else?"

"Yes," Arafrey asserted, straightening as she ran through her mental list. "If we hope to start mass production, we'll need space and volunteers to concentrate the nectar. They'll run the risk of infection; they should be made aware of this."

"We can use the dining room and clear the greenhouse for a nursery," said Galafrey, dipping his quill into the ink pot to begin a second note. "I'll send a squire to announce the position."

"We should send word to other cities also," suggested Valren. "Perhaps they can begin making their own?"

"Excellent idea," Galafrey agreed, passing the note to Valren. "Ara, have a list of instructions prepared for everything and we'll take it from there."

Arafrey opened her mouth to protest but stopped to stifle a yawn. "Thank you. Now, if you'll excuse me, it's been a long day."

* * *

Arafrey entered her room to find an elegant gown laid out for her, remembering instantly that she had been invited to an event that evening.

The priestess groaned in disgust and reached for the service bell, alerting palace staff that she was waiting.

It wasn't that late, and she had the time to get ready if she wanted to attend. Surely no one would begrudge her a fashionable entrance given her status, but it had been a long day.

The event was nothing formal, a party held by a noble she held little fondness for, and she quickly abandoned any plans to get into her dress. Besides, Yaldin's parties were notorious for overindulgence and drama, anything she missed would be sure to make it through the grapevine by morning. With any luck, everyone would be too busy gossiping to notice her absence.

The day's events caught up with Arafrey as she awaited her aide. Candles burned by her bed and upon the table, the light growing to sting her eyes. Her headache had yet to subside, and her legs ached from rushing around the city, but at least she had a decent excuse not to go to the party.

Arafrey crossed to her bedside and opened the drawer. She reached into her pocket, placing the Savulin Tonic inside, before closing the drawer again.

Ceal knocked before she entered with a plate piled with fresh fruit in one hand. She smiled but the fraying strands of mousy-brown hair escaping a hastily constructed knot suggested she was also having a long day.

"I brought you dinner, Your Grace." Ceal placed the plate on the wooden table. "Would you like assistance getting ready for the party?"

"No. Help me get ready for bed."

"Of course, Priestess." Ceal hurried over to begin unbuttoning the back of her robes.

Arafrey stood in silence as Ceal helped remove her robes, replacing them with a long-sleeved nightgown. She then collected the discarded garbs and hung them over her arm to take with her to the laundry room.

"Thank you, Ceal. You may leave the plate for tomorrow. You're dismissed for the night."

Ceal bowed before leaving and Arafrey waited for the door to click closed before rushing to blow out the candles on the table and retrieve her vial of Savulin Tonic.

She pulled back the covers and slipped between the cotton sheets, the vial clutched tightly in her hand. The bottle popped as she removed the stopper and, before the covers even had the chance to settle over her, she dropped the tonic onto her tongue. Arafrey replaced the cork, returned the bottle to her drawer and settled into her bed.

She sighed as the Savulin Tonic wrapped around her senses. The warmth spread down her throat as it seeped into her system. She rested her head against the pillow and sank into the mattress as her pain faded.

As she closed her eyes, it occurred to Arafrey that she had failed to check the potency of the new tonic, but she was finding it hard to care enough to do anything about it now. The pressure eased from behind her eyes. Her limbs grew heavy, and her mind became comfortably blank.

Finally painless, a serenity befell her. Words, thoughts and feelings were no longer a consideration as she drifted away from consciousness.

Pain-free and peaceful.

* * *

CHAPTER ELEVEN

Mika Rambush rolled from his bunk in the callous light of the very early morning and dressed in the dark, so as not to wake his sleeping comrades.

Originally from Horshcoast in the northern province of Freya, Mika was accustomed to the simpler things in life. Raised in a family with lots of children and absentee parents, he had joined the military ranks as a young man, determined to learn from the mistakes of his elders and make something of himself. This was when he met Gurrien, and later Reyla, becoming a lieutenant in time for the war before opting for a quieter life on the Palace Guard with his friends instead of responsibility and promotion.

The good life.

A simple life, with easy shifts and plenty of days off. That was the dream of all soldiers, wasn't it?

Mika met Gurrein in the corridor. He half smiled, then dropped his head with an apparent hangover acquired from the night before. Gurrein was from one town over from Mika but shaved his head and hid his accent to match the Ceynas locals. He was tall and wide when compared to the average Frey, but much of it was attributed to his arm and shoulder muscles and he had begun to look more like an upside-down triangle over the years.

"You must be getting old, Rein," Mika teased. "We only had a few, and the Hill's don't stay open that late on weekdays. We can't have been out that long."

Gurrein grumbled some unintelligible combination of words which were aimed to return the insult, but Mika only laughed.

"Come on, old man, let's grab these supplies and get on our way."

Mika patted Gurrien on the back and aimed them towards the depot. It was early enough for them to avoid the notoriously strict depot keeper, Map Flinley, allowing them to sneak around the counter and pilfer upgrades for their standard-issue short swords and shields. They also took packs and basic supplies, along with a travel cloak each, but retained their Palace Guard uniforms.

The sun was barely poking its head over the forest canopy when Mika and Gurrien arrived at the apothecary.

"Mornin'," came the soft voice of the Frey leaning against the apothecary wall. He was chewing a small wooden toothpick.

"You Illan?" asked Gurrien, his voice still raspy.

"Aye, that'd be me," Illan agreed, pushing off the wall. He nodded as Gurrien and Mika introduced themselves.

The apothecary's son's countenance was closer to that

of a feral creature than a man. His eyes were narrow and yellow, alert, catlike, and this likeness was further enforced as Illan sauntered through the forest on his tip-toes. Straight black hair sprung from his head like the crested feathers of southern cranes and it waved as he fidgeted on the spot.

"Don't know where we're off to, but you've got us for protection until we can find some of this nectar the Priestess is after," offered Mika, his long ponytail and thick accent instantly betraying him as a northern Frey who didn't know his way. "Don't suppose you know what's out there, do you?"

"Reckon it's just a bear or a nymph playing tricks on people. Heard rumour of a demon, but that's probably just this old Sudra who lives up near Grental. He likes to scare the kids away from his house whenever they get close," Illan explained, leading the two guards east to the city boundaries in a bid to keep moving. "Then again, since the sickness came in, there's been all sorts of wild tales coming out of the forests."

"I heard there's folks gone missing," Mika added, half hoping to be corrected. "Merchants not making it to their destination, even a few tales of dogs wandering off never to return."

"Not seen none of that, but them wolves are a might aggressive. Maybe the dogs decided to try it as wild uns a spell or the wolves got 'em all," Illan suggested with a carefree shrug. "We're off down near Old Wood, nothing up there but bears and rabbits normally, but mi dad's adamant that it's dangerous."

"Better safe than sorry," said Gurrien, the green returning to his cheeks as they travelled.

Mika agreed aloud but wasn't so sure the caution was necessary. Was there really a monster waiting for them in Old Wood? What could there be in the forests that was so terrible it kept people away? He looked away from the worn dirt track to the amber forest.

Autumn was here and the air was crisp but still warm enough to be pleasant. Many smaller animals zipped between brush and bloom collecting food in preparation for hibernation, and a family of deer grazed upon the fresh rosemary growing by the stream.

It all seemed perfectly safe and normal to Mika, but he was not one to grow complacent. He would do his duty, regardless of how boring it may be.

A shadow moved deep within the undergrowth as a bird burst from the brush and took flight. Mika didn't react. Birds didn't scare him. There was little that scared him these days.

He had not seen battle for many years but was a tried and tested warrior who held little fear of an enemy. Gurrien was not much different. The two of them served in the war against Sheya, making their way up the ranks the old-fashioned way. Neither had any hopes or dreams of becoming a knight and felt at home on the Queen's Guard, and they bonded further over their now rather monotonous routine and the days no one would ever miss.

"Just how rare's this flower anyway?" asked Mika.

The apothecary's son just laughed, leaving the two guards feeling rather unsettled.

"Can't be worse than boot camp, right?" Gurrien asked, turning to Mika for assurance.

Mika gave a deep chortle. "Let's hope not."

* * *

CHAPTER TWELVE

In the quiet before dusk, a hooded figure sat upon a lonely parapet, contemplating their position. Things weren't looking good.

Although she had readily accepted the praise her sisters had offered for her part in planning Elsafrey's assassination, she was unwilling to share her part in what had happened in the emperor's tent that night with anyone. How could she? If anyone found out they would surely run to Mother and she would be swiftly dealt with.

Regardless of her intentions, she had gone behind everyone's back and acted alone; against the will of the Sisterhood. Had the emperor perished, things would have been different. She would be able to call out their mother's failings and her sisters would turn to her for guidance.

But that's not how things happened.

The sun hung low behind her, painting the cloudless sky orange and red. Dark shadows stretched across the sand from square sandstone buildings, but Sudra still roamed the paths on their way between taverns and bed. In the distance, dots of light appeared in the sky as torches were set alight along the plateau.

Her heart ached as she longed to return to the palace and the temple below, but it was impossible. The Sudran palace was protected against unwanted entry and filled with empire soldiers; so it would be difficult to explain her presence if she were caught walking through the front door.

She had returned home that evening with hopes of finding some clarity – some sense of direction – but sitting alone on the city outskirts only exacerbated her isolation. There was no one she could turn to for guidance or support. Not her Mother. Not her sisters. Not even the Gods could help her now.

She released a long, hopeless breath. Her plan had been a complete failure. Her actions only worked to strengthen the empire and weaken her position. What could she do other than return to Mother and hope no one noticed her indiscretions?

Although she couldn't deny that the potion had worked for the most part. It had stripped the two leaders of their inhibitions and reduced them to their base urges as she had intended. Given Drazah's untimely demise, she had assumed that those urges would be enough to drive Nymati to do what her king could not, but, evidently, Nymati's appetite had outweighed her grief.

She picked at rubble she found on the parapet, bits of grit and sand blown up from the desert, until reaching a pebble she could throw into the horizon with her frustrations.

How could she have been so naive? She of all people should know not to underestimate Nymati or her appetite.

This oversight had cost her everything. Her chance at leadership. Her chance at freedom.

Even so, they could not continue under the leadership of their absentee mother. She had to do something before the empire became too powerful; before their mother drove their plans into ruin. Not that anyone could stop them now. Dark mana already filled the Manastream and the only thing standing in their way were two hapless Frey.

The cloaked figure rose from the parapet and turned to the horizon. This was not the time for moping around and licking wounds. It was the time for action.

Her sisters needed her. She couldn't just abandon them because of one oversight; because of Nymati. She wouldn't.

It was time for Alamantra to change, but she could change nothing as she was.

She drew in her courage, her eyes firmly on the palace as she found her resolve.

"Perictara."

With the cursed words she called upon her dark artes and returned to her master in a cloud of smoke.

But her time would come…

* * *

A Guard's Request

OBLIGATION

10 MONTHS BMF

* * *

Many times I paused to consider my duty.

It was my job only to watch.

I was not of their world,

but over time these mortals became my children,

my friends.

A Duran philosopher once asked

what mortals owed to each other,

but even now I wonder;

What do I owe them?

* * *

CHAPTER ONE

Sweat dripped from Mika's brow as he gulped down air, his shoulders heaving as he pressed against a rock face.

"This is madness," he hissed at Gurrien. "What kinda creature can take that amount of damage?"

A putrid black liquid dripped from Gurrein's sword. He had managed to get in a few hits before their retreat, but Mika hadn't even seen the beast to describe it. All he saw was the flash of bloody teeth amidst a giant shadow that descended upon their camp.

Mika peered around the rock, squinting. It was dark and deathly quiet. The canopy seemed to press down upon them like a cavern ready to fall in at any given moment. Fog blanketed the forest floor in a perpetual grey-blue haze that clung to his clothes and left the air so dense he could practically chew on each breath.

He had been to Old Wood Prison before, but camping in the wilds was something else. It was like living every scary campfire story all at once, but they had no choice if they wanted to find the hushin nectar for High Priestess Arafrey.

The trees in Old Wood were knobbly and twisted into

each other, making it impossible to see far. Their greyed barks ate any moonlight managing to break through the canopy and oozed with black sap that ran thick as tar.

The hair prickled at the nape of Mika's neck. "And here I thought Old Wood was already pretty creepy."

Gurrien grumbled. "Never saw owt like that in boot camp."

"I tolt you there's summat wrong out here. We should keep moving, it's not safe," Illan warned, blood splattered across his face.

"You said there was a flower patch near here, right?" Mika asked the apothecary's son. "How far?"

"If we keep north, we should reach another patch in less than an hour." Illan pointed.

They had already found some hushin nectar and seeds, but it was hardly sufficient enough to begin a full-scale operation. There had been a few more places they could have searched, but that was no longer an option since they had abandoned their camp and supplies.

Illan turned back, frowning as an ominous growl cut through the forest. "We can't keep this up much longer."

A high-pitched howl echoed through the forest and the trees shuddered about them. Mika ducked reflexively and searched for the source, but the fog clouded his senses. Whatever followed them was canine in nature, but it attacked without provocation and hunted relentlessly. It wasn't something they could just leave to roam Old Wood unchecked, but neither was it something they could deal with in their current position.

Mika swallowed as Gurrien sucked his teeth, no doubt having reached the same conclusion.

"Right, then. We make this the last one," Mika said finally. "These samples won't be any good to anyone if we don't get them back to the priestess. We can come back for this thing another time."

"Aye, we've not many options," Gurrien agreed.

"I say we make like Cheddicks and flit. Hopefully, it won't follow us out of Old Wood," said Illan. He was hardly unfit, but didn't have the stamina for prolonged combat and was already struggling to keep up. "Arafrey can't complain about what we've got. We're lucky we got any at all this late in the season."

"Then we're agreed. We make a run for it and rest up once we're out of Old Wood."

Mika adjusted his gear as he straightened. So much for their quiet life on the Palace Guard, he thought.

"Tails in gear," he rallied, patting Gurrein and Illan each on the back. "Shoot for gold, fellas. We can sleep for a week when we're safe at home."

* * *

CHAPTER TWO

Callius escaped the confines of his carriage to the marble stairs of the Duran palace. He breathed in the magnificent structure, glad to be back home in Rhoda.

The double doors opened, drawing his attention as Julius Gabris appeared wearing a navy tunic draped with an emerald toga. Julius held his arms wide as he approached.

"Cousin, you made good time," he called with a toothy grin. "It's good to have you home."

"It's good to be home," Callius replied as the pair embraced.

Julius was the first son of Callius' uncle, Marven, who had recently passed, making him second in line for the Duran throne. Without his support in running the kingdom, Callius would not have been able to leave on his conquest and build his empire, but their relationship had always been more of a working one; his cousin could never seem to remove the giant stick from his rectum.

"Could you tell the kitchen to prepare food and see Nymati's staff to their quarters?"

"Of course. I've arranged bedrooms on the second floor for your guests," Julius added, the reservation in his voice no doubt directed at the Sudra as he watched Nymati and her sons disembark from their carriages with a raised eyebrow.

Callius' heart filled his chest.

Nymati appeared to glow in the golden sun. She wore a plain linen dress, which wrapped around her body and trailed from her knees. Many layers of golden chains hung from her shoulders and waist, and golden bangles jangled over her wrists and ankles. Her breasts appeared naked without the giant ruby of her necklace and – while he wasn't complaining – Callius reminded himself to find a suitable jeweller when he found the time.

Amynus shirked over to Nymati and shrugged his features instead of saying anything directly to any of them. Callius found his brooding aura and likeness to Drazah unnerving. He would have to keep as close an eye on Amynus as he did Nymati, but at least he knew the latter wasn't actively trying to kill him at present.

Malaki, on the other hand, was more his mother's son, with raven hair and ruby eyes. He kept his head nestled into her waist as he wrapped around her. Callius wasn't familiar with children but he thought that Malaki's infantile nature seemed to be much younger than his age – although he was unsure how to approach the subject with Nymati.

"Should I have prepared the nursery?"

"No." Callius' chest clenched with sudden strain. He could allow no one to disturb the sanctity of that room. "But could you arrange for the council to convene first thing in the morning? We have much to discuss."

"Of course, Eminence." Julius bowed, flashing the balding spot on the very top of his head. He then returned to the palace.

Callius admired the alabaster structure, his sights drawn along the sash windows of the second floor to rest upon the nursery. He had preserved the room as it was, creating a shrine to those he lost and, while his proposal to Nymati would suggest he was already moving on, he wasn't quite ready to forget his past just yet.

"Your palace is magnificent," came Nymati's voice, calling his thoughts back to the present.

"Would you like the tour before dinner?" He forced a wonky smile.

"That would be lovely." Nymati smiled. Still marvelling at the architecture, she said, "Aeryn, I trust you can sort the luggage. Amynus. Malaki. Come."

Nymati hooked Amynus by the arm as Callius led them into the palace. Malaki ran ahead as they entered the foyer, looking back every so often like a pet dog checking to see he hadn't strayed too far from his owner.

They turned into the drawing room, allowing Callius to set the stage for their grand tour. Paintings of Gabris ancestors lined the walls, their majesty greeting their guests through the power of paint and Duran artistry. A low table sat between tall-backed sofas with crimson velvet upholstery where he and Tidus had hosted many a fine Duran lady in their younger days.

"We tend to greet our honoured guests in this room," Callius explained, crossing to the double doors. "That way we can easily show them to the trophy rooms."

He beamed with pride as the doors opened to reveal the first of two trophy rooms. This one he had dedicated to art and music, covering the walls with his favourite paintings and displays holding antiques and sculptures he had acquired on his travels. A particular favourite of his – a full-sized harp carved from polished Red Wood – filled one corner. The wood was imported from Freya and chiselled by Davinchus, one the finest Duran artisans of the era, and he made sure to tell Nymati as much as they passed.

The tour continued as he led them to the connecting hall. The double doors were propped open by polished brass doorstops shaped like roaring lions. Callius straightened as he entered and watched Nymati's reaction with heated anticipation of her Sudran fancies.

The displays were filled with grand armour, legendary weapons and hunting trophies of his ancestors. The relics and prizes of this room spanned many generations of Gabris history with some even dating back to the First Ones – if the plaques were to be believed anyway. In the centre, a stuffed lion raised above a pedestal: a taxidermy monument to the power of the Gabris lineage and a proven hit with the ladies.

Malaki marvelled at the mighty beast and reached out to touch its mane, only to find his hand smacked away by Nymati.

"It's okay, you can stroke him. This fella's been in here longer than I have." Callius found a lopsided smirk across his face as he ran a wide hand through the lion's mane, his heart a little warmer. "It's tradition to stroke his mane for good luck before heading into battle."

Malaki rushed to bury his hands into the thick hair and began combing it through his fingers. He turned up to look back at them, joyous, unlike his brother whose face seemed incapable of doing anything but frown.

"The rest of the wing is offices. But, if you'll follow me..." He encouraged them towards the corridor. "This is the throne hall. We host most of our social functions here."

The throne hall ran between the two wings of the palace: a wide hall with Duran banners of golden suns on a field of crimson hung upon the walls. Tall doors ran in pairs along one wall, which opened out onto the veranda, allowing the midday sun to enter. Mosaic tiles covered the floor in an intricate pattern that framed a bronzed sun that lay in the centre of the hall below a circular candelabra.

Callius was drawn to the gilded throne sitting solitary upon a dais of marble. Its high back swept down into wide armrests with ornate lions set into each. Padded cushions in rich red velvet upholstery filled the seat.

Callius pressed his lips. Normally the view filled him with pride, but this time he found it rather lonesome. Already, his stomach ran giddy, his thoughts racing to recover the throne's twin from storage. But he was getting ahead of himself again.

They left through terrace doors onto the garden veranda. The palace walls wrapped around the manicured flowerbeds. An ivy-covered trellis arched over paved paths connecting the wings of the palace. Golden honeysuckle and vibrant red roses filled their sights, their flowers blooming through the autumn chill.

Callius guided them deeper into the maze of red and gold. Here their paths crossed with a pair of familiar faces.

"Ah, Paullus, good timing," said Callius.

Paullus Fegril was a stout man with greying cinnamon hair that was slicked back to disguise the parts where it thinned. He was attached to the Gabris family through his mother, but had inherited neither their strong jawline nor broad shoulders. What he did have, however, was a nose for business – Paullus could smell an opportunity to make gold as if it were freshly baked cake.

His antithesis, the woman beside him – his daughter Antita – was a radiant beauty. Her hair sat in golden ringlets that swung forward as she bowed, returning to rest upon a thick teal palla she had wrapped around her arms to protect her from the cold.

"Allow me to introduce you to Nymati Tamun and her son Amynus." Callius indicated them with his hand. He would have introduced Malaki also, but he had lost sight of him in the posies. "Nymati will be joining the council from now on. Her insights into Sudra's economy will be invaluable going forward."

"Nice to meet you," replied Paullus, stopping himself as he reached for her hand. Nymati returned a tight smile but made no attempts to greet him. "This is my daughter, Antita." Paullus indicated her with his hand, prompting her to curtsey. She smiled, her eyes lingering on Amynus as she dipped and righted herself.

"Paullus is Master of Coin, so you'll be seeing a lot of each other," Callius explained.

"I look forward to working with you," said Nymati, her voice so even it was difficult to decide how genuine she was being.

They exchanged several further pleasantries before bidding the two farewell and continuing through the gardens.

"I think she liked you," Nymati cooed, pulling Amynus in playfully as they walked.

Amynus rolled his eyes. Having already been witness to it many times, Callius was growing accustomed to Nymati's teasing. Still, it wasn't his place to raise his concerns, so he remained quiet as they continued along the garden path.

"Maybe you should consider taking a Duran bride and settling down. It's certainly a step up from frequenting the whore houses down the Narrows," Nymati snipped, as Amynus quietly simmered.

Callius wasn't sure he agreed with Nymati's methods, but it was preferable to his father's cold combat-hardened shoulder. Not that his mother had been much warmer; her interests were limited to only his accomplishments that she could flaunt to her socialite friends.

"You know, perhaps it's for the best you've no crown to inherit. I've long dreaded the day your bastard child turns up at the palace doors looking for handouts."

"You know, I don't have to put up with this," Amynus belted out and scrambled from her grasp. He huffed and stormed off through the gardens.

Callius paused, unsure what to do. "Do you want to go after him?"

"No. Leave him be." Nymati shook her head in dismay. "At that age, a mother's scorn is far less effective than embarrassment. If he's uncomfortable talking about his actions, then perhaps he should refrain from doing them."

Callius smirked and watched as Malaki followed ladybirds and beetles around the roses. Again, he saw the logic, but was unsure about Nymati's execution.

"I've arranged for a tutor to come to the palace for Malaki. He's the best in the empire," he offered, hoping his generosity would ease the tension. "We also have the animal gardens here in Rhoda. You should take him."

"Thank you," Nymati replied, fluttering thick eyelashes in his direction. "I know you've no obligation to be so kind."

Callius rubbed the back of his neck as he floundered. "Would you rather I am unkind?" His ego smarted from the implication.

"No, I suppose not." She pursed her lips.

"You're not my prisoner. You're under no obligation to be here and the guards are under no orders to stop you, should you wish to leave. While this is a business arrangement, I'd rather prefer it if you were to think of this palace as a home."

Nymati wet her lips, but held her words.

The pair watched as Malaki rummaged through the flower beds. He pricked his finger on a rose bush and ran over to Nymati, his finger held out for her to see. It surprised Callius that he wasn't crying for attention or wanting it kissed better as he expected a child to do – especially one as infantile as Malaki. The boy showed his mother the mark with pride, the blood slowly oozing from his finger.

Malaki wiped his bloodied finger down his clothes as his mother praised him and returned to the flowers with a grin on his face. Callius was still trying to decide if it was a cultural difference when Nymati finally replied.

"I may not be under duress, but I do have an obligation." Nymati's voice remained solemn as she continued watching her son. "I have an obligation to my children, and to my people. However, it is a burden I bear with pride. I will do all I can to ensure the future of my children, and I shall accomplish my task by any means necessary."

Callius fought to keep his composure and remain placid, but her honesty cut like a knife. It served as a brutal reminder that perhaps Nymati didn't wish to be there in the first place. Despite all their dinners and idle merriment, he would always be the man who had bested her king and captured her kingdom.

Callius cleared his throat. "We should head to the dining hall, our food should be ready by now." He led them back into the palace. "Should I send someone to find Amynus?"

"He's old enough to fend for himself. Although I have long learnt not to underestimate my son's ability to attract drama, I at least have the hope that with no gold and no allies, he won't be too much trouble," Nymati replied, her nostrils flaring ever so slightly.

Callius couldn't help but wonder what kind of trouble an eighteen-year-old would be able to cause in Rhoda these days. He and Tidus had certainly found their fair share. At the very least, Nymati seemed disinterested in her son's outburst, so he supposed it was a common occurrence.

'The joys of parenting.' He smiled to himself.

* * *

Amynus stormed from the palace, planning on searching for a bar or whatever passed for a winery in the Duran capital – he had already forgotten the name.

By the carriages still parked outside, Saffia pushed onto her tiptoes, balancing on a wooden stool as she reached for the luggage above. Her tail swung out to hold her balance, her dusty-blonde ponytail swishing between her shoulder blades as the stool rocked unevenly. She strained as she pulled on a trunk and her balance wavered.

"Here, allow me," Amynus offered, rushing to shoulder the weight.

"Thank you." She smiled, their eyes meeting as she lowered to the stool.

Amynus turned away. The pair had not spoken since their meeting in the Dusty Lock. An uncomfortable silence hung between them as they took in the gargantuan palace. He wanted to ask why she hadn't sought him out while travelling. He was curious how she had managed to sustain herself so well when Feliss was practically ravenous. But he would ask nothing for fear of appearing weak or wanting in front of her.

"It's very beautiful, isn't it?" asked Saffia quietly.

"If you're into that kinda thing." He folded his arms across his chest.

"I hear even the poorest in Dura eat like kings. That their beds are made of goose feathers and their clothes the finest silk."

"Yeah, well, don't believe all you hear…"

Amynus was still unsure how to act around Saffia. He took some comfort in the fact his mother have been quick to chastise or tease him if Saffia had told her of their encounter. However, the wounds left by Taldi's betrayal ran deep, and he feared it was only a matter of time before Saffia would betray him too.

"I thought perhaps I would see how you were settling in later," said Saffia plainly. Amynus raised a brow as he turned to check her expression, but her malachite gaze gave little away.

"I'd like that," he replied hesitantly.

"I-"

They halted like naughty children, as Aeryn and Feliss emerged from the palace to collect their luggage, each wearing cream smocks and cotton gloves.

"I better get going." He smiled, turning towards the city.

As he walked away, Amynus wondered if he had made the correct decision. Although he had little choice if he wanted to continue his training – and he doubted the women in Dura would be willing to indulge him after hearing of their nature from Sabutok.

Amynus strained his ears to listen as Aeryn approached.

"What did he want?"

"Nothing. Be careful, that one's heavy."

Amynus breathed easy and looked to the skies. The sun was beginning its descent, giving him plenty of time to explore the city and decide what he was going to do about Saffia. Although, by rumble stirring in his loins, some parts of him had already decided.

* * *

CHAPTER THREE

Having first taken a boat from Alensya to Tepps, Reyla and Tharin had long left Sheya, following the trade route to Ruglor, cutting east through southern Agrana. The road was long and quiet as they entered the marshes, their days of travelling made all the more gruelling by the turbulence of the weather.

It had rained the entire time.

Reyla pulled her cloak close as a bitter wind cut the landscape. Short and spindly trees groaned, offering little cover as they swayed, their trunks strangled by creeping vines and moss. As Wilona had promised, a path allowed them safe passage through the marshes. While it was more of a dirt track, it saved them from wading through waist-high water-logged swamps.

Reyla found it disconcerting that they were yet to pass any other travellers. For a supposed trade route to be so quiet made no sense to her, there was surely more activity on the Freya by-roads than here in Agrana.

She tried not to think about it too deeply. The Agrana lived underground, so she and Tharin would be unlikely to encounter them on the surface, but there appeared to be some truth behind the rumours of missing merchants.

Reyla scanned the landscape for signs of life or disturbances as she tried to piece together an explanation.

It was always possible wild animals were to blame, especially given their aggression in Pudron, but they had seen no signs of anything bigger than a bird in days. Although the Agrana were not known for violence, they were known for being hostile towards outsiders and overly protective of their technology, so it wouldn't have surprised her if a few enterprising adventurers had decided to leave the path in search of a city only to become lost. Even so, for a well-known trade route to be left seemingly abandoned left a foul taste in her mouth.

Near two weeks after leaving Sheya, the mud path finally met the Agrana section of the Ballish, where a bridge stretched to the other side of the river. The stone appeared to grow from the ground in a similar way to how Frey architecture was grown from trees. It arced smoothly over the wide river with an impossibly square, stone frame.

Reyla ran her hand over the sleek stone as they crossed.

"I don't think I've ever seen Rugla artes used like this before, or even at all now I'm thinking about it," said Tharin. He shrugged, and inspected the designs again. "I guess it's alright looking, though I can't imagine their houses are very warm."

"I don't think they live in houses – at least that's what I

heard."

"Then what d'they live in?"

"I dunno, but it's not like they need roofs under the mountain, is it?"

On the other side of the river, they found a small shelter that had been raised similarly to the bridge. The three-walled structure formed into a pointed roof with a squared awning which covered a small fire pit. It wasn't much, but it offered the two weary travellers somewhere dry to make their camp.

Reyla checked the sun. "It's still a bit early, but I doubt we'll find a better place."

"We should remember this trick once we learn Rugla artes," Tharin suggested while dropping his gear to the ground. "Could come in useful."

Reyla did likewise and smirked. "Perhaps you should master the artes you have before making plans for the next ones."

Tharin chuckled and tossed her his water pouch before leaving the safety of the shelter to scavenge for firewood.

Reyla left him to it and delved into her backpack to check supplies. Their food rations weren't looking great: jam, potatoes, nuts and some sorry-looking apples. Unfortunately, there was little to scavenge from their path, the fruits and berries presumably picked clean by passers-by – wherever they may be.

Reyla collected the tin pot from her gear and their water pouches, then ran to the river to fill them up. The water from the Ballish ran south steadily but was dark and murky. She scooped water into the tin and lifted it to her nose for a sniff. Reyla's nose wrinkled at the smell, but she filled their pouches nonetheless – it wasn't like they had any other options.

She returned to the shelter and considered the difference in water quality compared to the crystalline rivers of Freya and Sheya and quietly pondered upon how she had taken them for granted. Although she had never been to Sudra, it was common knowledge that the Ballish provided water for much of their population. She supposed they also used that water to bathe and water their crops – but she resolved to boil the water and leave it to cool just to be safe. The last thing they needed was to become sick from the water while travelling – they were at risk enough from the weather and sleeping rough.

Tharin appeared with a stack of soaked timber in his arms and dropped it on the floor beside the fire pit as he took a seat. His socks squelched as he removed his shoes, and he sat them aside to dry while they set about making dinner.

Reyla started building the fire as a new wave of hail battered their shelter.

She despised the weather, but couldn't deny the practice it allowed them with their new artes. The many sores on their waterlogged feet they could soothe with

Frey healing artes. Their campfires were brought to life by Pudran fire, and they dried their drenched clothes by pulling the water from the fabrics with Shey artes. Although, Tharin often struggled to differentiate between his artes and had set his clothes alight more than once.

Now she had a feel for them, Reyla had no such issues, but still found her abilities lacking when it came to healing artes. They each started the same as mana drew from her core into her palm, activating her artes, but the colours changed depending on her intent. With Frey artes, the mana was cool and collected in the palm, the glow pure and white. Shey artes started the same but were blue and bitterly cold. They reminded Reyla of Frey artes as she used their power to extend her control over water and manipulate it with her will. Pudra fire artes were similar, except the mana burned hot and orange in her palm before sparking to life in her hands. While she could hold the fire in place, Reyla lacked any real control over the flames, and reserved their use for lighting their campfires.

Reyla piled a small collection of branches in a firepit. She held her hands over the pile, activating her artes so her palms glowed blue. The branches began to sweat as water rose to the surface. Defying gravity, the beads of moisture then collected beneath her hands in a floating ball of water.

Happy she had drawn enough water from the branches, Reyla whipped her hand to the side and cast the water past the boundaries of the shelter. She shook her hand as if to reset her artes before summoning fire to her palm. The base of the kindling crackled and popped as she held the flame close and pushed upon her artes to encourage it further.

"So, what's for dinner?" asked Tharin. His artes activated as he drew water from his clothing and flicked it away.

"We should fill up on apples." Reyla collected one from her pack and flipped it his way over the growing fire. "They're not going to last much longer."

"We still have some biscuit-bread saved."

"We can save that until last." Reyla wasn't fond of the stuff, but it was full of nutrients and seldom decayed. "We should prioritise perishables."

"You know, it's not so bad if you dip it in jam," Tharin teased as if reading her mind. "How long do you think we have 'til reaching Ruglor anyway?"

"Maybe a week," Reyla offered, looking to the black horizon to see nothing but clouds. "Assuming that river's the Ballish, the terrain should start going up soon. Just keep checking your ring."

She placed the tin of water on the fire to make tea, her feet tapping to the internal melody of her growing concern.

Rain was one thing but camping in adverse conditions was only going to grow more difficult as they reached the end of the year. Ruglor and Askana were the northernmost nations of Alamantra and each was known for their harsh winters. However, she noted, Ruglor was far easier to reach than Askana – finding a way to cross the sea may prove as problematic for them as entering the empire. Even more so if the rumours of Askana closing their borders were to be believed.

"How do you think everyone back home is doing?" asked Tharin, unhelpfully giving voice to the other thought Reyla was trying to avoid.

"I'm sure they're fine." She flashed a reassuring smile. "They're probably more worried about us."

He smiled back and his shoulders dropped as he breathed through his nose. His breath cast smoke on the cold air. It was already much colder than they were accustomed to and the chances of finding somewhere to purchase winter gear were growing slimmer by the day.

Reyla blamed herself for not thinking about the weather sooner. The oversight was a grave one set to hinder them in more ways than she could imagine, and she found no comfort in the knowledge that the first time they saw snow may also be their last.

"Here, drink up. We need to keep warm." She passed Tharin a mug of tea. "The weather's only going to get worse from here..."

* * *

CHAPTER FOUR

As autumn neared its end, the Kingdom of Freya gathered in prayer. Citizens bowed their heads within the embrace of the Life Tree and passed their wishes for a gentle winter as shrewd darkness set upon the forest.

The changing seasons brought an unusually cold wind, followed by torrential rain and rumbling thunder. Many festivals were cancelled due to the conditions, leaving morale even lower as the spreading sickness raged on.

The intense weather was but one of the changes drawing in as a result of the poison running through the Manastream. Crops didn't yield as much as they normally would have, leaving stores low. Rivers burst their banks and animals attacked for sport, leaving half-eaten carcasses strewn throughout the forests like carnivorous bunting. Sentries were stationed all over the city, in full armour, making their peaceful home feel more like a military camp. In Pudron, they had resorted to fencing off their villages in an attempt to protect themselves, something the Frey were considering.

As a small positive, Arafrey's balm did much to alleviate the suffering of those infected with the sickness, but there was nothing she could do to stop it from spreading. The leaders of the Frey warned their people away from using artes, but it was a thankless task and many refused to stop.

It all seemed rather hopeless. The whole of Freya suffered, and none felt it more than High Priestess Arafrey as she stood before the congregation, leading them in prayer.

"At times like these we give thanks to the Life Tree for watching over us," she projected to the courtyard, her eyes gliding over the hollow faces of those sitting in the pews. "However, as the Life Tree's colour turns, I ask that we give thanks to those risking infection to synthesise the soothing balm we have today. Give thanks to those working through their pain and pray that those working towards a cure shall find it soon."

The general public knew nothing of Reyla and Tharin's quest, but even so, she hoped they would hear their prayers. Although Arafrey had never placed much faith in the Gods, she believed in Reyla and Tharin. Knowing they were out there, searching for a cure, was the single remaining hope she clung to. If anyone could save Alamantra, it would be them, of that she was certain.

"Let us pray," she said, holding her hands together and bowing her head before continuing with the sermon for that day.

Arafrey passed on the teachings of Auldafrey with a heart of ice. She had no right to preach the words of the god she had once denied. Even the absolute proof of his being was not enough to repair the rift she felt between her heart and religion. She held no connection to the sermons she spoke. Each word passing her lips was as empty and sanctimonious as her supposedly salacious social life. Her people could look up to her from the pews for a thousand years and the fact would remain the same: *she was a fraud.*

Like all Frey, Arafrey respected nature and refrained from eating meat, but felt their collective values had changed over the years. While she took no issue with the teachings of Auldafrey on their own, she had long taken issue with the way her people chose to interpret them and was loath to perpetuate their misguidance.

'Besides,' she thought. *'What's the point in reciting his words to an audience who only heard what they wished to hear?'*

"You may collect the soothing balm from me as you come to the front. I ask that you refrain from activating your artes or connecting to the Life Tree as you pray," Arafrey announced after a moment of silence. She motioned towards the pool behind her, its mystic blue now more of a murky teal as it glowed within the roots of the Life Tree.

The temple aides brought out wicker baskets filled with small tubs of the soothing balm as Frey formed an orderly queue up to the manapool and down the aisle. They took it in turns to kneel, each casting their prayers into the glowing pool before moving on.

Arafrey greeted them each in turn, offering the balm

without question as they passed. Many Frey had visible streaks of black across their cheeks, and their eyes were sunken and dull. Some were unsteady on their feet and swayed as they queued. Others could barely hold their heads up, their eyelids hanging heavily as their pupils rolled.

Arafrey maintained her post as the queue shortened and the baskets emptied until there was only one Frey left.

He wore fine robes of chocolate brown with honey-coloured embroidery detail, leading her to believe he was a noble Frey. However, his hair was cut short like those of the lower class, the straight blackberry-coloured lengths barely covering his pointed ears.

"I'm sorry, that was the last of the soothing balm." Arafrey turned the basket apologetically as evidence. "If you come back tomorrow–"

"Actually, I was hoping I could speak with you," he chimed, sharp, fox-red eyes burning against his juniper skin as he smiled.

"Oh?" Arafrey stepped back, her narrowed eyes running up and down him to gauge his intentions, but his countenance was set and unyielding.

"The name's Miles Chadwin," he offered, extending his hand toward her.

"Ah. So, you're the merchant who's making waves," she mused, shaking his hand with the stiffness of several growing suspicions.

Arafrey righted herself to disguise the cold panic that grasped her lungs. She could think of no reason he would want to speak to her. She was certain she required nothing of him. Did her father put him up to this?

A smile formed as Arafrey's mask set back into place and bridled her thoughts. "It's nice to finally make your acquaintance."

"Likewise. I know you're a busy woman, so I shan't dance around the bush. I hear you may be in the market for hushin nectar." Miles grinned as Arafrey failed to hide her surprise. "I have an offer you may be interested in."

"You heard correctly. However, I'm afraid you'll have to speak with my father about that as Captain Valren is overseeing production," said Arafrey, the trace of bitterness in her tone aimed directly at the Captain.

Miles glanced to either side before looking back at her. "And I shall take my offer to him, but first, I have an offer for you."

"For me?" Arafrey asked, her suspicion rising.

"Yes, you see, I just happen to have sourced a fair amount, and I would be willing to give the crown my entire stock. Free of charge. Plus any more I may happen to source until the scourge has passed."

"And what would you have in return?"

He flashed a cheeky smile. "An evening of your time, My Lady. That is all I ask."

"I'm not in the habit of prostituting my time, Mr Chadwin," Arafrey hissed. *The audacity!* She turned to call upon her guards, but Miles swung around to meet her.

"I mean no offence, Your Grace. None at all," he corrected, his confidence never wavering. "Priestess, I assure you, I merely appreciate the valuable commodity of your time. One dinner, nothing more, of that I swear."

Arafrey's jaw clenched as she narrowed her eyes further. Did he seriously just use her people as an excuse to ask her out on a date? She didn't respond.

"Just think about it," Miles added, turning casually to leave. "But think fast, I won't withhold my stock should Captain Valren come asking."

Arafrey could have breathed fire as Miles Chadwin walked away. Her eyes glared with murderous intent at the back of his head in the hope that it might spontaneously explode if she wished for it hard enough.

If hushin nectar wasn't such a rare commodity she would have refused him there and then. But as the courtyard doors closed, she came to realise that it was an offer she could not refuse.

Which only made her despise him more.

* * *

Arafrey spent several hours checking on her patients

before returning to the palace.

Normally, she would ascend the polished staircase and return to her bedroom promptly, but today she turned to the dining room on the ground floor. It was still busy when she entered.

All the furniture had been cleared to make way for eight workbenches, arranged into two rows. Several Frey gathered around each, and the surfaces were littered with the materials and tools required to make the soothing balm. Baskets sat at the end of each row where the readied pots were placed.

"Ah, Priestess. To what do I owe the pleasure?" asked Captain Valren, coming to greet her.

"We're out of soothing balm in the temple."

"We have another batch ready for distribution, but King Rayner sent a request after their princess took ill," Valren replied, his long face tired and grey.

He looked ghastly, no doubt exhausted from months of shouldering the king's duties as her father mourned in his office. As she was standing there, she noticed that every so often his mouth would tighten when he moved, as if he were in pain. Arafrey had never noticed it before and thought perhaps he was afflicted with the sickness himself, but neither of these facts was enough for her to warm to him any as their rivalry blossomed.

"In that case, prioritise a batch for Pudron. It will take longer to travel than it will to synthesise a new batch."

"Indeed. Although, another synthesiser has taken ill and few unaffected are willing to volunteer," added Valren, much to her concern. "That makes six now."

"If it comes to it, we will have to skip synthesis and go with the normal soothing balm," she replied, although that would quadruple their hushin nectar requirements. "How are our nectar supplies?"

"At the current rate, we have only a few weeks' worth." Valren's brow wrinkled as his silver eyebrows pinched. "I've sent a few groups back into Old Wood, but it's becoming dangerous. We've yet to identify the creature roaming there."

Arafrey sighed. Even with the seeds and nectar brought back from Old Wood, they were a long way off cultivating enough to treat everyone in Ceynas. Despite her wishing the contrary, Mr Chadwin's offer was beginning to look quite appealing. The thought remained that she could always tell Captain Valren to seek him out should she choose to decline the offer herself – but that didn't change the fact that hushin nectar was rare and the cost was already straining the palace coffers. For all the good it would do for her people, what harm would it cause to have one dinner with Miles Chadwin? It certainly wouldn't be the worst thing she had ever done for her kingdom.

"I'll speak with the apothecary, I need to visit him anyway," she offered, quietly considering the depleted vial of Savulin Tonic in her bedside cabinet. "Could you inform me if we run out in the meantime?"

"Of course," Valren replied, nodding his head.

* * *

Arafrey ate dinner in her bedroom, alone.

She washed and readied for bed in silence, her thoughts deafening. No matter how she tried to ignore them, her thoughts consisted only of Miles Chadwin and his offer.

His face became imprinted on her mind, all pointed and smug. She could think of few whose very face made her boil with such fury, and thinking upon them all at once only added to her anger and frustrations.

Who was he to command her attention for so long? She had a great many matters she should be more concerned with, yet all she could think about was him. It was, in her mind at least, a great detriment to their kingdom that he would distract her like this during a crisis, and she could not forgive him for that, no matter his intentions.

"Anything else, Your Grace?" asked Ceal as she collected an empty plate from the table.

"No, that's all. You're dismissed. Thank you."

Ceal bowed and left the room, the door clicking shut behind her.

Alone, Arafrey released a heavy sigh of relief, her body

dropping with her facade.

The illusion of the perfect priestess was proving harder to maintain than ever before. The only time she found any peace was in the moments before bed, but it was a double-edged sword. It was easy to disguise among her staff and parishioners, but while alone her isolation stretched to fill the quiet of her bedroom, leaving her to consider all that she was missing. All she had lost.

As she crossed her bedroom, Arafrey found herself wishing her mother were there to tell her what to do. She wished Reyla were there to listen. She wished her father would give her even the smallest amount of affection. She wished for someone to notice, then wished for no one to notice at all, for she would rather be forgotten than have them find out the truth of who she really was.

Arafrey's heart grew heavy as she climbed into bed, the covers cold as she pulled them over her. Alone.

Even among her peers, she stood alone, but she would never let them know her pain. How could she? She was their light, their sun. A solitary star tasked with lighting their way through good times and bad.

She wondered what would happen to her kingdom should that light ever be extinguished…

Arafrey reached into her bedside table to retrieve her vial of Savulin Tonic. She had continued taking it before bed each night in hopes of deterring her headaches, but she was careful to take only two drops, being cautious of its addictive nature. So far, it had proven effective. However, should she miss a dose, her headache would return with a vengeance, and she would be no use to anyone the next day.

Arafrey placed two drops under her tongue and replaced the vial in her bedside cabinet. She dropped her head to the pillows, closing her eyes as the tonic entered her system.

Her thoughts returned to Miles Chadwin's offer.

Would it be so terrible to have dinner with him? He had only invited her to dinner, after all. She would owe him nothing if she accepted, yet, somehow, the idea made her feel dirty.

Her breathing shallowed and her cheeks warmed as the tonic took hold. It became harder for Arafrey to hold her thoughts as her head grew light and the image of Miles Chadwin became no more than a brown and purple smudge on her consciousness.

Each woe slipped from her grasp like seeds blown from a dandelion until there was nothing left but the darkness behind her eyelids and the determination that Miles Chadwin would pass her thoughts no longer.

* * *

CHAPTER FIVE

Emperor Gabris found his return to Dura to be quite a relief.

He had never enjoyed the administrative duties that came with ruling an empire, but neither did he enjoy allowing others to do it for him. Delegating tasks required a level of trust that he was loath to give the vast majority of his cousins, but therein lay the true labours of ruling – dealing with people. Thankfully, Nymati was around to cushion the blow as he returned to his work. Callius was even a little excited as he reclaimed his seat at the head of the council table that morning.

The council's meetings were held in the palace down a corridor off the throne hall, and next door to the emperor's office. A Duran banner, a golden sun on a bed of crimson, hung between the two sash windows and the back wall was lined with bookshelves holding official documents and papers. A long, rectangular table made from thick oak with a world map of questionable accuracy burned into its surface filled most of the room. Today, it was set with twelve chairs.

His council was composed of ten men, each with their

own branch of expertise. At every meeting, they would arrive with a list of topics they wished to discuss and the eleven of them would continue through lunch until no issues remained, regularly pressed for time. This time, however, was slightly different.

"Julius apprised me of the situation. But before we discuss matters, I have an announcement." Callius cleared his throat as his niggling doubts became raging beasts that snipped at his confidence. He would have to choose his next words very carefully. "You'll notice I asked Lady Nymati to join us today."

He turned to his left as Nymati smiled at the rest of the table. She had adopted Duran attire since their arrival, this time a cream tunic draped with an olive toga, but the neckline still plunged deep into her bosom. Nymati had also replaced her gloves with a pair in black lace that ran up to her elbows.

"I've asked her to remain in Dura and join us on the council to advise on Sudran affairs." There was a muttering of confusion among the council, but not the uproar Callius had expected, and his apprehensions simmered. "Now what's first on the agenda?"

Nymati remained quiet as the council descended into discussion, her lips tightly pressed as she listened. Callius imagined she found it all as overwhelming as he found Sudran affairs and was merely taking it in, but she soon broke her silence when they began discussing the issues surrounding their overcrowded prisons.

"I'm sorry," Nymati interrupted, her voice cool as a winter breeze. Gloved fingers cradled her face as she propped herself up lazily by her elbow. "I just don't understand why you have such a problem. Is crime such an issue here in Dura?"

"No, M'lady," replied Julius, one of several Gabris cousins on the council. "It's just with the emperor away there was a rise in petty thefts and–"

"Do you throw all your criminals in prison?" Nymati returned, her words edged in steel.

"Why yes. How else will they learn?" huffed Martel, Captain of the Guard, a large man who appeared to do more desk work these days than was probably good for him.

"So you punish your thieves by locking them up and feeding them for a few weeks–"

"Years," Martel interjected.

"Years," Nymati corrected, her brow popping.

"We increased sentencing in hopes of deterring criminals."

"That's clearly working out for you," Nymati mocked, causing Martel to sour – he had never appreciated authoritative women. "So am I to understand that you just lock away all of your criminals? Leaving them to rot in cells, on the edge of starvation, covered in their filth, in shame and without honour?" Nymati looked to each of them in turn, but they looked away.

She scoffed, amused. "How barbaric."

"And what, pray tell, is it you Sudra do with your criminals?" asked Tolis, Minister of Science. Callius rather liked Tolis. He was a mouse of a man who weighed no more than a bag of flour when wet, but he wasn't afraid to call others out on their errors and always stood his ground.

"We have no need for prisons in Sudra," Nymati explained to everyone's surprise. "Those who break the law are sent to fight in the coliseum or are sentenced to hard labour so they may earn their right to be members of society again."

"The coliseum?" gasped Ermis, Minister of Education, a round man with unkempt straw-like hair. "But they are untrained and will surely be killed."

"They should have thought about that before breaking the law." Nymati's eyes cast daggers as she sneered.

"So then, what of repeat offenders or those who commit more serious crimes?" asked Callius, his interest piqued in more than just the topic at hand.

"We don't tend to get many repeat offenders. I suppose it depends on the case, but I would have no qualms about taking out anyone I felt was too dangerous myself. A life for a life as they say." Nymati shrugged nonchalantly. "Drazah also sentenced more than his fair share of criminals, mostly murderers or those deemed too dangerous for rehabilitation. It's not a task we take on lightly, but it's certainly far preferable to burning them like witches; the smell clings to your clothing."

The councilmen sat silent, stunned with outrage and confusion. Their faces twisted and clenched as they processed, but Callius smiled, rubbing his jaw as he formulated a plan.

"You know... The Gladiator fights have lost much of their appeal of late and attendance is way down." Callius flicked his eyes over to Christos, Entertainments Manager and Master of the Coliseum. "It could be worth throwing an event to test the waters."

"Certainly worth a try," agreed Antonis, forever sucking up.

"We could announce Lady Nymati is in attendance and charge two silver for entry," added Paullus while rubbing his hands together.

"It wouldn't cost us anything to try." Christos shrugged to downplay his investment.

"Then make it so," Callius instructed and sat back with a sense of accomplishment. If the council were so willing to introduce Sudran customs to the coliseum it was more likely they would be able to accept Nymati as their empress. Still, he planned to hold on to news of their engagement until he was certain.

The councilmen began planning the festivities and divided the chores among themselves before continuing as they had before. Paullus raised concerns over the cost of supporting Sudra going forward and Julius mentioned plans to cultivate much of southern Estra – apprising the council that there had been delays due to a few Estra clans who were unwilling to accept their new regime. The Puwhar were mostly harmless and gave few objections to the empire's intrusion, but their gentle natures and childlike statures gave them few utilities outside of their artes. Tolis also suggested sending an excursion team to explore the indigenous plants and animals of Puwhar before making any plans to raise the jungles for lumber. Callius agreed to this, but insisted they kept their costs low.

"As for your return celebrations, we'll hold a banquet this evening, then a formal event at the end of the month. Say three weeks?" asked Christos, waiting for a nod from Callius before continuing. "Anyone invited from outside the city would just be a courtesy message and won't be expected to attend anyway."

"Very well. I–" Callius stopped as the cathedral bells chimed in the distance. "Right. Christos, get the invites done and delivered. The rest of you already have your assignments. I shall see you all tomorrow. Meeting adjourned."

The councilmen filed out of the room, presumably off to their own offices to implement the changes they had just decided upon. But Nymati remained seated, watching everyone leave until there was only the two of them left.

"It was good to see you get involved today," he

complimented. "Surprised it took you so long. I never imagined you would be one to be nervous."

"I feel more cautious than nervous." Nymati smiled her appreciation. "You rule so many, I'd hate to say something to affect them negatively. Although, if I am nervous, I suppose it is because I have yet to tell my sons of our coming nuptials and the window for me to do so myself is fast closing."

"I'm afraid I have little experience with children." Callius cleared away the papers he had left out on the table.

Sunshine beamed through the windows as the clouds shifted outside, catching on the ruby of Nymati's necklace. The sparkling gem called his attention. It was almost as beautiful as the individual wearing it and the return of the brilliant gem earned him much acclaim from its owner.

Callius' eyes then followed the plunging seams of Nymati's tunic, up her neckline, where Nymati's eyes caught his. He started.

"Do you think we could have a child together?" she asked bluntly.

Callius recoiled, nearly swallowing his tongue. He hadn't given it much consideration, not seriously anyway. Certainly, their having children together was a possibility he was very much hoping for, but in his experience, what a man wanted was rarely the reality of his situation.

Callius recovered his wits and prayed to the Gods for

his mouth not to betray him. "In theory, it's possible, although I have never met anyone who is half Sudra. I met a man who was half Frey once. Had his mother's ears and height but the tan complexion of a Duran."

"Could he heal?"

"I believe so."

Silence.

They held still. Both were thinking the same thing, but Nymati was the one to give it a voice.

"You know there's no guarantee our child would have Sudran artes even if we had one. Would that matter to you?"

"I don't imagine it would." He was almost certain, but Nymati's tone suggested she didn't feel the same way. "Besides, it's not like I have any need for magic and far too many rely on their artes over their brains these days."

"You certainly didn't need them to take Sudra," she returned pointedly, her eyes fixed on him. "I hear I missed quite the battle."

Callius hesitated. He was still struggling to figure Nymati out. She was always so serene and indifferent; her body language gave nothing away. He hoped to be able to read her subtle tells as they grew closer, but Nymati's guard was as impenetrable as his own. Except, even he didn't carry his sword on him at all times.

"Did you know Drazah had not fully transformed for

many years before your duel?" she asked. "He was challenged many times in his reign and retained his role without ever drawing upon his true power. It speaks volumes to know that he went all out against you."

"Tell me," Callius started with a hint of trepidation as he tried to summon the courage to continue. "If any of the challengers would have won, what would become of you?"

"I would have been given the chance to defend my crown and follow the new king – should he want me." Nymati held silent a moment, the ruby of her eyes flickering as she followed her thoughts to their conclusion. "Although, even then, I suppose there would be no guarantee I would be able to win a tournament a second time."

"And this has happened before?"

"Oh yes," she replied proudly. "Over the years there have been several challenges won for the crown. Many queens abdicated without a fight and died soon after, heartbroken. A few defended their titles but hadn't the strength to carry on.

"There was one queen who went through several kings," Nymati added with perhaps a little too much admiration in her tone for the emperor's liking. "Although she may have killed a few of them herself..."

"And, had a Sudran bested your king, and he gave you the chance to defend your title, would you?" Callius wasn't sure he wanted to know the answer and regretted it almost instantly.

Nymati snorted.

"That's something I have been left wondering myself." Her voice was so soft he could hardly hear it. Nymati breathed with remorse and looked away sadly. "I spent much of my life protecting our heritage. Putting merit in strength and valour. Keeping our bloodlines strong and pure. And yet here I am with you, a man of proven strength, who bested our best, wondering if I would feel any different if you were Sudra."

Nymati gazed up at him with such vulnerability in the wide sparkling rubies of her eyes that it made him feel like a monster.

"Perhaps if you were Sudra, I wouldn't feel like I am betraying my people so much." Nymati tilted her head, a crooked smile cracking over the side of her face. "Although, I can't be the only one who is curious to see what would happen."

* * *

A Guard's Request

WROUGHT IN STONE

9 MONTHS BMF

* * *

As the seasons changed,

so too did the Manastream.

Bruises formed over the atmosphere where corruption clotted the natural flow of mana.

The Manastream was helpless.

I was helpless.

Cursed only to watch,

I prayed,

but no one was listening.

* * *

CHAPTER ONE

Reyla Fenwilt had never been one to complain. From an early age, it was impressed upon her that every Frey had to do things they didn't wish to. Adults had jobs to attend, and children had chores. That was just how it was. Yet even she could not help but complain about their journey through Agrana.

She was miserable. The road was uneven and boggy. There was nothing to forage and animals appeared to avoid the area at all costs. Rain fell continuously upon them in an endless cycle of torrential downpours and that really fine stuff that soaks you right through.

Reyla didn't blame any merchants who might choose to trade closer to home rather than risk the trek. They would have likely starved or died from exposure if not for their artes. She supposed this could account for some of the missing travellers Wilona had mentioned and tried not to worry herself with it any further.

Crossing the border into Ruglor offered Reyla new concerns to worry herself over as the temperature dropped and the days grew short.

Winter was coming in fast. Hail dropped in random

bursts, and the harsh winds of the mountain bit their skin leaving them cold, wet and raw. It was altogether depressing and uncomfortable. She was beginning to understand why those in Ruglor and Agrana lived underground, but there was practically nothing on the surface. There were no structures and no pavings or roads. The merchant pass simply vanished into the dirt leaving them to trail paths left by animals and Rugla hunters. Sometimes, it felt as if she and Tharin were the only two left on the entire planet. Together they forged through the lowlands and into the Ruglor foothills, joined in their mission and misery as they set their quest against the magnitude of the mountains. It was unnerving and liberating all in the same breath.

It was just past midday when Reyla turned to look over the foothills behind them. The endless waves of green and brown forestry skirted the base of an incredible mountain range which spanned much of Ruglor. She craned her neck as she returned to the mountain before her, the peak hidden among clouds.

"I keep looking up, expecting the clouds to get closer, but they just keep on going," groaned Tharin. "With legs so small, you'd think the Rugla would've installed a trolley or at least some kind of horse rental somewhere."

"I'm not sure how often they come down this far. They're not known for leaving their Stronghold."

"I don't blame them," Tharin remarked, bracing himself against strong winds that seemed to come from all directions.

The trees creaked against the gales, their branches bare and barks dry. Reyla found it strange to see the trees so naked. In Freya, the trees only shed their leaves in spring to make way for the new buds. If she focused, she could sense that the manaflow of the trees was slower too, as if they planned to sleep through winter.

The mountains then howled as rain turned into hail and hail into sleet. All of a sudden, everything fell quiet and dark. Clouds swarmed above, blotting out the sun as the temperature dropped even further and snow descended upon them.

"Look at this!" Tharin cheered, holding his palms to the skies. Neither had ever seen snow before.

Reyla pulled her cloak tight. She was unable to share Tharin's elation and suspected it would soon run out as snow settled over the landscape.

Reyla tried not to dwell on her previous oversights as her cheeks turned raw. Already, their leaf-leather shoes were worn through. Their leggings and tunics were thin and poorly insulated, and the wool of their travel cloaks collected water droplets upon the fibres.

She picked up her pace, hoping to reach the Ruglor Stronghold before freezing to death.

"You think the weather is why they live underground?" asked Tharin, wiping the sizeable chunks of ice from his cloak.

Reyla just snorted. A few weeks ago, she would have mentioned how she had wondered the same thing, to which Tharin would then have responded with something to the sounds of, *"no way, get out of my brain"*. However, they had spent such a large amount of time together that it was happening more often.

It was negligible at first. They had picked up each other's mannerisms without meaning to, but eventually, they had started to think more alike and even adopted each other's sense of humour. It was as if at some point they stopped being individuals and had become a team again. Although, it felt like something more than that.

Something tugged within Reyla's chest as she pondered. There was something there which hadn't been there before. It held residence alongside her demons but held no hostility. Pondering it caused her body to tingle right down to her core and she determined that perhaps it was something to do with the blessings, but that only brought her more cause for concern.

Could the blessing be changing them somehow? Sure, she felt stronger, but she didn't feel different.

Did she?

* * *

Thick fog blanketed the mountains overnight, bringing with it a bitter frost as snow continued to fall.

By some stroke of good fortune, they stumbled upon a worn path with fresh tracks running in either direction. It was a coin toss as to which direction to take, so Reyla chose the way which continued up the mountains, with hopes of finding the entrance to the Rugla Stronghold. Then without warning, the tracks vanished with little explanation as to why.

They found another track headed north with the steady incline of the terrain, following it for days and huddling into the rocks for shelter at night. By the fourth or fifth morning, Reyla was beginning to doubt they even followed a path and stretched her senses as far as she could, in hopes of finding life beneath them, but there was nothing.

She thought of the shrines and the ring on her finger. Like a child holding their parent's hand through the city centre, the gentle tug of the twisted silver band assured her as much as it guided them. The static wrapped around her joints and pulled her towards the heart of the mountains. They just had to keep moving.

Reyla gritted her teeth with every step. She was frozen, soggy, and aching from head to toe, but she pushed on through blisters and backache as the trees thinned and a large crag jutted out of the mountainside. Her spirits jumped as high as her icebound limbs would allow.

The morning sun beamed upon a giant stone gate. It grew seamlessly from the cliff face reaching high above them, with a thick stone archway around a double door with carved detailing. The top panels were of the mountains with gold depicting the snowy peaks. Lower panels of cascading black and white stone made an opposed diagonal banding, fanning away from the thick spherical golden door handles. The middle panels were taller than the others, with intricate carvings of Rugla men mining. To the bottom, the same geometric panel repeated as above and all of it was framed by thick stone and delicate golden borders.

Their jaws slackened as they gazed in awe at the impressive structure before them.

Reyla stepped back, looking for a way in. There was nobody around, and no discerning opening or knocker. Tharin pounded his fist against the feature, but no one answered.

"I guess we wait?" Tharin shrugged.

Reyla stretched her senses but was too tired to catch wind of anything. "I guess so. We should take a break anyways."

"What's the plan if they don't answer?"

Reyla turned. Her mouth opened, but no words came out. She had no idea, but it was unlikely they would survive another night on the mountains as dark clouds shuffled on the horizon. It would only take one wrong turn in a storm to put their quest to its end.

"Let's hope someone answers then." Tharin chuckled despite his worry. "Tea?"

The pair dropped their gear and collected wood to rouse a fire, then huddled around it for warmth. They had lunch and relaxed a little, but after a few more hours, still, nothing had happened. Tharin grew impatient and banged on the carved door a few times but quickly gave up before returning to the ground beside the fire.

"You ever seen one of the Rugla?" he asked, holding his hands to the flame.

"No, but I've heard the stories." She left it at that. As far as Reyla was concerned, the Rugla ran on trade and mining and had a reputation for greed and negotiating slippery contracts that swayed in their favour. They were short and square by most accounts but not to be underestimated. They did, thankfully, have a good history with the Frey, so there was hope they wouldn't be too hostile to their entry.

"Here's hoping they're not all true, eh?" Tharin smirked. He stretched against a fallen tree, stopping as something shuffled in the bushes.

"Show yourself," Reyla belted as the pair rose to their feet, swords drawn.

"Don't mean no 'arm," came a rough voice as a short figure emerged from the undergrowth. "Jus' on mi way back to the gate. I–" He started when he saw the two Frey. "What're two Frey doin' way oot 'ere?"

The Rugla were among the shortest in Alamantra, with this one standing at most three and a half feet tall. His skin was light beige with patches of dark, stone-like flecks covering his temples and joints, but these were hidden under layers of dirt and grime, making it hard to tell which was which.

The two Frey were rather confused but explained themselves.

"This ain't the gate." He chuckled, holding a hand to the plate armour across his stomach. "This is the Pa'alen. The Gate's further up."

"Oh, right." Tharin sighed, his eyes returning to the tall mountain, dismayed.

"The name's Jip. I can guide ye there," the Rugla offered, flashing a wide smile that showed several gold-plated teeth. "Fur a price, naturally."

"You want us to pay you?"

"Well, unless you Frey have some other way to compensate a man for services rendered," said Jip, his hands to his hips. "Though you're no' likely to get far. He's none too keen on visitors oor Goldstorm y' know…"

"Fine." Reyla huffed, rolling her eyes.

She fumbled around in her backpack to find her coin pouch. She then pulled out a couple of bronze coins and placed them into the Rugla's waiting palm. His fingers snapped shut and the coins hastily stowed away in the man's pocket.

"Grab yer gear and douse the flames," he chirped.

"We'd better get oor shifty on if we wanna hit the gate by nightfall."

The two Frey hurried to collect themselves. They shouldered their packs and followed after the short man as he led them further up the mountain.

"Well, that worked out." Tharin smiled at Reyla. "Should we?"

Reyla forced a smile to disguise her apprehensions.

"Yeah, let's."

* * *

CHAPTER TWO

Amynus was lounging over his bed in the Duran palace, staring at the ceiling, when Saffia entered.

"Your mother's called for you," she cooed, her hands behind her back as she slunk over.

"What's she want?" he asked and swung his legs to the floor.

"No one knows. She's been keeping to herself a lot recently." Satisfaction stretched her smile. "It's really getting to Aeryn."

The pair sniggered. He and Saffia had spent many nights together in Dura and discovered they shared a mutual hatred of Aeryn. They spoke of little else – assuming they spoke at all.

Amynus was never quite sure what made him dislike Aeryn so much. Perhaps it was for her part in Taldi's betrayal, or the troubling notion his mother would make him marry her someday. Either way, it was nice to have someone share in his distaste for a change.

Amynus rose to meet her. He slipped his hand around Saffia's waist as he leaned in. Her ebony lips warmed against his as he stole a kiss.

"I had fun last night." His lip curled to the side, aware of her gloved hands as they brushed against him. "Where is she?"

"Her bedroom." Saffia released a heated breath. "I'll be on call later should you need anything."

He traced the line of her jaw to her chin, his smile cheeky and full of intent. "Good to know."

Amynus left his room, a grim countenance setting across his person as the door closed behind him.

Vast oil paintings were hung upon the wall, each depicting great battles in stunning detail, and cabinets were pressed into alcoves, every shelf filled with fine ceramics and fineries he had no name or use for. Duran power and history burst from the affluent displays as if to remind him of his place. Not that he needed reminding.

His shoulders raised and bowed his back as the pitiful embers within his core stirred. He could think of no good reason his mother would call upon him and counted through his transgressions to ready his defences.

Amynus knocked on the door and pushed it open as his mother called for him to enter.

This bedroom was much grander than his own. She had a four-poster bed, which was piled high with plush pillows and thick duvets. A cream lounging chair and a polished cedar dresser with a tall vanity mirror sat along one side.

Even the curtains were of a higher calibre than his own, with thick crimson fabric that reached the floor and hung upon polished gold-plated railings.

His mother sat on the bed with a stoic expression on her face that caused his lungs to tighten. Malaki was seated beside her, swinging his feet as he dangled his legs over the edge, his face alight with youthful ignorance.

"You sent for me." Amynus huffed, mentally preparing himself for the coming offence.

"I have something I wish to discuss as a family." Nymati smiled but her tone forced Amynus' back to straighten. "The emperor has asked me to remain here in Dura to become his empress."

Amynus' breath caught as if someone had just stabbed him in the back. His brows pressed as he opened his mouth to protest, but Nymati raised a single finger to warn him away.

"I am not here to garner your approval. This is not a marriage of love and devotion. This is what's best for our people. It is a business arrangement, nothing more."

Amynus held in place, a fury bubbling within his core unlike anything he had felt before.

Malaki's ruby eyes sparkled with his ignorance. "Does that mean we get to go to the coliseum, Mamma? Saffi says they start bullfighting in the winter. Can we go?"

"Of course we can, sweetheart," Nymati replied as if

talking to an infant. "Whatever you want."

"What about what I want, huh?" Amynus' nostrils flared as he summoned his courage. "I don't want to stay here. I want to go back home."

"You watch your tone."

Amynus drew back into himself. She didn't even need to raise her voice for him to cower and fall in line. It reduced him to a child again. He was weak and powerless. Hopeless and pathetic. There was no point in him trying. What could a weakling such as he do when faced with the might of Sudra's Demon Queen?

"If we leave, we have no home to return to," Nymati warned. "You need to think of the bigger picture, my son."

"Whatever. You do what you want."

Amynus scoffed and turned to leave, but Nymati flew across the room. She grabbed him by the arm, her gloveless fingernails pinching his skin as she held him still.

"Listen to me," she growled, her eyes so dark and narrow they turned blood red. "You may not appreciate it, but we don't have the luxury of choice."

"He killed my father!" Amynus burst out. "Doesn't that mean anything to you?"

Nymati shot a look at Malaki, fire burning in her eyes. It was likely he understood much of what was going on, but Malaki had not been told the full truth about his father's untimely end. Amynus didn't think it fair, but he wasn't about to be the one to tell him either.

"Some things are far greater than we are," Nymati sneered, her hold growing tighter as she spoke. "You're a grown man and I won't stop you if you want to leave, but you more than most should understand how important it is that we protect our people and their secret."

His blood ran cold. What did she mean by that? It was a terrible taboo even to mention their secret in passing. Why mention it now?

Did she know? How? How did she know?

Did Saffia tell her?

"Crown or no crown our people need us to carry on," Nymati insisted. "They look to us for strength when they have none."

Amynus turned away as she activated her artes against him. She did it reflexively, unable to stop herself. A mother's charm didn't have the same effect as it would upon a lover, but it was still a betrayal every time she tried to sway him as she would others. Nymati would rather have a puppet than a son, of that he was certain.

"We are their hope, their compass," she continued, preaching to him as she did their citizens. "I will not abandon them now and I would be remiss if I allowed you to walk away from your future because you were unwilling to yield – if only for the time being."

Nymati released his arm and returned to the bed beside

Malaki. She wrapped Malaki into her side, and he hugged her back, one serving as a miniature copy of the other. This hurt Amynus most of all, but he was unable to explain why.

"So, how does this change things?" he asked.

"It doesn't," Nymati replied, as if it were so simple. "We keep on going as we always have. We protect our people. At all costs."

Amynus sucked his teeth to give himself space to think. He wasn't fool enough to expect a straight answer, but he had hoped for a little more than that. His mother never did anything without purpose. She usually held ulterior motives but was a master of keeping them to herself. Not that she would ever share them with him willingly, of course, he was always the last to know.

Although it hit him bitterly, his best move was to lay low until he figured out what game they were playing.

"When's the wedding?" he asked.

"There will be an engagement announcement to make it official, soon." She sighed, her brows raising with the efforts of her parental concern. "Look, I know this isn't what you want. It isn't what I want either."

Her voice wavered and stressed in all the right places, but Amynus was beyond caring. There was nothing she could say to sedate the fire in his core, nor alleviate the sting of her betrayal.

"We just have to make the best of it," she insisted. "Play your cards right and you could be sitting on the Sudran throne within two years."

"Fine, but I'm not going to the wedding."

Amynus didn't give her the chance to refute his decision. He turned on his heel and returned to his room without another word, leaving a storm cloud in his wake.

His mother could marry the emperor all she wanted, but Amynus would never stop his quest for vengeance. He just had to bide his time…

* * *

CHAPTER THREE

Snow blanketed the ground and the moon glowed pigeon-grey as Reyla and Tharin followed the Rugla, Jip, up the mountain.

Reyla's cheeks burned. She had never felt a cold like this before and was ill-prepared for the strain it had upon her body. Her joints were frozen to the point of numbness and her eyelids felt heavy as she traced Jip's dawdling pace.

The air was thin, too thin. Her lungs strained through cold and deprivation. The hours slipped by as she fell into lethargy and focused solely on Jip's footprints in the snow.

"Almost there."

Reyla looked up as Jip pointed to something in the distance before increasing his speed, leaving Reyla behind as Tharin kept pace with him. She drew a deep breath and pushed on her manacore, but she was running on empty and only managed to weaken herself further.

Pushing through each step was a test of her willpower, but finally, Reyla reached a plateau. She braced weakly against the wind as flat sheets of pure white snow carpeted their path to the real entrance of the stronghold.

It was much smaller than the fake Ruglor Gate but still impressively large, she thought, considering the size of the inhabitants. Two doors of thick wood over twenty feet tall covered the tunnel's entrance, each with solid steel strips running from giant hinges. One of the doors was pushed open enough to allow someone to pass through and a small guard booth sat on the right side, a stone structure with a wooden roof and no door.

A guard hid from the elements in the booth. The short man perched beside a bonfire in a metal bin, his hands wide as he held them over the heat. Reyla rushed over to join him, rejoicing as she entered the proximity of the flames.

"Jip!" called the guard, his steel armour clinking as he jumped to his feet. "What's this you've brought me?"

"These loonies thought the Pa'alen was the entrance." Jip chortled. "Thought I'd show 'em the way."

The guard eyed the two Frey with a suspicious amber gaze. He had black wiry hair that poked from under his metal helm. The raised freckles upon his face were a lot darker than Jip's but were hidden by a thick black beard that reached over his chest plate.

"You got papers?" he asked. They didn't. "'Fraid yer no getting past 'ere without any. Y' need permission t' get past me."

Tharin turned to Reyla, worried.

Jip flashed a wide smile at them. "Sorry, kiddos, looks

like this is as far as I can take ya. I'd better get moving." He waved a paper to the guard. "Good luck."

Reyla grumbled goodbye as Jip disappeared down the tunnel. So much for taking her to the king; it appeared she was going to need to keep her guard up around the Rugla.

"So what now?" asked Tharin, his brows pinched.

"Lemme think," she replied quietly, rubbing her hands over the fire and taking stock of the guard. Until that moment, she was hoping that Rugla's greedy reputation was an exaggeration, but it seemed that was not the case. It could, however, work to their benefit.

Bribing the guard was the clear option, but bribing him to do what? That was her main concern. Even if they asked him to let them pass, they still had to find their way to the shrine and there was no telling how many checkpoints lay ahead. The truth could get them far, but that held its own problems.

Static wrapped around Reyla's finger and pulled her towards the heart of the mountain – this was surely the way. Her lips formed a thin line as her expression fell blank.

"Is there any way you could pass on a message for us? We have a message for the king and have come an awful long way to deliver it. It would be such a shame to be turned away now."

"Oh, I don't know," the guard protested. Reyla couldn't decipher his tone through his accent.

"Our message is of great importance," she stressed, reaching into her pocket. "We would, of course, be incredibly grateful if you would just inform your superiors of our arrival."

Reyla pulled a silver coin from her pocket. Holding it between her thumb and forefinger, she flashed the surface toward the guard. He straightened, his armour clattering as he eyed the coin. She smirked internally, wondering what his reaction would have been if she'd pulled out a piece of gold; it wasn't her proudest moment.

"I'll make a call," the guard agreed, rushing over to collect the coin. "But no promises."

"No promises," Reyla affirmed, releasing the coin into his small grubby hand.

The guard returned to his post. He reached for a rope that hung from the ceiling, pulling it down to cause it to tighten down the tunnel. Attached to the wall was a small box with two funnel-like receivers, one was stuck to the box, but the other he pulled away and held to his ear.

"But, Reyla, we don't have a message for the king," Tharin whispered, huddling closer into the fire.

"Don't worry about it. If this works, I'll come up with something, but we have to get inside first."

Tharin nodded his head in agreement but was likely too cold to argue. They watched intently as the guard seemed to talk to himself, often looking over his shoulder to them, before replacing the funnel.

"Yer in luck." The guard grinned as he joined them. "Mi Captain's at the second gate. Ee's offered to escort yous to King Goldstorm."

"That is most fortunate," Reyla agreed.

"Jus' follow the tunnel down 'til you reach the gate. Don't stray from the path though," he warned. "If yer not at the gate in half an hour they'll send guards after ye, so I'd get a move on if I were you."

"Thanks," Reyla grumbled. The Rugla's reputable hospitality appeared to match the rumours also. She turned to Tharin. "You got everything?"

"Yeah, let's do this."

* * *

The two Frey were well out of earshot of the guard when Tharin queried Reyla.

"So, what's the plan?"

"We do whatever they ask of us and get an audience with the king," she replied, darted hazel eyes surveying the rock tunnel as she walked. "This place is a fortress, we're not going to get anywhere without permission."

The tunnel walls were perfectly smooth and square, likely formed with Rugla artes, with a well-trodden dirt floor. Their path was lit by torches held in brass sconces, spread evenly along the stone. It was much warmer within the tunnel and the air was stale but easier to breathe. Every so often there would be a small arch leading to Rugla-sized corridors branching away from the main path, but there was no indication of where they went. Smooth metal rails and wooden sleepers tracked into tunnels through some of the corridors, but they had yet to see anything pass on them.

They must have been walking an hour when Reyla caught sight of a giant wooden barrier in the distance. She slowed their pace. Before it, several Rugla guards gathered, each clad in steel armour and helms, and holding a variety of axes and spears. Their short stature made the barrier behind them all the more impressive. It was a door set within the wall of the tunnel which appeared to drop from the ceiling. The Rugla seemed to have been waiting impatiently for their arrival and fell in line upon seeing the two Frey approach.

Reyla steadied her nerves, trying to relax and seem as non-threatening as possible while standing two feet taller than her opposition.

"We were told we could meet your captain here," Reyla offered, placing a hand across her stomach as she bowed. Tharin followed suit.

There was a rustle of metal as the Rugla guards tightened their grips around their weapons. Reyla counted them as she tensed. There were twelve guards, although their armour was all different, so it was hard to determine if one of them was their superior.

"Let me through," called a deep voice as a figure appeared from a tunnel near the gate.

A Rugla man walked towards them, his golden armour lined with silver chainmail which gleamed from its impeccable upkeep. A pointed nose stuck out of his wide face and a two-horned helm rested upon a thick brown brow.

"We've been expecting you," he stated, his nose exaggerating his movement as he looked each Frey up and down. "I'm Captain Lubren and 'al be escorting you to the Core."

"Thank you, Captain, we are most grateful," replied Reyla.

"However," started Captain Lubren, his pause causing Reyla's anxiety to spike. "If you wish to go any further, you'll have to relinquish your weapons and gear."

Reyla sighed as the threat to her wallet subsided, and readily agreed. She removed her waterlogged gloves then dropped her pack to the floor and released her sword belt. Tharin did likewise, each quietly collecting their coin pouches into their pockets as neither of them had much faith in the Rugla.

Reyla paused as she released her knife belt. Her hardened fingers brushed the leaf-leather sheath as if to say goodbye to her trusty blade. She had worn it almost as long as she had known Tharin and setting it aside felt akin to chopping off a limb and leaving it behind. Her knuckles grew white as she reached to hand the Rugla her most prized possession and released it to the will of the Universe.

"We'll keep it safe fur ye," assured Captain Lubren before instructing his men to collect their belongings into a chest. "Jus' pop in on yer way back out."

Several Rugla collected the chest and ran off down a tiny corridor.

"Now then. Raise the gate," he called, prompting the men in the line-up to turn.

They squared off before the giant gate, their hands to the floor and glowing as they activated their artes. The ground trembled as the men lifted their arms and the gate groaned and began to rise.

Reyla's jaw loosened as pillars of stone grew from beneath the gate. There was a pillar for each of the Rugla as they worked in unison, pushing the giant barrier up and into the ceiling.

"Follow me," ordered Lubren, marching down the tunnel.

A flurry of doubt ran over her chest as Reyla stepped under the gate. It was a defence beyond any wall or parapet and made from a plate of solid, arte-formed wood. If they were to displease the Rugla king somehow, there would be no way for them to escape.

"This way," Lubren beckoned. "Only nine gates to the Core."

* * *

CHAPTER FOUR

The deeper Reyla and Tharin followed Captain Lubren into the mountain, the busier the tunnel became. Carts frequently crossed the tunnel, often unmanned and burdened with ores and supplies, and guard patrols passed into the path before disappearing into the side tunnels.

They had travelled for some time before reaching the second gate. This one was already open with eight stone pillars holding it in place. No one tried to stop their passing and there didn't seem to be any guards maintaining it, but Reyla supposed security was much less of a problem beyond the first gates.

It was much warmer this side of the gate, for which Reyla was grateful, but she slowly grew more aware of her body as it began to thaw. She wet her cracked lips and fumbled for her water-pouch. The water was still frozen, and she chewed on the slush with some hope it would quell the pains wrapping her empty stomach, but there was little she could do for her poor, throbbing feet.

They passed by seven more gates over several hours. Reyla figured that they had walked through the night and into the morning as the smells of fresh coffee and fried meats wafted in from the side-tunnels and their route grew busy with Rugla going about their day.

At first, the citizens paid them no mind, but suspicious eyes soon noticed their presence and followed their path. The Rugla wore tattered leathers and matted animal furs with metal plates and helms that shone like a tavern bar. Reyla righted herself in preparation for any confrontation, but no attempts were made to meet them.

With ten gates and many miles between them and the snow, Reyla and Tharin emerged from the tunnel, coming out in a giant natural chasm that must have spanned over a kilometre wide. Thick chains held luminous orbs that hung like miniature moons and cast a pale, yellow light over them.

"Welcome to The Core," said Lubren, opening his arm to the sheer drop before them.

The Stronghold's Core was a giant mass of stone suspended in the very centre of the chasm. It looked like a giant beehive made of stone that extended deep into the ground. The rock face grew up into an angular stone palace with six tiers, each level rimmed with gold-plated parapets.

Reyla peered over the chasm edge. The core appeared to go down forever with large steel and gold supports along the width every few levels. Long stone and iron bridges crossed the great chasm to the palace gates. These were twinned with manned sentry towers on either side, their guards watching with curiosity as they crossed to the palace. It was a fortress beyond measure.

Golden statues of Rugla warriors loomed from the roofs of the sentry towers, their weapons battle-ready. If the stories were to be believed, the statues were dormant golems said to awaken in times of crisis. Some believed them to be sentient, but logic dictated to Reyla that the Rugla likely controlled them with artes somehow.

Tharin moved in closer to Reyla as they passed over the bridge, sweat upon his brow.

"Relax," Reyla hissed with a stern side-eye.

"I never expected we'd ever be so high up underground." Tharin walked as close to the centre of the bridge as possible, his eyes on the palace ahead.

"Since when do you have a problem with heights?"

"Since always," he claimed, his voice strained. "Dunno if you've noticed, but Freya's pretty flat. It's not like we go climbing the Life Tree or anything, is it?"

Reyla chuckled as Captain Lubren instructed the guards to open the palace doors and allow them passage.

The interior of the castle was equally as extravagant as the exterior. An amber crushed velvet rug ran down the middle of the square corridors, but the ceiling was low and barely tall enough to allow the two Frey to pass comfortably.

Captain Lubren marched right down a corridor, their

path decorated to a garish degree with cabinets, paintings and tapestries. The majority of the visible surfaces were piled with gold, candlesticks, suits of armour, weapons, *everything*, causing the halls to shine magnificently as they walked quietly behind.

Two guards pushed upon the doors as they approached the end of the corridor. The polished brass hinges whined as they swung into the throne hall. Here the ceilings expanded to three storeys high, stretching over a long rectangular hall. No pillars or columns held up the ceiling, allowing the sleek marble stone floor to flow seamlessly from one end of the room to the other, the surface polished to perfection. Crystals hung from a barely visible web in concentric circles that spanned the ceiling and reflected the lights above to cast soft spotlights in all directions.

Captain Lubren continued forward, the hard rubber of his boots squeaking against the floor. Before them, a stone throne dominated the back of the hall. The angular monstrosity reached higher than most trees, with a solid stone base that seemed to box in around the severe-looking man seated upon it.

It was King Goldstorm. Reyla recognised him from a history book and scrambled to remember everything she could about him. Every inch of his body was clad in gold – from his boots and armour to the crown wrapped around his head – and each was encrusted with diamonds and gems in intricate patterns. Glossy black hair ran down past his shoulders, meeting a thick braided beard which covered most of his face and was tied with golden rings about his chest.

An assortment of Rugla gathered behind the throne. They all wore bright armour and steely expressions, except for one, a woman in overalls with a bright expression. She seemed to be younger than the others by some years and had her burgundy hair tied back in a ponytail that ran past her knees. The smiling face shone upon Reyla like a beacon of hope, comforting her sleep-deprived and exhausted self.

Reyla flashed Tharin her trademark reassuring smile as they each took a knee before the throne.

"I am Rubalix Goldstorm the third, son of Rubalix the second and grandson of Merose Goldstorm the first. What business have you in my mountains?" boomed the Rugla king, his voice echoing off the stone walls.

"Your Majesty, we come with news from Freya," Reyla began, her eyes on the floor.

"Ah, yes. We heard of dear Elsafrey's passing. You have my deepest condolences," offered King Goldstorm.

Reyla's heart tugged with sudden emotion, but she was mostly grateful his accent wasn't as thick as the rest of the Rugla – it was going to make her task much easier.

"If only that were the reason for our visit, Sire," Reyla replied, looking up to meet the king's golden stare. "Our people have been afflicted with a terrible sickness. Before her passing, Queen Elsafrey ordered us to travel to each of the ten nations and seek out the temples of our ancestors, with hopes of finding a cure."

"There is no sickness here," Goldstorm snapped. "You won't find answers here. You may as well just go back home."

Tharin frowned. "Please, you have to let us—"

"I don't *have* to do anything," the king sneered, rising in his throne.

Reyla's insides clenched. He had a point, and Tharin quickly backed down, looking to Reyla to carry on for him. Her pulse rattled her eardrums, but she swallowed her nerves, returning the king's mettle with some of her own.

"Sire, this sickness may not be here now, but it's only a matter of time," she asserted, raising her chin as if to strengthen her position. "We've already been through three other kingdoms and there's sickness wherever we go. We believe it started in Pudron, reaching Freya and Sheya by mid-summer."

"That may be so, but even if it held the answers you seek, our temple is sacred, and you are not permitted to enter."

Reyla sighed, her shoulders falling with her optimism. She had hoped self-preservation would work to persuade the king – and was fast running out of options. She was certain she didn't have enough gold to bribe him.

"What do we do now?" Tharin whispered.

Reyla pinched her lips and clasped her hands, debating their next move. If they could not get permission they would have to break in, but the Rugla's security was beyond anything she had seen before, and escape would be difficult if they were caught.

She turned to her ring for guidance, and it responded, the pull the strongest it had been since entering Ruglor as she thought of the shrines. Deep in thought, Reyla rubbed her hands and twisted the silver ring around her finger.

"Can it be?" gasped Goldstorm, leaving his throne in a flurry of motion.

He snatched Reyla's hand in his and pulled her arm to his face. Fighting panic, confusion and the compulsion to rip her hand away, Reyla froze, her nostrils flaring as the Rugla king inspected the ring.

"Where did you get this?" he demanded.

Reyla shuffled uncomfortably as his fingers curled around her hand, fingering the ring as if getting ready to steal it away. She held his gaze, aware as Tharin readied beside her.

"You know what this is?" asked Reyla, her eyes narrowed as if to accuse him right back. "Then you know why we're here."

"We shall see." The king huffed and released her hand. He returned to his throne without explanation as his features dropped back into the same sullen expression as before.

"Fine," Goldstorm grumbled. "I will allow you entry on

the condition that you pay the toll and present a gold coin to Gatruk Goldstorm, the first of our kind. We will provide you with beds and escort you to the mines once you have rested."

Reyla and Tharin breathed joint sighs of relief. They didn't understand what had caused his change in attitude but decided not to argue.

"Ruby," Goldstorm called over his shoulder. The young Rugla woman answered him. "Make sure our guests are taken care of and know all they need to know."

"Yes, Father." She beamed at the two Frey.

"Be sure to make haste, young Frey," warned the king. "I don't have time to be chasing fool's errands and don't wish to have you in my mountains any longer than necessary."

Reyla and Tharin gave him a low bow.

"You have our word," Reyla promised.

* * *

They followed the Rugla woman from the throne hall and along another cluttered corridor.

"I'm Rubalix Goldstorm the fourth, but everyone just calls me Ruby," she said, her eyes like polished jade as she tossed a smirk over her shoulder.

Reyla noted the lack of royal monicker added to Ruby's titles but considered bringing it up impolite and chose not to mention it.

The two Frey introduced themselves.

"Don't mind my father," chirped Ruby. "He's no' much of a mornin' rock and we don't often let strangers into the mountain."

Unlike the rest of the Rugla Reyla had seen, Ruby wasn't wearing armour but a beige tunic and grey overalls with black leather boots, similar to a handyman. Her burgundy ponytail swished as she walked, with the pat of her hard shoes echoing the movement.

"Yeah... Almost didn't get in here at all," Tharin admitted.

Ruby laughed it off and led them down a flight of stairs, deeper into the Stronghold Core, and along another corridor. This corridor was much thinner than the previous ones and shorter too, causing the two Frey to slouch. It was also less cluttered – as if all their wares were exhibited in the palace above.

"I'll take you to the mess hall in a bit," Ruby explained. "It'll be pretty busy about now, so best to leave it a while. Ah bet yer both knackered walking down from the gate all night. Yous can rest up in here with me."

Ruby pushed on a door, stepping into a workshop of some kind. It was filled with workbenches and shelves stacked with boxes of tools, materials and trinkets. A long-armed brass magnifying glass was attached to one of the workbenches, where it loomed over a mess of cogs, cables and metal rods. Papers with blueprints and sketches of half-released contraptions covered a wide easel that hung from the wall, each scribbled with annotations in illegible handwriting.

"Pick a pew, and I'll pop the kettle on," said Ruby gesturing to the stools.

The stool Reyla sat on was not made for someone so tall, making it uncomfortable, but it offered her feet some much-needed relief. Now they had stopped, she fell, exhausted, her feet throbbing after so many hours of walking. Reyla's body slunk even further at the thought of searching out food. They hadn't slept and she was unsure she had the energy to get back to her feet. Her stomach grumbled in protest.

What time was it anyway? She looked around for a sign, but it was impossible to tell so far underground.

"Tea?" asked Ruby.

She dipped behind one of the cupboard doors, returning with ceramic cups. She then placed them on a workbench by an hourglass-shaped contraption.

Reyla's head tilted towards the strange machine. The main hourglass was bronze with a spout at the top and a nozzle on the bottom, all raised on wooden legs above a mana-crystal. Ruby pressed something on the base of the instrument, causing it to light up. Reyla watched the machine in amazement as Ruby pulled a stool over to the workbench while the hourglass warmed and steam came from the spout as the contents boiled. With the cups under the nozzle, Ruby decanted the contents into each before joining the two Frey at the workbench.

"So, how're your smelting skills?" asked Ruby, passing them each a cup of mud-coloured liquid.

Neither Frey was overly confident.

Ruby chuckled. "To get into the temple, you're gonna have to go into the mines, collect some gold and bring it back to the temple. There, you must melt the gold into a coin to offer to Gatruk Goldstorm." Ruby took a breath to blow on her tea. "Don't worry I'll guide you through it. Hardest part will be finding the ores."

"Does the size matter?" asked Tharin, his face a lighter shade of green than normal.

"Does it ever?" Ruby smirked.

Reyla sipped her tea, the taste bitter and earthy to the point she wondered if the Rugla just watered down mud.

Despite King Goldstorm being about as forthcoming as a hunk of stone, she couldn't deny the hospitality. Ordering his own daughter to escort them was surely a sign of his interest, but it was anyone's guess as to how long that hospitality would last. With any luck, the temple would hold their trial, but if not, they would have to find some other excuse to explore the Stronghold.

Tired, Reyla lost track of the conversation. She sipped her bitter tea as she disconnected, her idle eyes drawn to blueprints pinned to an easel. At first, she didn't think much of them, her thoughts blank as she pieced together the various designs. From under the many layers of scribbles and notes, she picked out the shape of a stern, plans for a helm, and calculations of wind speeds and resistance.

"Is that a ship?" she burst out, surprising herself with the sudden volume.

"Not just a ship. An airship!" cheered Ruby. She jumped to her feet and rushed across the room.

Static filled the room as Ruby pulled at the blueprints, discarding them to the floor to uncover one that spanned the entire easel. It had a design similar to that of a boat but had a large balloon on top and exhausts along either side. The pencil marks were faded in places and there were smudges and stains from many hours of hard labour making much of it hard to see, but sure enough an airship it was.

"It's my grandest invention, but I've never gotten much further than the planning stages," Ruby admitted. "Managed to get the engine and guidance started but the hull's a bit big to fit in the workshop. Besides, mi dad would never let me test it out."

"Do you really think you could fly?"

The idea was absurd to Reyla. She didn't enjoy riding

boats or carts and would prefer to have her feet on the ground – but to soar through the skies, travelling as the crow flies. It seemed rather magical. Could they really fly? And if so, could they fly to Askana?

"If I could get some supplies, sure – in theory anyways." Ruby shrugged with a strange sense of melancholy. "Mostly I'd need some more mana-crystals. The ones I have now are low on energy. Some reinforced silk thread perhaps too – you Frey could do that, right? Then there's cotton and wood… See, it starts to add up real fast."

Reyla marvelled at the plans further still. It all seemed a little too perfect. The Aska were said to have closed their borders years ago and she doubted anyone would dare take them by boat. But if they flew? Would the Aska even be able to stop them?

"What if we get you the supplies?" Reyla offered with a sudden degree of urgency. "Could you do it?"

"Well, yeah, of course, but–"

"And if you can fly, would you take us to Askana?" Reyla pressed her heart, already envisioning the sight.

Ruby paused, a smile cracking over her face as an idea flashed behind the jade of her eyes.

"I shall make a list…"

* * *

Once they had finished their muddy tea, Ruby showed them to the mess hall, collecting a small notepad and pencil from one of the workbenches as they left the workshop. Ruby scribbled notes onto her paper as she walked, leading them deeper into the Core, not once looking up to see where she was going.

"You Frey look like you haven't eaten in years," she said in jest while pushing a door open with her shoulder. "Eat as much as you like, won't see anyone go hungry while under our roof."

The mess hall was a wide stone room with a curved outer wall, the windows overlooking the chasm. Long stone tables ran along the length in three rows, each set with wooden benches on either side. On the inner wall, a large clock with brass hands counted over wooden counters burdened with metal trays filled with roasted meat and vegetables.

Reyla tried to hold her disgust as the clock hands ticked into the afternoon. She hadn't been this sleep-deprived since her time on the frontlines and she stifled another deep yawn. It didn't help that the atmosphere was so subdued – it was certainly nothing like the ruckus Reyla was accustomed to in the Frey barracks. Many of the Rugla digested on the benches, quiet with food and beer, and a single guitar played in the corner by a fire, the tune soft and folksy.

"Help ye sen," said Ruby, passing them each a plate

and indicating the buffet.

Reyla braced herself over the buffet and gingerly collected bread onto the ceramic plate as she surveyed what was on offer. Her nose curled over the remains of some unknown animal carcass, forcing her to grimace. Much of the food was roasted and likely covered in animal fats, but she was hardly in a position to complain and took what vegetables she could before joining Ruby on one of the tables.

"So how come you're off to Askana?" she asked, more focused on making notes than clearing her plate.

"We've gotta go everywhere." Tharin pushed bread into his mouth to avoid saying more.

"No one's sure why they closed the borders. Time was they'd trade with us over all sorts of things, but no more. Been years since we've received any correspondence too." Ruby still scribbled into her notebook. "Perhaps it would be worth me coming with you as well."

"I hope yer no filling our Ruby's head with thoughts of flying again," came a voice as the notebook was whipped from her hands by an older Rugla man. He held the book away from Ruby as he read it. "I tolt you. Ain't no chance yer Dad's even gonna let ye fly that thing. Besides ye need more mana-crystals b'fore you even think 'bout getting anywhere."

"Either sit down and contribute or leave," Ruby hissed, snatching her book back. He sized up the two Frey and was on the verge of leaving when Ruby added: "Of course, if you do leave, I will have to find a new pilot…"

The Rugla then joined them at the table and Ruby smirked at her victory.

"This is my uncle, Cidric Goldstorm, youngest son of Rubalix the second, fifth in line for the throne." Ruby introduced him proudly.

Reyla noted once more the string of titles and wondered if she was addressing Ruby incorrectly.

"Cid," he insisted, greeting them. The rust-coloured flecks around his temples squeezed as he grinned, the familial resemblance between him and Ruby suddenly apparent. A pair of brass goggles rested upon his head, the wide band flattening his dry, honey-coloured hair like a helmet.

"He also used to captain the ships between 'ere and Askana. Best captain we had."

"Ah, shucks, but even flattery won't be enough to get ye to Askana," Cid warned. "The wind's bin blowin' awful bad these last few months, you'll have a hard time getting through that on the sea as it is. Doubt a balloon would last in it all that long."

"I keep telling you, it's not just a balloon. You let me worry about the construction and start figuring out how we're gonna get this all past mi dad."

"Now that's on you." Cid laughed loudly. He caught

himself, a twinkle appearing in his eye. "Although, you know the Swiftbow is still in storage."

"The Swiftbow?" Ruby repeated, frowning.

"What's that?" asked Tharin, although Reyla wondered the same.

"It's an old prototype of mine," Ruby replied. "I wanted to design a ship that was fast enough to make it to Freya in just a few days, but it never made it to the water."

"Maybe not," said Cid. "But it's got a small hull and no guff on the inside. If you used that you'd only have the balloon to worry about."

"If we used the Swiftbow, the balloon wouldn't need to be so big either," Ruby agreed, pouting as she stared at her uncle with a contemplative intensity. "D'you think you can get it to the Western Cove without notice?"

"The Western Cove? I can try."

"Then I guess we'd better eat up," chirped Ruby, finally releasing her notepad. "Seems we've all got our work cut out for us."

* * *

Reyla and Tharin joined Cid and Ruby in their planning, but lack of sleep and potential frostbite left them weary and of little use.

The pair were given a room on a floor deep within the Core. Ruby referred to this level as barracks, but it was no more than another string of plain stone corridors with brown fir doors, and Reyla doubted she would be able to tell the difference.

"Try not to worry about the noise. There'll be a lot of folks coming and going," Ruby told them before returning to her workshop. "We Rugla are not governed by the sun like the rest of you."

Reyla was too tired to determine her meaning and passed on her thanks before closing the door behind her.

The room itself reminded Reyla of her room back home in the barracks. It was equipped with the bare necessities, two tiny beds and a table between which held a burning candle, but nothing else. She assumed only the Rugla soldiers lived in the Core but still struggled to imagine how the citizens lived.

Reyla sighed as she dropped to the mattress, her rear below her knees as the frame hung closer to the floor than she expected. She activated her artes and rubbed her shoulder, glad to be sitting down once more.

Tharin threw himself on the bed fully clothed, his feet hanging over the edge of the frame.

"I don't care that it's stuffed with feathers and two feet short, I'm so glad to have a bed to sleep in," he whined, his voice muffled against the mattress and bedsheets.

"We have been roughing it a while now," she agreed,

dropping her head to the flat pillow.

Reyla considered removing her gear but had become accustomed to sleeping in it while travelling. They bathed where possible but had refrained from removing their gear in the cold of Ruglor, as such, they were both beginning to feel a little ripe. She assumed the Rugla had showers or some other means of cleaning themselves and made plans to request one before setting off again, but she imagined they may fare better with buckets and a rag.

"You think Ruby's going to build us a ship?" asked Tharin, turning his head to look at her.

"Somehow I don't think she's building it for us." Reyla smirked. "I get the feeling she's wanted to build it for a while now."

Tharin chuckled and turned back to his pillow. Reyla stretched her arms out and behind her head, then closed her eyes. Her entire body throbbed like a stubbed toe as she released an almighty yawn and tried to settle.

"How're we going to pass a trial without our gear?" Tharin asked through the pillow.

"We'll figure something out."

"Yeah." He yawned. "We always do…"

* * *

CHAPTER FIVE

High Priestess Arafrey left the temple a little after midday.

Gurrein was the guard assigned to her, and he marched behind, wearing the green garbs of the Princess' Guard. Both he and Mika had been reassigned to her guard after returning from Old Wood, filling spaces left by others who had become stricken with the sickness. Arafrey liked them well enough. Mika was perhaps a little too cocky and Gurrein tried too hard to impress others, but they were kind and diligent. They were excellent guards, but Arafrey feared there would be no filling the hole left by those missing.

Arafrey arrived at Grownwell, a cafe not far from the temple, where she planned to meet the twins.

The oak-grown structure was more akin to a gazebo with large pane-less windows that opened out into the forests. Round arte-formed tables seated happy couples and gossiping ladies in fine robes. A counter wrapped around a large fireplace where the owner displayed freshly baked sundries.

Arafrey's stomach rumbled at the scent of fresh

cinnamon buns in the air and her feet burned as she rested, suddenly exhausted.

Her morning had been a whirlwind of sermons, treatments and administrative duties which awaited her return. It wasn't so much the tasks which troubled her, more the sheer volume of them. Arafrey had never realised just how many things were involved in managing and maintaining the temple. It was a wonder her mother had ever got anything done.

Arafrey relaxed deeper into the chair, her eyes glazing over as she awaited the twins' arrival.

She had often visited Grownwell with her mother after sermons before returning to the palace. It was a tradition that had faded into obscurity as Arafrey strived for independence – something she sorely regretted in hindsight – and she considered it a waste to meet the twins there. Although, with both her mother and Reyla gone, she really couldn't afford to be picky about where she got her social interaction from.

"Ah, there you are, Ara." Lierin's shrill voice returned Arafrey to the cafe. "Of all the places to choose. You know we can have tea at ours? We're always happy to host."

Arafrey begrudged waking that morning as the twins crossed the cafe to join her, their noses held high. This day they wore sepia robes, their drab hair clipped on alternate sides with amber and gold clasps – perfectly presented in all the ways they considered most important.

"I like it here, it's peaceful," Arafrey replied firmly, more for the owner's benefit than Lierin's. "Besides, I needed a change in scenery."

"How are you? It's been so long since we've had tea," Lierin stated, without giving Arafrey the chance to respond. "You know, I don't think we've ever been here…"

Tierin greeted Arafrey with a weak smile as the pair took seats.

"… it's so terribly quaint, isn't it?" Lierin turned her head without really looking.

The waiter arrived to take their order, a young man with a beige tunic and dull leggings under his coffee-stained apron.

"Two strawberry teas," Lierin barked in his general direction.

"Green for me, please," added Arafrey, her brow creased apologetically.

"You're *always* working now," Lierin complained, her mouth opening so wide it forced her head back. "Isn't the point of being the boss to get everyone else to do the work for you? That's what Father's always saying."

"This is hardly the time to be relaxing," Arafrey chided. She rubbed her neck as the muscles between her shoulders grew tight. It had been foolish of her to think the twins could be anything but a test of her willpower and patience.

"Perhaps once the sickness passes, I can think about delegating tasks and attending social events."

"Let's hope that's soon." Lierin ignored the waiter as he arrived with their tea. "Your social life has already taken a huge hit. There's so much you've missed already."

Lierin continued regurgitating all the gossip she had collected since their last meeting, clucking continuously, with Tierin chirping occasionally to agree or add even juicier titbits. Arafrey limited herself to one-word answers and let the twins voice their opinions without her input, making sure to join in when they laughed. Thankfully, Lierin was quite capable of carrying a conversation herself.

Arafrey's eyelid throbbed as a shot of pain wrapped around her skull. She wished she'd had the forethought to cancel their appointment when her headache threatened that morning. The twins were hardly the most agreeable of Frey, and Lierin's acute voice cut right through her at the best of times.

She counted the hours since she had last taken her tonic and cursed herself for not deciding to take it pre-emptively. Pride and stubbornness wouldn't allow her to take medicine unless she needed it, which always resulted in her downfall. At least she was able to find comfort in the knowledge that a vial awaited her in the temple. All she had to do was suffer a single cup of tea and then she could excuse herself...

Arafrey stared at the untouched teas and willed them to evaporate so she could leave. It had been so long since she had sat down and socialised with people who were not staff or patients that she had almost forgotten how to hold a simple conversation.

Was the Summer's Night Festival her last social occasion? The last few months had gone by so fast. So much had happened in that time, it hardly felt like any time at all, but at the same time, she had never felt more tired, making it feel like years.

"Oh! And did you hear?" added Lierin, the sparkle of juicy gossip catching upon her lips. "There was a party at Yaldin's where Salden drank his body weight in wine and decided to start dancing on the tables. Anyway, he falls on his backside, flips the table and causes a right old mess. So then there's a rush of servers to the broom cupboard to start cleaning it all up and you'd never guess who they found in there with one of the male waiters."

Lierin paused for effect, causing Arafrey's entire body to go cold. Her breath caught. She knew it as her heartbeats quickened, but still managed to gather her strength enough to ask: "Wh- Who?"

"Bodair Asrich. Can you even imagine?" Lierin nearly burst from her satisfaction, throwing her arms up as she released a cackle. "And to think father wanted Tierin to marry him."

Arafrey gasped, her temple pulsating. She pressed her fingers against them and pushed the pain aside; she didn't have time for a headache now. "What of Bodair?"

"I suppose it's gotten to his parents by now. Wouldn't be surprised if they kicked him out, a prominent family like theirs." Lierin shrugged before changing the subject, but Arafrey's heartbeat never slowed.

It had been weeks since Yaldin's party. Tears held behind Arafrey's facade causing it to tremble. She wondered where Bodair was, sickened to realise she had not seen him since her coronation—and even then it had only been at a distance. She supposed he was forced to keep a low profile after the incident, but her heart ached, wracked with guilt to think she hadn't noticed his absence.

By the time they had finished their tea, Arafrey's headache had grown from an annoying pulsation behind her eye into a sharp crack that ran through her skull. It was like cold fire stabbing through her consciousness and into her brain. Black spots ran through her vision and halos wrapped around the candle lights as her stomach churned in rebellion.

Taking forcefully slow, deep breaths, Arafrey pushed herself to her feet.

"I should get back to the temple," she announced with enfeebled urgency. "It's been lovely seeing you."

Arafrey didn't hear their goodbyes as she piled silver coins upon the table and left. She merely assumed Gurrein followed her and rushed back to the temple, marching unevenly, and held up by willpower alone as the forest spun around her. Each footstep echoed through her body and rang through her skull like alarm bells as she struggled forward, desperate to reach the temple without anyone seeing her.

Entering the temple was as much of a blur as the journey there. Arafrey hurried past the staff and slammed the door to her office before any of them had the chance to speak to her. Sweat dripped from Arafrey's brow as she threw open the doors to the medicine cabinet and snatched up the Savulin Tonic inside like a frog catching a fly.

Disregarding all caution, she removed the lid and drank from the bottle greedily. Her actions were reckless, but she didn't care. She would rather that than allow others to see her weakness, her position demanded as much. Her citizens were as fickle as they were pious and she would have little success in leading them if they were to discover the truth of her indiscretions.

Arafrey staggered away from the cabinet to her desk chair, her limbs betraying her as she found her seat. There was nothing she could do now except wait and accept the merciless assault on her senses. She was hopeless – but Arafrey knew that already.

She was hopeless, helpless and sorely unsuited to the roles designated to her by the advent of her birth. Her people deserved better, and she felt it as much of a disservice to them as to her that she should be their only option.

Arafrey closed her eyes and waited for the tonic to take hold. The warmth of the Savulin Tonic washed over her senses and eased her heartache and pain. Her thoughts became whispers as she lost herself to the darkness behind her eyelids.

And there she remained for the rest of the day.

* * *

CHAPTER SIX

After sleeping in bunks made for someone much shorter than they were, Reyla and Tharin were awoken by a guard and shown back to the mess hall for breakfast. Once they had consumed their fill of jam on toast, the guard escorted them back through the Core to the palace level.

Reyla felt like a child being marched home to be scolded as she maintained their pace. The guard blustered through the palace, his face pressed into a permanent look of disdain as if escorting them were some kind of punishment. He grunted to the bridge guards as they left the palace, but held his silence as they continued to cross the chasm.

From their position beneath the glowing orbs suspended from the ceiling, Reyla deduced they were going north, although there was little else to support her theory. The tunnel meeting this bridge was much smaller than the one leading in from the surface, however, and was framed with wooden beams. Several Rugla were already gathered deeper inside the tunnel, loitering around a row of wooden boxes filled with tools.

"Help ye' sen to tools. Al be waitin' 'ere fur when ye done," said the guard, with little ceremony before setting his back to the tunnel wall. He notched his thumb further down the tunnel. "Mine's that way."

"Um, thanks." Reyla pushed her face into a flat smile but was unable to match the sentiment.

She pulled a pickaxe from the box and swung it over her shoulder. Tharin followed as she ventured into the mines. The other Rugla seemed largely contented with ignoring them, but a lifetime of abject cruelty from her would-be comrades and countrymen left her suspicious.

Reyla pressed her thumb against the silver ring on her finger as her apprehensions increased. Collecting gold to create a coin was all well and good, but what would they do if the shrine lay somewhere else?

Reyla's ring tingled and pulled to the call of her concerns. She frowned down the mines and thought of the shrines once more. To her surprise, the pull seemed to be growing, becoming stronger and more regular as they walked away from the Core.

She decided to wait until after they had passed the Rugla before mentioning it to Tharin.

"Yeah, I feel it too," he replied, swinging the pickaxe over his shoulder. "That means it must be down here somewhere, right?"

"I suppose, but we should still collect the ore and complete the ceremony anyway. We don't want to upset our hosts..."

Tharin sniggered his agreement and together they began searching for gold veins, venturing deeper and deeper into the mines.

While she had no desire to return to the snow, Reyla found their path agitated her instincts in a far more sinister way. It felt unnatural to her. The cold, bare walls seemed to close in around them and grumbled against wooden brackets with the threat that they might soon fall. Balls of light were suspended in glass orbs from the ceiling to combat the darkness, but they flickered and dimmed the further they went from the entrance.

Unlike the tunnel leading down from the Stronghold's main gate, the mines were uneven and often dipped where the earth had proven too stubborn to move. Half-filled carts waited upon cast-iron tracks beside piles of rock and ore as the main path continued branching off into a labyrinth of winding side tunnels and mining spots.

Reyla followed the pull of her ring, making note of numbers etched into the rock face at each intersection. The number of branches decreased until they eventually came to a dead end. They checked their rings.

"So, we dig?" asked Tharin as he eyed the wall.

"Guess so."

Reyla swung her pickaxe over her shoulder before bringing it down against the wall. The metal made contact, the force echoing through the handle and into her arms before carrying off down the mine. Pins and needles filled Reyla's arms as she stepped back to see the pitiful impact she had made.

"Lemme try," offered Tharin, drawing his pickaxe above his head.

The pickaxe made contact with another metallic clink that echoed down the tunnels. A scattering of pebbles broke away as he pulled the pickaxe from the wall - but the impression left behind was minimal. Tharin breathed through his nose as he tried again, and again, putting as much weight as possible behind each swing.

"It's no use." He sighed. Reyla had long made the same conclusion but decided not to say anything. "What do we do?"

Reyla ran her hand over the wall, just thinking of the shrine causing the ring on her finger to hum. The pull was strong and consistent, letting her know that they were certainly in the right place. She continued along the wall and back again, scanning the surface and paying close attention to the direction the ring pulled her.

"There must be some kind of trick to it. It must be hidden like the one in Freya."

"We only saw the third when Wilona prayed too," added Tharin.

"That's true. Activate your artes."

"What?"

"Maybe it reacts to artes. Use them against the wall." Reyla spread her fingers as wide as possible and drew on her manacore. She willed the mana into her hand, activating her artes.

Tharin followed and the pair ran their hands over the solid surface.

"Jackpot! Found it!" Tharin cried, snatching his hand away as an emblem etched into the wall.

The emblem burned bright, causing them to shield their eyes as cracks formed in the wall. Light pushed through the cracks as they spread to the ceiling and floor, before crumbling away to nothing, revealing a door. It was made from white stone with the emblem embossed in gold just as they had seen in Freya, except now the emblem had four teardrop wings on either side.

"We're going in?" Tharin gasped as Reyla reached for the golden handle. "We don't have any gear."

"What did you think was going to happen? Besides, we might not have the opportunity to come back."

"Right." He nodded, tightening his grip on the pickaxe. "No choice. Just how we like it."

Tharin led the way, pushing on the heavy door to reveal a narrow, ragged tunnel. It was dark but a soft glow came from somewhere further inside, calling them forward. Fearing one of the miners would follow, Reyla closed the door behind them, blocking out the light from the tunnels. She held her arms out to the walls, following the sound of Tharin's footsteps as he shuffled towards the glow.

The pair stepped out into a cave, the ceiling home to hundreds of tiny luminescent rocks. Gem-filled stalactites and stalagmites created a glittering maze that guided them further. Thick veins of ore ran through their path and overhead as they continued, the air cold and damp.

"Surprised the Rugla haven't dug this place up already," Tharin commented, gazing up at the precious gems littering the walls.

The maze of stone thinned as they came across a golden statue of a man, or at least a representation of one as its features were poorly defined and lacked any detailing. It stood on a stone podium, almost seven feet tall with legs and arms that were thick as tree trunks. It was frightful but sad at the same time, almost as if it were unfinished. Reyla wondered if it was intended to be representative of the first Rugla as there was little of anything else in the cave.

"Hello?" Tharin's voice echoed around the cave before coming back to them. "Guess he's still sleeping…"

As if in response, a loud creak came from the statue as its golden limbs groaned into life. It heaved its enormous mass off the podium, hurling arms towards Tharin with little prompting.

Tharin dodged with only seconds to spare as its clumpy fist smashed into the ground. The Frey scattered to opposite sides of the cave, giving the statue a wide birth.

"Careful. I think it's a golem," warned Reyla, her eyes on the creature as it straightened back up.

"Like from the stories? Can't be, they're made of stone."

"You can cover stone, I–"

Reyla was unable to finish her sentence as the golem turned and ran towards her. She slid from its path, ducking under its swinging arms to safety.

"So how d'you defeat it?" asked Tharin.

The golem cut through her response, ramming into Tharin. He rolled out of the way as its arms crashed into unsuspecting stalactites, showering him with precious gems.

Reyla launched at the golem as it turned on Tharin. She grasped the handle of her pickaxe and jumped as she pulled it back. Sparks splintered as she hammered the metal against the golem's golden surface. She recoiled from the ricochet and the golem stumbled forward.

"Golems aren't sentient," Reyla finally managed. "We just need to break the stone at its core."

"In the gold?" Tharin gasped and eyed up the golem. "That's a lotta gold!"

Reyla circled the golem, its arms swinging to the side as its whole body rocked under its enormous weight. It was difficult to gauge what the golem was thinking – if it thought anything at all – as it wavered between them. Its expressionless golden face loomed head and shoulders above them, haunting, threatening.

All of a sudden, the golem somehow made eye contact with Reyla and stared her down. It squared off its shoulders, ignoring Tharin as he prepared to flank the thing.

Before the golem made its move, Tharin ran at its back. With his pickaxe held firmly in both hands, he swung at the base of its skull where the tip held firm. He was forced to abandon the pickaxe as the golem reacted to his attack, swinging its whole body.

"Well, that didn't work," said Tharin, watching the tool now embedded in the golem's neck.

"Then it's time we try something else," Reyla deduced aloud as she discarded her pickaxe and summoned fire to her hand. "If we can't crack this thing open, then we'll just have to melt it instead."

Reyla threw the ball of fire at the golem's back. It clenched as the fire landed, spinning on its heel to face her. The golem then bounded for Reyla, its feet unsteady as it stormed forward.

"Guess he didn't like that." She grinned and ran in to meet it head-on.

An unlikely game of chicken ensued, the golem fast closing in. Reyla pressed on, lifting her lead foot to the heel just before they collided, causing her to fall backwards and slide. Momentum carried her forward as she leant back on her foot and slid between its legs, blasting fire from her hands as they crossed.

Reyla rolled to her feet as the golem stumbled forward and turned again to face them. Its chest dripped from a molten pool of gold where her fire had landed. She grinned to Tharin as they shot looks of confirmation, a plan developing within the silence.

They each summoned fire to their hand, as the golem rebounded with newfound speed. Rocks flew into the air with each heavy golden step, crashing into the gem-covered walls as the Frey dodged from the golem's path. Reyla released her fire at the creature's back, catching its shoulder, while Tharin skimmed its leg, but it quickly recovered.

Reyla's boots skidded across the cave floor, swinging her around to stare down the faceless monster. She rushed in, pushing off the floor as she summoned fire, aiming for its head in hopes of finding the core.

She smashed fire into the golem's would-be face. Its body twisted to respond, pendulum arms swinging in her direction. She ducked under an arm, avoiding the attack – but failed to account for a second as it smashed into her. It knocked Reyla into the air, hurtling her into the cave wall where her vision went dark.

Gems rained down as Reyla landed on the floor. She didn't get back up.

"Reyla!" Tharin cried, clenching his fists.

An almighty surge of energy bubbled from within

Tharin's core. It burned through his body and into his hands where it burst into flames. With a primal roar, Tharin charged the golem, ploughing his flaming fists into its body. The golden surface slicked away like butter, the surface melting away with every swipe. Sweat leaked from Tharin's body through heat and exhaustion, but he gritted his teeth, relentless, never giving the golem the chance to land another attack.

Over and over, Tharin repeated his assault. Gold splattered over the cave, as he continued furiously beating away the soft metal until his fist made contact with something solid. He jolted. Right in the golem's centre, he found a heart of stone. With a flurry of excitement, Tharin brought his fist around for one final punch.

The stone cracked down the middle and shot free of the golem's body in a burst of molten gold. What remained of its torso held still, and its melted limbs dropped to the side before falling lifeless to the floor.

"Reyla," Tharin burst out, abandoning the golem to the bundle on the floor.

Her eyes fluttered open as he pulled her around to face him. A trickle of blood ran from her temple to her cheek.

"I'm fine, I'm fine," she assured him, her voice slurred as she came around. "What about the trial?"

"I think- I think I did it," replied Tharin nodding to the melted golem.

"I think you did too." Reyla smiled, patting him on the

shoulder.

Tharin's chest puffed with pride. "So then, where's–?"

"I'm here, I'm here," huffed a crusty voice.

The spirit of Gatruk Goldstorm, the first of the Rugla, appeared unceremoniously before them. He was a round man with thick grey hair. Although he was translucent, the gems set into his crown and armour still sparkled to a garish degree and multiple chins pressed up against his chest plate, forcing him to speak a semi-coherent mix between a groan and a mumble.

"Well done. You won, let's get this over with," he grumbled, stretching his hands towards them as a sudden wave came over them. "Now take the blessing and leave me alone."

"Is that it?" Reyla demanded, equal parts confused and insulted.

"What do you want from me? You have your blessing, go control the earth … yadda yadda yadda. Just leave me be. I'm old and dead. I want no part in whatever chaos my siblings may cause."

"Thanks, I guess," said Tharin.

Gatruk Goldstorm mumbled something at them under his breath, before fading away to nothing as unceremoniously as he had arrived.

Tharin turned to Reyla, his mouth ajar.

"Come on, let's go find some gold," she said.

"Can't we just use that?" asked Tharin, indicating the melted torso on the floor.

"You wanna explain why it's all melted?"

He snorted. "No, I guess not."

* * *

CHAPTER SEVEN

It was dark out when Arafrey finally awoke, her back stiff from sprawling over her desk. Her head was foggy and the world shone in a haze of Savulin-tinted lights.

She left her office to find Mika waiting in the quiet corridor. He followed, making no comment or judgement that she had missed the guard change.

Arafrey shivered. It was dark and unnaturally cold. Normally, the warmth of the Life Tree growing around them was enough to combat the winter cold, but this year was proving difficult all around. Steam rose from the manapool and the pews in the courtyard were frosted over – something she had never seen happen in all her years - but there it was. Yet more evidence of the sickness plaguing her kingdom.

Arafrey braced herself for the cold winds outside as Mika opened the door, but nothing prepared her for what came next.

"Bodair," she cried, dropping to a bundle in the entrance.

There was a slurred response as Bodair's eyes rolled behind his eyelids. Arafrey bundled him into her arms, scrambling to sit him upright on the temple stairs. His clothes were dirty, he reeked of alcohol, and he was cold, so very cold.

How long had he been out there?

"Quick, Mika, take him inside," she ordered, prompting Mika to take action. "There's a bed in the staff room."

Arafrey directed them to the room tucked away at the end of the corridor by her office. It was a small room with several bunks so the medics could rest in peace. Sister Francis was already awake for the night shift, so it was empty.

Mika dropped Bodair onto one of the bunks and returned to the corridor by her order, leaving them alone. Arafrey pulled a bed sheet over Bodair and dragged a stool to his bedside. She collected a bowl of water and a cloth before taking a seat.

"Oh, dear Bodair," she whined, brushing soaked hair from his face. "What have they done to you?"

He was so cold and pale, and his breathing shallow as he lay unresponsive. She wiped dirt from his face as gently as possible, although she doubted anything would wake him in his condition.

"We're not so different you and I," she whispered while dabbing his brow.

Arafrey wondered how her parents would react if it was her who was exposed. Perhaps her mother would have been happy for her, but her father was another matter entirely. Would he cast her aside as Bodair's parents had?

"It's all so horrible how they're treating you and there's so little we can do about any of it."

Arafrey's lips trembled, tears falling from her emerald eyes as she considered the hopelessness of his situation. The hopelessness of her situation.

Her heart broke further as she thought of Reyla and their last moments together. Arafrey had always hoped they would be able to figure it out someday, but that hope was as long gone as her beloved guard. It seemed Reyla was right all along; there was no hope for any of them. None at all.

A lump caught in the back of Arafrey's throat as she swallowed, a notion occurring to her.

"Except… There is something I can do," she corrected, drawing a deep breath as she set upon her determination. "Perhaps not now, but once I am queen."

Arafrey's body shook with sudden drive; the will of her promise rekindling something deep within her. It was time for her to stop indulging in childish fancies and face the harsh realities of her situation. She was done hiding from her future. Whether she was ready or not, her people needed her. Bodair needed her.

"You can't hear me, but I swear to you Bodair, when I am queen you will be able to love anyone you wish. Under my rule, I won't allow anyone to be treated like this, ever again.

"I promise you, I will change their ways.

"It's time for all of us to stop pretending and finally grow up."

* * *

CHAPTER EIGHT

Reyla returned to the mine entrance to find Ruby waiting for her.

"How'd it go?" she asked.

Reyla held up a gold nugget, victorious. It was about the same size as her fist, with a smooth and shiny surface.

"Tharin not back yet?" She scanned the tunnels.

"Not yet. Once he's back, I'll take you to the shrine so you can pay the toll."

Reyla tried to retrain her features as she decided how she felt about the whole thing. Smelting coins seemed easy enough in theory but she was hardly practised in such activities. Neither was she familiar with Ruglor's religious practices and was contented to continue ignoring them as she did her own. Besides, it wasn't like they needed to visit the shrine anymore.

Tharin arrived a while after, sweat pouring from his brow as he carried an ore in both hands. It was the size of a small child, but the surface was bumped and filled with holes.

"What d'you call that?" Ruby exclaimed. "Just how

many times d'you plan on visiting Gatruk?"

"What? I thought you said size mattered?"

"I'm sure it does to you tall folks." Ruby sniffed, winking.

"What's that supposed to mean?"

Reyla rolled her eyes as Ruby chuckled.

"Looks full o' impurities. Gee it 'ere," Ruby instructed.

Tharin dropped the gold to the ground allowing Ruby to swing a pickaxe upon it. The ore cracked and broke into several smaller pieces and Ruby threw one up to Tharin.

"That'll do ya," said Ruby. "Come on. The shrine's this way."

They followed Ruby back to the Core, her burgundy ponytail whipping behind her as before. They returned to the palace, walking the wide corridors and amber carpet to a section they had not seen before.

Ruby led them into a room with a burning furnace that extended up through the ceiling. A solid wooden workbench lay covered in heavy metal tools. There was a door in the wall facing them made from stone and carved with a square pattern, and beside it, a golden chute came up from the ground with a coin-sized slot in the top.

The temperature rose as soon as the door closed behind them.

"All you 'ave to do now is melt yer ore and pour it into

the mould," Ruby instructed. "Easy enough. Though I'd better take some of the impurities outta yours, Tharin."

Tharin handed the ore over to Ruby.

She activated her artes as she accepted it, brushing her fingers over the surface causing it to ripple. As Ruby pulled her hand away, small flecks of stone came with it to collect in her palm. The gold moved around the impurities like liquid, the nugget shrinking as it reformed to accommodate the large chunk of removed minerals now residing in Ruby's hand.

"That should be enough," she said, casually handing back the nugget and discarding the scum in a bucket. "Just pop yer gold in the crucible and shove it in the furnace. Once it's hot enough, pull it out and pour it in the moulds."

Reyla half-listened as Ruby went on to explain the methods the Rugla used to melt and purify the ore in great detail. Ruby then gave them a full history of each of the tools provided before explaining how they were used. She found it amusing to see how excitable Ruby got about anything even remotely technological, but it reminded her of another inquisitive woman whom Reyla was trying to forget.

Tharin took his gold to the crucible first, carrying it to the furnace using metal tongs and thick gloves provided. He stepped back as Ruby held the door open and a gust of blazing hot air escaped its belly. With the crucible placed inside, Ruby closed the door, allowing Reyla to follow suit.

With their ore melted, the two Frey took turns removing their crucibles from the furnace. They each poured the molten gold into moulds upon the workbench, the gold hissing as it made contact with the cold surface. As they poured, Ruby activated her artes before the crucible spouts, pushing any remaining impurities back so they didn't fall into the mould.

"Just pay the toll and on ye go," said Ruby pointing to the slot in the golden chute by the door. "I'll be here when you're done."

Reyla wondered where all the coins went as she dropped hers into the slot. She listened as Tharin released his, but was unable to hear either of them land. Something told Reyla that it was unlikely the Rugla were willing to leave such valuable offerings to collect within the ground undisturbed. Then again, given the decoration of the true shrine in the mines, it was always possible that Gatruk had devised a way to collect it himself.

Reyla pushed on the shrine door, closing it behind them as they entered.

The room had a golden statue of Gatruk Goldstorm in the middle – or at least that's who she assumed it was supposed to be, as the Rugla they met ever so briefly carried fewer muscles than this statue suggested. Fire burned in golden spheres in each corner, the flames an unnatural red that filled the room. Each of the walls were adorned with thick tapestries, embroidered with golden thread that glittered in the light.

Reyla dropped to the floor, resting her knees upon a thick cushioned mat and her bottom on her shoes. She brought her hands together, clasping them in prayer, and closed her eyes.

"What're you doing?" asked Tharin.

Reyla looked up, opening one eye to pinched brows as Tharin returned her gaze.

"We paid the toll," she replied, shirking her shoulders. "May as well pray whilst we're here."

Tharin snorted, but considered her response before joining her on the mat.

Reyla drew a deep breath and closed her eyes. It had been her idea, but now she was praying she regretted the decision as her thoughts returned home. She wondered how her people were coping with the sickness and imagined the ways it would affect them.

There was no doubt in Reyla's mind that with Elsafrey gone, Princess Arafrey would have been forced to marry; she would have to before taking the role of high priestess. Her heart grew heavy and her stomach ran stale as she wondered *who*. Who would Galafrey strong-arm the princess into marrying? Which undeserving nobleman got to spend his wedding night with *her* princess?

Reyla fought against the tide of her emotions and pushed them back into the dark waters of her past.

'*It's better this way,*' she told herself. But the mountain would sooner swallow her whole than give her the peace she required.

* * *

"All good?" asked Ruby as they left the shrine.

"All good." Tharin grinned, raising his thumb.

"Then follow me," Ruby replied, guiding them back down into the Core.

Reyla walked silently behind them, quietly reorganising her thoughts and emotions. She was the one who had said it was time to grow up. She had been the one to end things. So why couldn't she just move on?

"Which one of you wants to reinforce some thread for me?" asked Ruby.

"Not me," replied Tharin. "Was never any good at that kind of thing."

"I can do it," offered Reyla, happy for a task to keep her mind occupied.

"That's what I was hoping to hear," said Ruby as they entered her workshop to find Cid waiting for them. He was hunched over a small spindle-like contraption.

"It's been a while since I've seen one of these," said Reyla.

She sat before the wooden spindle. A full ream of cream silk thread sat on one side; Cid had already wrapped it around the wheel for her. The wheel sat above a foot pedal which turned the empty spool connected to the other end of the thread.

"How strong do you want it?" Reyla asked, testing the tension with her finger.

"It needs to hold the fabric airtight together, but we still need to cut it," Ruby explained.

"Gotcha," Reyla replied, having no idea what that actually meant.

Reyla held her hands around the thread. She pressed on the foot pedal, her hands glowing as she activated her artes and began reinforcing the silk. The thread grew darker as the molecules combined, coiling around the empty spool to Reyla's busy beat.

Cid inspected her work. "You're pretty good at that."

"Reyla's pretty good at all kinds of things," bragged Tharin as if the compliment were his own. "She used to be the princess' personal aide."

"You worked for the princess?" Ruby marvelled. Reyla bobbed her head in agreement, saving her focus for the spindle. "What's she like?"

"We both did, one time or another," said Tharin. "She's not as shiny as Elsafrey, but she's still pretty smart."

"Shiny?" Cid frowned. "What d'ya mean?"

"I dunno how else to explain. Elsafrey always had this glow about her, but Arafrey always seemed kinda… I dunno… Sad… Kinda like she didn't want to be there, you know?"

Reyla looked up from the spindle so fast that she nearly choked. She had always assumed she was the only one who knew how Arafrey felt. It worried her to think Tharin had noticed. Did anyone else? *Did he see through her too?*

"So, where you off to next?" asked Ruby.

Tharin went to answer, but soon turned to Reyla.

She gave it some thought. As they had received no directions from the spirit, they would have to decide where to go themselves.

"Agrana will be our best bet," she replied, still rhythmically pushing the foot pedal. "We should try and source your mana-crystals."

This was only half true.

It occurred to her that the trials they had already faced gave them artes; the gift of healing, then control over fire, water and earth. That left only two other elemental arte users, the Agrana and Puwhar. Their rings would confirm her theory when they passed the border.

"Well, I've got te head up that way tomorrow, so I'll take ye back to the gate to grab yer gear," said Cid. "Afraid the mines are undergoing maintenance or we'd get ye a lift. I don't begrudge you walking down them mountains in this weather."

"Don't worry, we'll see ye off right," Ruby assured. "We don't want you getting lost to the cold. There's enough dangers out there without worrying about the weather."

* * *

CHAPTER NINE

Callius entered the throne hall the night of the return celebrations to applause as the herald announced his arrival.

He waited for the applause to decay before crossing toward the throne. His citizens turned to extend their gratitude and well wishes as he passed. Callius smiled and exchanged pleasantries, then snagged a filled goblet from one of the serving staff before taking his seat.

Alone upon his throne, Callius watched over his people as they gathered around the edge of the hall. Many danced in pairs below the candelabra to the music from a lyre and harp. Others picked at the lavish buffet running along the wall, a vast platter of meats and cheeses piled higher than some of his guests.

The hall continued to fill and the atmosphere warmed with idle chatter as the festivities progressed. Servers circled the crowds with wine and the people called on them greedily. It was truly a momentous occasion.

Callius swelled with pride. As mundane as these events had become, he always felt such satisfaction in seeing his people so joyous.

"Now entering, Lady Nymati Tamun and son Amynus, of Sudra," announced the herald.

All eyes turned to the herald and the room fell into a soft tremor of murmurs that rumbled beneath the music. The Duran lords and ladies studied the two Sudra with burning intensity, curious to see what they did.

The pair were dressed in the finest Duran attire: Nymati a flowing ivory gown cinched with a golden waistband and Amynus a beige tunic that cut above the knee. Callius imagined neither Sudra was overly fond of the thick fabrics and undergarments, but they hid it well, along with any other apprehensions they might have been carrying.

Callius' violet gaze followed as they circled the hall, the crowd parting around them as they collected drinks. Even from across the hall, he could see the frown on Amynus' face, although he was rarely without it. Nymati ignored him, as always, her arm hooked tightly around his as she guided them through the socialites.

Callius tried not to be obvious in his observations and watched through his periphery as their path crossed with Councilman Martel. He and Nymati had already come to disagree on several occasions, but it seemed the pair were beginning to warm to each other. They appeared to exchange pleasantries, while Amynus brooded, before parting on good terms.

A flutter ran through Callius' stomach as he spotted other keen eyes upon the Sudra, who judged the interaction for themselves. He had expected their curiosity but was unable to gauge their reaction from such a distance.

There was no doubt in his mind that Nymati was exactly what his people needed. Whether they would accept her as their own was still to be determined. She may have done well pleasing the council, but that could soon change once marriage put Nymati between them and the crown.

Callius drummed his fingers against the throne arm. It was a risk, but one that would change the course of history if executed properly. With Nymati by his side, the Sudra would grow as loyal as his citizens, and the empire would become an unstoppable force. Together, he and Nymati could unite Alamantra and bring about a new era of peace and prosperity – he could see it so clearly.

The emperor continued observing those around Nymati as she and Amynus finished their circuit, waiting for the right moment to begin his speech.

He rose to his feet as the song finished and the dancers bowed, raising his drink into the air. The musicians paused, a still coming over the hall as the patrons turned to face him.

Callius cleared his throat, then did it again for good measure. Never before had he felt so nervous to face them.

"Welcome." Callius held his arms wide as if to embrace them. "Tonight, we celebrate as I return from my expedition to Sudra successful."

"For the empire!" cried the crowd with a round of applause.

"The Sudra are a formidable people who are sure to strengthen our empire even further," he continued, treading carefully so as not to offend Nymati. "Already my dream of uniting Alamantra is coming to fruition and I have you, my loyal citizens, to thank for that."

Conducting his crowd came as easily to him as breathing. His booming words filled the hall, and his citizens swayed to the timbre of his imperial aria.

"And how shall I repay your loyalty?" he asked, spreading his arms even further. "Already I have given you gold…"

There was a cheer from the hall.

"Power."

They cheered again.

"And land."

More cheers.

"What more could I give you?" asked Callius, pausing as excited whispers polkaed around the hall.

"And so I asked myself: what is it our empire is missing? What is the one thing I have yet to provide my people?" he teased, taking great pleasure in their growing excitement. "Then it dawned on me. I have yet to provide you with an empress and heir to lead us in our new age of prosperity."

The murmurs returned as heads turned to see if anyone knew what or who he was talking about. Callius scanned them with delight as greedy eyes lit up, each quietly hoping it would be their name he called out.

"Which is why I asked none other than Nymati Tamun to become my wife and empress," he announced with pride to many suddenly stunned faces. "I can think of no one better to stand by my side than the legendary Demon Queen herself."

The councilmen led the celebrations as Callius gestured for Nymati to come to join him by the throne. It was their job to fall in line, but they needed little prompting. *Excellent.*

"If we are to make Alamantra whole, then we need to embrace those we welcome into the empire," he called over their response, placing a tentative palm on the small of Nymati's back. "And how better to welcome our new Sudran brethren than to hold a tournament, following Sudran rules, to celebrate our engagement."

Callius simpered. The crowd seemed to like that one too, their elation only growing.

"And, once we are wed, I shall return to Halda, where I will gather our armies and prepare to take the west. With Agrana technology arriving as we speak, Freya and Pudron combined will be no match against our will."

"For the empire!" the crowd roared.

Callius basked in their adoration with Nymati by his

side, his hand still lingering behind her. He breathed with a sense of accomplishment, truly excited about the future for the first time in many years.

Nymati sighed beside him, frustration pinching her features as Amynus slipped by the herald to the exit.

"You needn't worry about him so much," Callius assured her. "I checked with the guards, and he's hardly left the palace all week."

"That's what worries me," she hissed, her contempt simmering. "My son could start a forest fire in a snowstorm."

"Then it's a good job there are no forests nearby." Callius snorted, a smile cracking across his square jaw. "Could come in handy invading Freya though."

Nymati chuckled, her tail flicking behind her. "That's not such a bad idea."

* * *

Amynus stormed through the Duran palace, but quickly realised he had nowhere to go, and returned to his bedroom.

He kicked open his door with fury, causing Saffia to jump as the door bounced off the furniture.

"Shouldn't you be at the party?"

Amynus released a guttural roar, his anger, betrayal and frustration all bundled up into a single primal retort.

"It's official. Mother is marrying the emperor," he fumed loudly, slamming the door behind him.

"Are you okay?"

"I'm fine, it's just– She acts as if it never happened," he raved. "It's as if he never killed my father. Like she doesn't care."

"Now, you know that isn't true," Saffia replied softly, taking his hand in hers.

Although her hands were gloved, they were still warm as she activated her artes against him. He sighed, releasing his fury as his shoulders dropped. The effects were lessened but welcome. He was even willing to admit that he might hold true affections towards Saffia but could never be certain she wouldn't betray him eventually.

"I just hate it here. There's nothing to do. Nowhere to go. I wish we'd never left Sudra."

"Well... I hope it's not all bad," Saffia cooed, moving closer.

"No, I suppose you're right," he replied, his earlier mood replaced with something much more devilish.

Saffia stroked her finger along the collar of his tunic. She smelt like bread and dish soap; like comfort and warmth warped into a single touch. Just being near her was enough to soothe his temper and kindle his appetite.

"What would you do now?" Saffia asked, the hushed syllables patting towards warmer climates. "You know your mother wouldn't be very happy if you killed the emperor and ruined her plans."

Amynus growled as he pushed her away. "Perhaps that would make her consider bringing me into the fold." He was always the last to know anything. "What do I care anyway? The emperor will be a far easier target once Mother gets her claws into him. No Duran will be able to resist her charm or quench her appetite."

"And in the meantime?"

"Perhaps I shall join the army," Amynus replied, turning back.

He stroked a soft thumb across Saffia's cheek, summoning his most charming smile as he cocked his brow. Her cheek warmed beneath his touch. His pulse throbbing, he slipped his hands around her waist and stared deep into her malachite eyes.

"Of course, I'll need to continue my training," he breathed, with no need for any charm as Saffia fell into his embrace. "There's no point in me getting sloppy just because my prey does."

Saffia nuzzled into his neck, tracing his jaw with the tip of her tongue. She kissed his ear and whispered, "I kinda like it when we get sloppy…"

* * *

Nymati excused herself from the party as soon as she could manage. She rummaged through her ivory layers to find her cigarette tin as she slipped from the hall onto the quiet veranda. It was out, and a cigarette was placed to her lips before the door had closed behind her.

She struck a match, inhaling greedily as she leant back against the palace wall. Nymati exhaled, aiming the smoke at the night skies as she admired the crescent moon and enjoyed her moment of peace.

"Is it true?" a voice accused from the shadows.

Nymati flicked her eyes to the source. Aeryn's stony stare glared back at her.

She returned to her cigarette with a scowl, drawing deeply as she considered her position.

After being poisoned with the emperor that night, Nymati was cautious of her staff and had kept much to herself. The traitor was certainly among them, but Aeryn? Would Aeryn, of all her girls, be the one to betray her? Even so, was it worth the risk to trust her?

Nymati remained silent.

"I don't understand. Why didn't you tell me you were marrying the emperor?"

"Should I run everything by you?" Nymati's eyes shot back to Aeryn.

Nymati finished her cigarette and flicked the end to the ground. Aeryn looked away, wincing as if it were her Nymati had discarded.

"I didn't think so."

"But he killed Drazah," Aeryn pleaded. "Was– was this all part of your plan?"

"No, but plans change, they adapt. As should we," replied Nymati, catching her temper; the emperor would be unhappy if she made a scene. "Besides, I am as much to blame as the emperor. Drazah should never have challenged him." Nymati curled away from Aeryn, resetting as she brushed down her layers and cleared her throat. "Now I'll have you remember your place and I'll hear no more questions from you."

"But–"

"But nothing. It is only by my will that you are not tossed to the streets," Nymati scolded, the rigidity of her stance reflected in her posture. "You'd do well to remember where you came from."

Aeryn retreated and bowed her head. "Yes, M'lady."

"Inform the rest of the girls we will be staying in Dura for the foreseeable future. I'll hear no more on the matter. Understood?"

"Yes, M'lady."

"Now leave me be. I have politics to tend."

Nymati blew past Aeryn before she could respond,

leaving her alone with her anger and betrayal.

An action Aeryn swore she would live to regret.

* * *

CHAPTER TEN

Arafrey returned to the temple the next morning to find Bodair still sleeping in the staff room. The temple aides had left him be and carried on their duties as normal, so Arafrey decided to do likewise and set about her routine.

It was around midday when a rather blue-skinned Bodair shuffled into her office, his face mournful and defeated.

"Oh, Priestess!" he cried, collapsing into the chair across from her. "I'm beyond sorry for being an inconvenience to you. You have my deepest gratitude for taking care of me."

"What happened?"

"I have been cast aside! Thrown out!"

Even hungover Bodair had a flare for the dramatic and draped over the office chair as he whined.

"They've cancelled all my plays and discredited my papers. I've been living with friends but last night… Last night…" He wiped his hands over his face. "I decided I would hold my head high and attend the party at my parents' house. Oh, Ara, you should've seen their faces!"

Arafrey held her breath as Bodair retold the events of the previous evening to the best of his hazy recollection. Her stomach tightened with a fast-rising fury. *How could anyone treat their own child so poorly?*

"And now, my only friends want nothing to do with me. They fear their reputations will be sullied by association. My life is over! Whatever shall I do?"

'What would he do?' she wondered. His parents were prominent enough that few Frey would be willing to cross them and would likely cast Bodair aside as they had. He would have to leave Ceynas to have any hopes of finding employment.

"I just..." His voice cracked and he sighed. "I just. I thought they cared enough." He looked away, wiping tears from his coppery eyes.

Arafrey pressed her hands together, unable to find the correct words. Her heart broke for him. It broke for herself and all the Frey like them who were forced to hide their feelings. She wanted to cry with him, but would not allow herself. It would do neither of them any good. The time for tears had long passed. She needed to be strong enough for both of them.

"How's the hangover?" she asked, her own head still hazy from Savulin Tonic.

"It's no more than I deserve, quite frankly. I've no job and I wasted the last of my coin in the tavern."

"You know, we have an opening here in the temple,"

Arafrey offered. "I have yet to appoint a personal aide if you'd be interested."

"An aide?" he repeated, sitting up in the chair.

"It's a lowly job to be sure, but I can give you a room at the temple and a small wage." She regretted each word to this effect, he deserved so much better than she was able to offer. "You would have to clean and manage my schedule."

"I'll take it. Of course I will." His eyes gleamed. "How can I ever repay you?"

"Just go collect your things and get settled in the staff quarters."

Bodair jumped to his feet, the green returning to his cheeks. His smile widened so much it warmed her lonely heart.

"And while you're at it," Arafrey added. "I'd like you to take a message to Miles Chadwin."

"Chadwin?" He turned, surprised. "Sure. What's the message?"

"Inform him, I would like to accept his offer."

* * *

CHAPTER ELEVEN

Reyla was woken by a loud knock as Cid and Ruby burst into their room.

She had barely opened her eyes and swung her legs over the side of her bed when Ruby dropped heavy sacks on the foot. The mattress shook from the weight, rattling her bones.

"Scavenged what we could from the kitchen," explained Ruby. "Should be enough to get you down the mountain."

Reyla gave her thanks while rubbing her shoulder awake.

"You'll be wanting these," added Cid, dropping a mound on Tharin's bed. "They're made for Estra but should keep you warm. They don't wear shoes but pulled together some leg warmers that'll go over yer boots nicely."

Tharin picked up a bracer but recoiled as his fingers touched fur.

"We couldn't possibly," he protested.

"Afraid y' don't have much choice, lad," Cid warned.

"The snow's no' stopped since you arrived. Surprised y' dint freeze to death on the way up here."

Reyla couldn't refute his logic. They didn't have much choice. Surely the animals and Gods would forgive them if it meant completing their trials and saving the planet.

"He's right. Gear up," she told Tharin, nodding at the pile. "It's better we stay warm."

Cid and Ruby waited as they switched their gear. They replaced their leaf-leather bracers with fur-lined ones that ran up to their elbows and had metal plates set into the leather. The leg warmers were thick with rabbit skin and strapped around their ankles and knees. About their waists, they tied pelts into skirts that covered their thighs, leaving a slit down one side so as not to restrict their movement. Finally, they were given hats of grey wolf fur that pulled down over the pointed tips of their ears.

"It'll have to do," said Ruby, taking measurements in her notepad. "You'll need proper gear before going to Askana though. Their summers make oor winters seem pleasant."

"We'll keep that in mind," Reyla assured her, already nauseous from the smell of animal hides.

Equipped and loaded, they returned to the palace level of the Core and prepared to cross the chasm.

"Take care not to get lost in Agrana," warned Ruby as she waved them off by the bridge. "I'll be eagerly awaiting your return."

The two Frey waved back, and Cid showed them to the entrance of the Stronghold.

* * *

A wave of relief washed over Reyla as she shouldered her backpack and was reunited with her blades. She stroked the leaf-leather sheath of her trusty knife, as if to apologise for leaving it so long, and swore never to do so again.

"From the entrance, follow the path down 'til it splits in three, then head directly west. You'll reach the border within a week," said Cid, his face red from having walked so far. "Stay true from the fork. If ye head west too early, you'll miss the northern bridge and have to get wet or walk around."

"Right," said Reyla, mentally preparing herself to begin travelling again. She turned to Tharin. "You ready?"

"As ready as I'm gonna be," he replied dourly, looking up the tunnel and pulling his shoulder straps tight. "Let's do this thing."

"We'll be back soon," Reyla assured, the pair waving their goodbyes as they continued to the exit and out into the winter snow.

* * *

A Guard's Request

THE GUARD'S REQUEST

8 MONTHS BMF

* * *

I never imagined things would deteriorate so fast.

I watched from my void,

certain Alamantra was in good hands.

That my world would be saved.

What a fool I was…

* * *

CHAPTER ONE

Winter reigned supreme as Reyla and Tharin descended the last leg of the Ruglor foothills.

The morning sun hid behind a sky of white clouds, leaving the landscape perpetually grey and dismal. Before them, the frostbitten landscape levelled and the trees grew short. Snow crunched beneath their feet. Birds flew between the leaf-bare trees in search of food, but there was little on offer.

"Now, I'm not saying I agree with killing animals for food. I just appreciate the fact they didn't put anything to waste," explained Tharin, examining his new bracer with his arm held high. "And, once you get over the smell, these duds really aren't all that bad."

"They are kinda comfy," Reyla agreed, enjoying the warmth her new gear provided. They surely wouldn't have survived the return trip without them.

Reyla glanced over her shoulder. The mountains of Ruglor seemed so far away as the snow-covered peaks hid behind a band of thick clouds. She wondered if they were close to the Agrana border and looked to her ring for guidance, but there was no reaction. They weren't far off though and were making good time as their blessings offered them the additional energy needed to push forward at unnatural speeds.

With only Tharin to compare to, it was difficult to tell, but Reyla could no longer deny it. The blessings didn't just unlock their artes, they were changing them. The only question was, how?

Reyla returned her sights to the landscape ahead, her enhanced vision catching upon mice as they foraged through the frozen foliage. She noticed other things too, things she would not have before. Her pointed ears twitched at the smallest sounds, able to isolate the crackle of a blackbird's talons as they wrapped around crisp branches from a distance. As she breathed, she could taste the damp decay of the marshes they had yet to enter and smell the freshwater of a stream running nearby. Everything was loud and raw, yet the power at her disposal left her strong and invulnerable.

It was all quite extraordinary, exhilarating even, but she stilled, worried. They were not even halfway through their journey and had already seen such a change. What more would these blessings offer them? And how much more would they change?

"What do you suppose the Agrana trial will entail?" asked Tharin, side-stepping to avoid a slush puddle. "I don't know all that much about Agrana artes."

"That's not surprising, they're pretty protective of their tech." Reyla's knowledge was limited to a few brief interactions and what she remembered from Arafrey's studies. "Agrana artes control electricity like the Pudra do with fire — not that we faced the Pudron trial for comparison."

"So, it's like summoning lightning to their hands?"

"Exactly. And they use this to power all kinds of machines," Reyla explained to a wide-eyed Tharin – the lecture returning her to a state of normality. It also brought her a strange sense of accomplishment and she fancied that, if she ever retired, she could make a good go of it as a teacher as she didn't half mind imparting her knowledge to such an eager audience. "I hear they can draw mana directly from the Manastream to trap it inside mana-crystals."

"That's pretty cool," said Tharin, flexing his fingers as if imagining sparks between them. "Still, I can't think of no electric creatures. An eel maybe? Or is that too similar to Najra? Whatever he was."

"You're getting ahead of yourself. There's still no guarantee that Agrana's our next trial."

As the pair continued west, the snow melted into slush as the temperature rose, turning the soil to mush and leaving their shoes waterlogged. Their new gear kept them warm and their artes allowed them to raise shelter each night, but Reyla had long grown tired of sleet and snow and longed for the forests of Freya. She was altogether miserable and dreaded the cold weather awaiting them in Askana. Equally, she was grateful for her companion's cheery disposition as it broke through the darkness and held her demons in check.

"Looks like you were right," announced Tharin excitedly, prompting Reyla to check her ring. "The next trial is in Agrana."

"Then that's where we'll go," she replied looking north-west with the pull on her finger. "Let's just hope the spirit there is more helpful than the last."

"Ha! That won't be difficult."

* * *

Rain returned to the Agrana skies as they slogged through the overgrown marshes. The rain dissolved much of the snow and ice overnight, causing the marsh waters to rise.

The northern terrain was more unforgiving and denser than the southern trade route they had travelled before. It was not all bad though. Wild berry bushes cluttered the thick treeline, and they scavenged a great bounty of green parsnips and kale-like foliage to fill their bellies.

They had yet to meet a single soul in Agrana, but every few days they would cross over the vast networks of mana sources likely belonging to their people. Reyla knew there would be an accompanying entrance to the underground cities within their vicinity, and made sure to steer clear from them.

It was still morning when they found a wide river blocking their path. The surface lay thick with algae that gathered around the banking, but in the middle, the current ran fast, streaking south under the surface.

"Guess this means we missed the bridge."

"Hmm. The Ballish should thin at some point, but it's not guaranteed to be close." Reyla sighed, her thoughts running as she scanned the murky water.

It was impossible to tell how deep the river ran but ducks gathered in pairs, vanishing as they dived in search of food. The Ballish wouldn't end until they reached an ocean and there was no way for them to tell how far they missed the bridge by, or which direction it lay in.

"Do you think there's another bridge?" asked Tharin, straining to see downriver. "We could always try raising one ourselves. I don't fancy swimming."

"No, me neither," Reyla continued searching their surroundings for a solution.

"What if we make a raft and use our artes to push them?"

"Well, if we're using our artes we may as well…" Reyla began as if to tease him, but trailed off as something occurred to her. "Have you ever seen Shey walk on water?"

"Walk on water?" Tharin repeated, his nose wrinkled.

"They used it to ambush us during skirmishes on the border," she explained. Her face scrunched as she struggled to recall such long-buried memories. "I'm not sure how they managed it, but it looked like they were skating across the surface."

Tharin scoffed. "And you think we're going to do that?"

"Have you another solution?"

He didn't respond.

"We have these blessings; we may as well use them. We should probably even try mastering them if we expect to pass these trials."

Tharin huffed his agreement. "So how do we do it?"

"Damned if I know. Maybe it's like synthesis. Try pulling the surface together to increase the density."

"Oh, Reyla! You know I'm no good at synthesis."

"And I'm no good at healing, yet my shoulder's given me no bother in weeks," Reyla returned. "Just shoot for gold. We're not getting across otherwise."

"Shoot for gold." Tharin snorted as the pair stepped up to the water's edge.

Reyla activated her artes in her right hand, summoning the mana from her core as her hand glowed softly. She imagined the water coming together, the molecules growing tighter, as she would when manipulating organic matter. Her fingers tensed, casting ripples over the surface as the water collected below her hand, creating a translucent plate.

Breathing a silent prayer, Reyla lifted her boot over the plate, hesitating as she imagined her foot stepping through. As her boot touched the water, the plate dipped. The water bent under her weight, pulling on her activated artes. She pushed on her mana reserves to counter the resistance, fighting the tension as her muscles trembled and threatened to fail.

"So far so good," Tharin encouraged, watching patiently from the safety of the bank.

Spurred on by his words, Reyla activated artes in her left hand, collecting the water as she had before. With a second plate fully formed, she prepared to leave the bank. Holding her breath, she stepped from the safety of the soil onto the watery plate. It pulled on her arms as her weight forced the plate down, but she pushed on her mana to compensate, clenching her fists as she strained to hold herself still.

Balanced upon her plates with her feet wide, Reyla turned over her shoulder to Tharin. "Well, come on then."

"Sometimes, I really wish you'd just suck at something," Tharin complained and tightened his gear as he prepared to try himself. "What's your plan for moving?"

"Um…"

Reyla frowned at her feet, wobbling as she shifted to

maintain her balance. She breathed through her nose, her shoulders dropping as she centred her weight. Calm and steady, Reyla slid her right foot forward, moving her hand with it as she pulled the water below. She pushed on her artes, affirming her control over the watery plates and repeated the motion with her left foot.

Reyla inched forward, shifting her weight from one foot to the other. Behind her, Tharin followed suit, his arms held wide to maintain his balance.

"You make it look so easy." He scowled, throwing his arms out wide as the plates dipped below the water.

"It gets easier if you keep moving," Reyla instructed, falling into a rhythmic to and fro.

Reyla's confidence grew as she slipped closer to the centre of the algae-covered river. Her speed increased as she pushed her artes against the water. Propelling forward, she swayed from one foot to the other with natural grace. She flexed her fingers to affirm her control over the artes, the activated mana slowly sapping away her extensive energy supply.

Water hissed at her feet as Reyla looked back to check on Tharin. He strained to catch up, water soaking his lower half as he sliced through the water unevenly, his caramel hair slicking back as he gained momentum.

As Reyla returned to the river ahead, something appeared on the surface.

Her heart jolted. Unable to stop, Reyla squinted her

eyes forward as a leathery stone shone among the algae. She pushed on, skating over the water as another stone appeared beside it. And another. It was then the stones opened their eyes, their cold reptilian stares striking fear into her chest.

"Don't panic," Reyla shouted without breaking contact. "But there's something in the water."

"There's what?"

"Some kind of–"

Reyla started as the water broke before her. A set of wide teeth-filled jaws appeared in front of her. She swerved, water spraying behind her as she struggled to stay afloat. More jaws appeared from beneath the water, snapping shut as fast as they opened, before crashing back down, causing the river to wave.

Tharin veered away as they gained their first clear view of the creatures. Fearsome beasts, some near three metres in length.

"Alligators! Whatever you do, don't stop!"

"Wasn't planning on it!"

Heart pounding, Reyla pushed on her artes, rushing for the riverbanks. Water crashed around them as jaws snipped at their ankles, the beasts missing by mere inches. Steam gritted through Reyla's teeth as she prepared to face the swarming alligators head-on.

She didn't have the time to mind what Tharin was

doing, as the alligators raced toward her. They climbed over each other in a frenzied attempt to reach her first, their tails flailing like clubs. Drawing on her mana reserves, Reyla blasted water from beneath her feet, but no amount of velocity would help her as a wall of alligators blocked her path.

With nothing but a hope and a prayer, Reyla gave one final push on her artes and leapt into the air. Her gear weighed her down but momentum carried her forward as she stepped over the first gaping maw and into the line of another.

Reyla reactivated her artes, arcing over the scrambling alligators. She pulled water into a tall, narrow wave around them to meet her feet. Reyla focused her control into a single plate, her left hand holding it still as she moved the river with her right. Waving above the confused alligators, she surfed upon her plate to the water's edge, the wind breezing through her chestnut mane as she reached the bank.

Reyla gasped for breath, rejoicing as soil squelched beneath her feet. She released her artes, her body burning from her hands to her mana core from overuse. Her palms stung and her legs wobbled as she staggered to safety. She gulped down another breath as Tharin stumbled in beside her.

"We'd better keep going," he suggested, inclining his head to the fast-approaching alligators.

"After you," she managed, and the pair set off in a jog.

* * *

It was just after midday when the two Frey finally slowed their pace. Reyla's limbs cracked and creaked as they came to a halt, her lungs raw.

"I guess now we know where all those merchants went," mused Tharin, dropping to his knees with the heavy thud of his gear against his shoulders. "I heard alligators were big, but that was something else."

Reyla snorted, still short of breath as she leaned against a tree for support. When–

THWACK.

Reyla recoiled as an arrow landed firmly in the tree trunk. In unison, they turned to the source as a barrage of arrows arced towards them. Exhausted, Reyla launched herself behind cover, pressing as close to the trees as possible.

Reyla chanced a glance around her tree but saw nothing among the overgrown marshes. "You see anything?"

Tharin strained around a tree. He was just shaking his head in the negative when another volley of arrows rained down upon them, whistling and thumping into the marshes.

Reyla closed her eyes and cast her senses as wide as she could manage. Her ears caught crunching and her nose picked up leathers, but it wasn't enough. She focused further still, the flow of mana around her brushing against her consciousness as she reached out to those around her as if connecting to the Life Tree. Her stomach dropped.

They were surrounded.

"We're gonna have to make a break for it," Reyla instructed. "Follow the rings and aim for the shrine."

"Right."

"On my count, keep your head low and run. Ready?"

Tharin nodded his head, bracing against the tree as he prepared to run. Reyla waited for another assault of arrows to soar before shouting:

"Now!"

The pair turned north and ran. A fourth volley of arrows ricocheted off the shield attached to Reyla's pack, but she couldn't stop. Head down, she pushed into a sprint, arrows flying past like warring birds.

"There's too many of them," Tharin called out to Reyla. "Should we?"

She already knew his thinking. "Let's."

The two exchanged a final glance and separated. Reyla went left, Tharin right.

Reyla focused on the marshes ahead, stretching her senses in hopes of catching signs of the figures now following her. Arrows whipped through the air, missing by the smallest of margins, but it was only dumb luck. Each harried step echoed through her limbs. Her energy was long depleted, but her legs kept moving, propelled only by adrenaline and fear.

Reyla dared to believe she was doing well. Given the number of arrows still being released, it seemed the number following her had dropped from five to two. Even without her blessings, Reyla reckoned she could outpace most Agrana, but they were more accustomed to the terrain and a few gained on her.

Each step became a battle of attrition between her heart and mind. Her muscles were annihilated. Cramps ran the length of her body as she ducked and wove between the trees, but it was a strain in all regards. She wasn't sure how much longer she could keep it up.

Reyla summoned the energy to avoid a fallen tree, launching over the trunk as arrows battered off her pack. Her foot came upon the ground, but as she sprang, the floor gave way beneath her.

Reyla dropped helplessly as the ground swallowed her whole. She fell into a deep hole, landing with a crack as her head bounced off the very bottom.

Her vision blurred, Reyla looked up as silhouetted heads poked over the sides.

Panicking, she scrambled to pick herself up and fend them off. Her heart beat against her chest as she clawed at the muddy walls. Her knees buckled with little prompting and she crumbled to the ground. There was nothing she could do.

She had no more to give.

She was trapped.

Everything went dark.

* * *

Subject 236 – Log Entry No.1

The specimen was brought to my attention after a routine farming expedition. Subject, Frey, female, late-twenties, excellent condition. She withstood chi-harvesting and produced a white chi-crystal.

Initial observations turn up nothing and all personal belongings have been confiscated.

The subject has sustained a substantial wound to the head and remains unconscious. I decided to leave it and see her reaction.

The subject was confined to the facility for further research.

* * *

CHAPTER TWO

Christos Gabris basked in the mid-day sun, his blood boiling with anticipation. He sat atop a podium in line with the public stalls, the sun shining off his head as he observed the crowds.

Of late, his gladiator fights had drawn little attention, leaving a sizeable hole in his pocket. Most men had been drawn into the empire's conquest, taking his audience and performers with them. Those who returned were sick of battle or too broken to attend, and again Christos suffered a blow to his profits. It had become rather depressing to perform for such a small turnout, but this would do nicely.

He grinned, mentally counting the proceeds from such a successful event.

The grey stone coliseum was perfectly round. Filled stalls stepped up, away from the arena towards an open roof. A well-trodden mix of sand and dirt made up the arena floor that ran off down tunnels to the back rooms and was blocked by thick wooden gates.

Christos looked over the audience once more as Callius and Nymati appeared from the tunnel entrance together. The patrons rose in droves, clapping and cheering their affections. There were even a few Sudra and Estra among their numbers, which surprised him, as they were uncommon guests within his walls. But he would count their coins all the same.

He sneered as the couple took their seats and the crowd grew quiet. They could fill the stalls all they wanted, the Manastream would run red with blood before he would ever accept a Sudran whore as his queen. And he wasn't the only one. This wasn't the time to make waves though.

Christos pushed up the long sleeves of his toga as he rose to his feet. He cleared his throat, all eyes falling upon him as thick tension filled the arena.

"Today we hold a tournament in honour of our Empress-to-be, Lady Nymati of Sudra. Following Sudran traditions, ten men will be given the chance to prove their worth and win their freedom before your very eyes."

His voice projected over the arena, his arms moving as if conducting an orchestra as he rallied the crowd.

"These men, these criminals and delinquents, will draw from a lottery the name of the gladiator they shall face in combat. Should they win, they will be given their freedom. Should they lose, however, their fate shall be left up to you, the people of the empire!"

"For the empire!" the stadium roared.

"Let's welcome our fearless gladiators to the arena."

The crowd erupted as five gladiators entered. They

flexed their massive muscles and raised their shining weapons, showing off for the crowd as they walked. Each gladiator was clad in the finest Duran armour and guards, their gear as primed and polished as the formidable men wearing them.

Christos had hand-picked them himself, purposefully choosing men of varied strength for the crowds' excitement. The first two, Hercule and Bardent, were seasoned fighters, trained in the finest schools with only a handful of defeats between them. Behind, Nero and Danlin were less experienced but had accumulated a good fifty wins between them over the last year. Finally, there was Elrin, an amateur with hardly any training, but he was skilled enough to hold his own for a few wins here and there.

The gamblers already raged in the stalls, foaming at the mouth. It was anyone's guess what would happen. Any challenger who was to draw Elrin could have a decent chance of winning, however, those who drew the lottery later had a hope of fighting a tired opponent adding to his chances.

"And now for our challengers!"

Christos encouraged the spectators as ten challengers were escorted to the arena, boos and jeers following them as they reached his feet. Some of the criminals looked as if they had seen a fight or two, but were weary and thin. Old pieces of equipment had been salvaged from the coliseum stores for each, unusable tat abandoned by former gladiators that offered the illusion of protection for the sake of those placing bets. Everything was ready. The stage was set.

"Now, who is ready to fight for their freedom?"

The crowd went wild.

* * *

Across the arena, Callius sat watching Nymati, ignoring much of everything else.

Nymati's ruby gaze had been fixed on the arena since they entered. Her tail flicked behind her as she leant forward, chewing on her nails. She hadn't spoken since their arrival but had seemed so invested he chose not to interrupt.

For all the time they had spent together, this venture felt more to him like a first date than a public affair. They had travelled together in the carriage and made polite conversations while on route, but they had yet to bypass their reservations and still struggled to let down their defences. Their comfort would surely ease with time, but Callius was determined to make a good impression whenever the opportunity presented itself.

Back in the arena, the first challenger had fallen within moments and the gladiator held him still, a sword point resting under his chin. Christos called the match to an end, holding his arm with his thumb outstretched. All eyes then turned to Callius, Nymati's included, his pulse racing as he held the fate of the challenger in his grasp.

Callius paused, puffing his chest as he cast his considerations over Nymati. If he allowed the man to live, would she think him weak? Or would she consider him a barbarian to order him slain?

Her eyes shone with a glittering eagerness. Her chest heaved with each bated breath, saliva catching in the corners of her ebony lips as she awaited his response. What would she do in his position?

Callius thrust his arm forward, flexing his muscles for Nymati's benefit. A cool shiver ran through his shoulders as he turned his thumb to the ground – and the gladiator swung his sword. The stalls roared with applause as the challenger's head flew from his shoulders, blood spraying over the compact sands and rolling away. Nymati rose with them, pursing her lips as she whistled.

Accomplished, Callius sat back in his chair, eager to make his next move. If blood and battle was enough to make his empress warm to him then blood and battle she would get.

* * *

Around the sixth match, Nymati sank back against the hard-backed chair. Her lips parted as if feasting on the moment and she remained transfixed on the fighters below.

Callius wet his lips and summoned his courage. "Is everything to your satisfaction?"

For a moment, Callius feared Nymati would not answer. Every doubt and fear lingering in the back of his mind arose in that moment. They had not exchanged a word in over an hour and there was every possibility she had forgotten he was sat there entirely. If this were a first date, he was failing miserably, and he thanked the gods they were already engaged to be wed, for he would surely be doomed to failure otherwise.

There was a break in the fighting below as the men circled, and then Nymati turned to answer. "Very much so. Your gladiators are trained well."

Callius gained inches, his fears forgotten as Nymati returned to the battle below with a sultry smile. His pulse throbbed with his renewed sense of vigour. If he had known that barbarity was all it took to win Nymati's favour, then he would have done this much sooner. Still, even he had his limits, and he had yet to experience the full extent of Sudran sensibilities.

"Well, most of them are well-trained." Nymati smirked as a gladiator fumbled his way to victory.

The gladiator held still as the crowd held out their arms and decided the fate of the contender, dispensing justice quickly. Iron lingered in the air in a slurry of blood, sweat and pain.

"It is making me hungry though." Nymati inhaled deeply, her eyes closing as she released a deep, satisfied groan.

"Would you like something brought?" Callius fussed and looked over his shoulder for loitering staff. "What would you like?"

"No, no. Not that kind of hungry." Nymati chuckled. "It's what we Sudra call our... cravings." She flicked her brow in amusement, her lips parting with a fang-filled smile.

"Oh... Oh!" Callius stumbled, realising what she meant. He cocked his brow right back. "Well, I'm sure we can do something about that too."

"Don't worry," Nymati assured him, chuckling as she waved him off with a gloved hand. "There are protocols set in place for when the king is away or unable to share his mana for whatever reason. Why else did you think my staff is comprised of so many?"

"Your staff?" he asked, his brows knitting. He had always thought the Sudra needed to be intimate to feed, but Nymati's staff were all women, suggesting that was not the case.

"Maybe I'll show you sometime." Nymati winked as if reading his mind.

Callius was afforded some time to recover as the fan

favourite, Bardent, stepped up to the latest challenger. Having already taken out two previous competitors, he showed little fatigue. Opposing Bardent, the challenger held his battleaxe naturally but was over a foot shorter with little muscle to speak of.

"I hear Amynus is doing well in training," Callius offered, predicting an easy win for Bardent. "No doubt he'll be on patrol by the end of the month."

"I heard something similar. Although, I can't quite believe it myself," Nymati replied, shifting her attention as Bardent stumbled, losing the upper hand. "I was beginning to worry he would never leave his bedroom."

Nymati leant forward. The challenger side-stepped as Bardent swung his long sword in a vertical arc. It crashed into the sandy floor, dust rising from its point as the challenger ripped his battleaxe around to meet Bardent. A metallic clang rang through the arena as the battleaxe bounced off Bardent's bronze chest plate, forcing him backwards. The challenger followed through without hesitation, delivering a second catastrophic blow to the gladiator's chest.

Bardent crashed to the ground, unable to move as the challenger placed a foot upon his chest. He squirmed, utterly defeated as the challenger raised his battleaxe high above his head.

"And the challenger wins!" cried Christos stepping down from his podium.

The arena boomed as Christos beckoned the challenger to meet him. Bardent slammed his fists into the arena floor, his face as red as his cloak. Nymati joined them in applause as she turned to Callius to share in his surprise.

"In accordance with the traditions of Sudra, the challenger has now proven himself and earned his freedom," Christos continued. He held the challenger's arm to the sky, unaware as a furious Bardent collected his sword and rose to his feet. He charged at the challenger, his sword aimed at the challenger's back as if to take him off-guard.

What happened next was so quick anyone who blinked would have missed it, Callius included. However, in that second, Nymati had launched herself over the balcony.

Wings erupted from her back. Wide spans of black leather fanned, casting a dark shadow over the arena stalls before snapping back. Nymati hurtled toward the arena floor in a nosedive. Fast gaining speed, her hands held out as she grabbed the gladiator by the throat. She dragged him into the air where she held him still.

Nymati hovered above the stunned arena, her wings flapping to maintain her altitude as Bardent's legs dangled helplessly.

"How dare you display such dishonour in front of your emperor?" Nymati roared, her voice filling the arena. "I will not tolerate such disrespect in my presence and nor should any of you here today."

The colosseum spectators dropped to their seats, cowering as all eyes fixed upon Nymati. She dug her fingers deeper into Bardent's neck. He released a choked groan of pain, his limbs flailing at Nymati unsuccessfully.

"Hear me now, if I am to be your empress this kind of back-handery will not be accepted," she warned, a blood-red aura emanating from her fury. "We stand on the eve of a new dawn. A new world within our grasp."

"You..." Nymati's eyes trained upon Bardent as she appeared to stare deep into his soul. "You are not worthy of our new world. And so, I leave your fate to the crowd."

"What say you?" called Christos to the crowd. He thrust his arm forward, his thumb held out firmly.

Bardent's face went from red to white as a sea of thumbs turned to face the ground, his fate decided.

Callius leant forward, unblinking, a flurry in his chest as Nymati pulled Bardent's face to meet hers. He held his breath as Nymati opened her mouth wide and inhaled. A stream of pure mana burst from Bardent's lips, bridging the gap between them. Bardent convulsed, releasing a pained cry along with the last of his mana.

Nymati hurled his lifeless body into the ground without remorse. His limbs crumbled on impact, his innards splattering against the hard sand.

The stalls shook, the crowd unable to contain themselves anymore. They cried and cheered. They jumped and waved.

Callius caught himself staring in disbelief. Nymati had just torn the life from a man before their very eyes, and his people applauded her for it. They loved her for it, and he was beginning to believe he felt it too.

Nymati basked in their adoration before floating down to rejoin Callius in his booth.

He grinned. "Well, I guess that works too."

* * *

CHAPTER THREE

Arafrey was dreaming of streams and lavender fields when Ceal woke her.

"Time for breakfast, Your Grace," she whispered with a gentle nudge, but Arafrey ignored her and returned to her fields.

It was peaceful there. It was her favourite place on the planet. She wasn't a princess or a high priestess. She was free, but she was also sad. The shadowy figment of the love she had lost still lingered in their secret place, hanging like a spectre among the flowers, calling her back to reality.

"You've to go visit your father before heading to the temple," Ceal continued, soon followed by the creaking of hinges as she collected something from the wardrobe for Arafrey to wear.

Arafrey had yet to open her eyes. With each passing day, waking only continued to grow more difficult. The weight of the kingdom rested upon her shoulders as she summoned the will to leave the shelter of her duvet, and prepared to carry their burden for one more day.

"Porridge for breakfast." Ceal smiled, opening navy robes before Arafrey to encourage her movement.

Arafrey rose to her feet with the speed of a grazing turtle, her head low as she stepped into her robes. She scowled at the walls as Ceal managed her buttons and wrapped a wide leaf-leather belt around her middle. It was, by Arafrey's inclination, an insult and injury that she should have to leave her bed at all that day, but her duties would have to come first.

"Would you like me to have a bath prepared for your return?" Ceal asked quietly as Arafrey reached her breakfast. She knew not to press the priestess while in these moods. "Or perhaps a change of clothes?"

"No. I haven't the time to return to the palace before my appointment." Arafrey grumbled and glared into her porridge. "Do you know what my father wishes to speak about?"

"I'm afraid not, Your Grace."

Arafrey sighed. That was never a good sign.

* * *

Arafrey was unsurprised to find both her father and Captain Valren waiting as she entered the king's chambers.

She had seen Captain Valren more than her father of late. He had always been an incredible aide and confidant to her family, but he rubbed Arafrey the wrong way entirely. Much of it had to do with his ignorance regarding

Reyla's treatment within his ranks, but she feared he was beginning to enable her father's disposition and had become more of a crux since her mother's passing.

The morning sun beamed through the tall stained-glass window behind them. It shone over Galafrey's high-backed chair, enveloping him as it cast an ominous shadow across the desk. Captain Valren stood beside him, his long face set in stone as she took a seat.

"I've just been informed you hired a new aide," said Galafrey, his monotone voice striking fear into her heart so effortlessly. "The Asrich boy, Ara? Really now?"

Arafrey's brow raised as she restrained her features; *it took him long enough.*

"I wasn't aware the temple staff fell under your jurisdiction," Arafrey chided, slitting her eyes in Valren's direction – it was surely him who had told on her. "Not that it matters, I won't cast him aside as the rest of you have."

"Don't be so dramatic. You know the role of aide to the high priestess is traditionally fulfilled by women."

"It was also tradition for our ancestors to shed their clothes and dance beneath the moon in oils each month, but I don't see either of you baring your naked skin to the starry skies," Arafrey countered, her tone rising as her fuse ran short.

There was nothing she hated more than her people using tradition to justify their bigotry. Their traditions.

Their religion. It was all fake. A way to control the masses. Her father knew this as well as she, yet he hid behind them like his mother's uptight skirts.

"If you'd like, I could collect our scriptures and you can show me where our ancestors dictated the gender of my aide," she offered, seething and serious as she posed against them.

"*And,* as for any indiscretions Bodair may be accused of," she added before either could breathe. "It is my role as high priestess to guide and protect all of our people, not just the ones whose life choices I agree with. For if that were the case, I assure you, I would gladly rain almighty damnation upon your so-called noble elites."

"Are you quite done?" huffed Galafrey, the muscles in his face taut as he threatened to frown.

"Quite. Unless you have something more you wish to discuss," Arafrey replied, daring them to test her further, but neither responded. "Now, if you don't mind, I have a temple to run."

Arafrey turned on her heel and marched triumphantly for the exit with her small yet long overdue victory.

"Actually," called Galafrey, causing her to turn as she reached the door. "Will you be attending the Faldin wedding this evening?"

"I already have plans," she replied with an air of smug satisfaction and left.

A Guard's Request

* * *

Arafrey was still in a foul mood when she left the temple that evening.

She and Bodair had spent much of the afternoon in her office rearranging the staff rota after more had taken ill with the sickness. Bodair was already proving himself worthy of her defence, but it only added to her frustrations. It was apparent that no amount of good deeds or work ethic would clear the slate that would otherwise be clean and respected, but she was determined to find a way.

Arafrey turned north from the temple into a residential area of Ceynas, with Mika close behind her. Here the houses were more uniform and grown closer together, from fewer trees, and rarely had more than a few feet of garden to speak of. Giant pinella trees grew in this area, their greyed trunks tall and their thin branches bright with orange leaves. The light of the Life Tree still reached them here and its browning glow dappled over the forest floor as it beamed through the canopy.

The Chadwin estate was indistinguishable from those around it, except for a redwood door and holly bushes that grew in hanging baskets below the window frames. Arafrey knocked on the polished wood, drawing in a deep breath as movement creaked on the other side.

"High Priestess," came Miles' voice as he opened the door wide. "Welcome to my home. Please, do come in."

Although Miles presented himself as a noble Frey, his home was nothing to the like. Arafrey found herself in a reception room of sorts, but it was essentially just a narrow space that seemed to run the length of the building.

Tree trunks protruded from the walls they had grown, their arms arte-stretched and formed into beams that hugged the interior of a stone fireplace. A hearty fire crackled and popped over thick logs, warming a pair of tall leaf-leather armchairs that sat in front. They were the kind that Arafrey imagined an elderly couple would favour – although perhaps not any of the elderly couples she knew.

Family portraits littered the walls, hung close together like creeping ivy leaves. Some were barely the size of her hand, others were wide as sunflowers, their paint cracked and their frames mismatched.

"Your home is lovely," said Arafrey, admiring the assortment of knick-knacks spread over antique shelves and cabinets. It was nothing like she had expected.

"Thank you, it's a family home. Would your guard like some refreshments?" Miles looked at Mika apologetically. "I'm afraid I'm not well-practised in royal etiquette."

"Would you like anything?" Arafrey asked Mika, but he just shook his head.

"Well, you're welcome to take a seat. Get warm by the fire and–"

Miles stopped as an elderly Frey shuffled in, plum-coloured robes hanging off his withered frame. Confusion passed over his wrinkled face, which turned into a bright smile as his eyes refocused and he truly saw them.

"Queen Elsafrey in my own home," he marvelled, hurrying over to greet her.

The mention of her mother caused Arafrey's heart to sink. While she may have inherited Elsafrey's features, that was where their similarities ended. Arafrey would never be the queen or priestess her mother was, but nor did she ever wish to be either.

"It is such an honour," he professed, a shaky hand held to his chest as he tried to bow.

"Father, this is Princess Arafrey," Miles corrected, projecting his voice as he rushed to support the old Frey. "I thought you'd gone to bed."

"No. No. The princess is hardly a toddler," the old Frey argued. "Dear Elsa, that rub you gave me for my knees worked a charm."

"Father, you're confused," Miles assured him, looking to Arafrey as if to explain. "How about we get you settled in your chair?"

"I am about as confused as I am your father, young man. Now, stop being rude to our Queen." He righted himself as if winning the argument.

A younger Frey with an apron wrapped around her middle rushed in from the same door. She started as her eyes set on Arafrey, but she went to attend to the man all the same.

"I'm so sorry, Mr Chadwin. He must've went for a wander while I was setting the table," she pleaded, pleated auburn hair swinging down her back as she wrapped the elder Chadwin into her arms. "You're all good now, Sir. How's about we get you a cup of tea and a nice book?"

"That sounds lovely. It was ever so nice to see you, Your Grace." He smiled and followed the woman away.

"Thanks, Jena," said Miles. His face showed a vision of pale indifference as he spoke, but his voice was soft and appreciative in a way Arafrey had known few nobles to achieve.

The elder Chadwin clutched onto Jena's arm as they left the way they came. It was only as the door closed that Arafrey caught the concern on Miles' face. Then she saw something else set upon his pointed features, something bittersweet that she couldn't quite place, and yet, it hurt her heart all the same.

"You'll have to forgive my father, his memory isn't what it used to be," Miles apologised quietly.

"It's quite alright," Arafrey assured, fearing she may have judged Miles too quickly. But her fears were short lived.

Arafrey pressed a tight smile as her thoughts turned into suspicions and her hackles raised.

Was this his plan? Did he orchestrate their whole

evening to expose her to his humble house where he cared for his father so tenderly? But to what end? Why be so vulnerable around her when they were just trading for materials?

Arafrey didn't appreciate thinking that way and endeavoured to wait until judging her host further. After all, there was only one way to discover his true intentions.

"Now, if you'll follow me to the dining room," offered Miles, motioning toward the door.

"I'll call if I need you," Arafrey told Mika before following Miles into the corridor and crossing into the room beyond.

The dining room was shorter than the reception room but equally as narrow. A thin rectangular table sat below the smallest chandelier Arafrey had ever seen and was set with burning candles and two place settings. Platters of fresh fruit, cheese and bread covered much of the surface. Two plates, each covered with a silver cloche, sat before the place settings at one end of the table.

"Is it just you and your father who live here?" asked Arafrey as she took her seat.

"Jena also lives here. My father needs full-time care, and my mother is no longer with us."

Miles removed the cloches from their plates to reveal stuffed peppers with a mushroom risotto.

Arafrey's taste buds rejoiced. She had eaten nothing all

day, so it was surely welcome, but it was warm. Warm not just in temperature, but in the patience and care taken to make it. The taste of something Arafrey had long forgotten: the warmth of a loving home.

"Jena is an excellent chef," he praised, setting himself at the head of the table. He continued to sing the praises of his staff as if they were brethren. "Although, she may have overdone it a little to impress Your Grace."

He collected a wine bottle from the table, pouring generous measures into their glasses. Taking the lead and serving himself was not a common practice among the Frey in Arafrey's circles, but she was happy to drop the pretence if it meant eating more of the delicious offerings in peace.

"Well, you can let her know I am thoroughly impressed," Arafrey replied, her mouth watering as she inhaled the steaming vapours.

Arafrey relaxed, the tension in her shoulders releasing with every morsel. Her face softened, lifting the stressful months from her features and returning the youth she had been denied.

She thought it refreshing to see a Frey so proud of their staff, although it would be unfair to judge Miles as she would a noble Frey. Everything about him and his home was modest, causing her to regret her earlier hostility toward him. Yet her suspicions remained firm. He had to have some reason for inviting her there.

Miles wiped his mouth on a napkin before breaking the silence that fell as they began eating. "Concentrating the hushin nectar was a stroke of genius. What was the inspiration?"

"A book on plant anatomy I read several years ago," she replied, being sure not to remember it too clearly as she reached for her wine. "It's easily the most boring book on the planet, but it left an impression."

Miles chortled. "I'd imagine you read a lot of boring books."

"My studies introduced me to all manner of authors, but none have ever struck me quite as hard as that one," she insisted, waving her fork before returning for another serving. "If it wasn't for Re–"

Arafrey stopped herself from sharing any further, her breath shaking as she pushed past the sudden pain striking her chest. She panicked to see that look on Miles' face again, the same expression as before. *Was it pity?*

"Let's just say I won't be reading it again," she said firmly before forcing a smile across her face.

Miles laughed in response, returning his attention to his plate without pushing her any further for details.

It wasn't until after Arafrey had finished her wine that she found the courage to finally confront her host. "I hope you'll not find me rude, but what do you hope to accomplish by inviting me here this evening?" Her voice naturally conveyed her royal authority as she tried to remain even. "Did my father put you up to this?"

"I'm sorry, I don't follow," Miles replied, a deep frown pressing lines across his forehead. "I've not had the opportunity to exchange much more than a few words in passing with His Majesty."

"Then why invite me here? Do you hope your generosity will earn my favour?"

"No. Not at all," he insisted, dropping his utensils to place a hand on his heart. "I had full intentions of donating the hushin nectar to the crown regardless of your attendance this evening."

"Then why? Why bother with any of this?"

Miles sat back in his chair, his face sad and serious as he studied hers. He tapped his fingers on the table with deep contemplation and sighed.

"It was the look in your eyes," he finally replied, causing Arafrey to turn cold.

"My eyes?" Her heart raced as she feared the worst.

"Your composure is wrought in oak and stone, but your eyes… Your eyes give you away." His voice deepened as it slowed. "They are the eyes of someone suffering a great loss. I know those eyes. They are the same eyes I saw in the mirror when my mother passed."

"Excuse me?" Arafrey scolded, her lungs filling with ice as her back straightened. "What exactly is it you are accusing me of Mr Chadwin?"

"Nothing, please, I mean no offence. Only–"

"First, you come to my temple, flaunting your good fortune like an adolescent peacock," she flamed, clutching her hand into a fist. "And now this!"

Never before had she felt so violated, so vulnerable. Her temple pulsated as panic contorted her chest and pain cracked through her composure. She couldn't bear the idea that someone – anyone – could see her for what she was. A failure. A disappointment. A poor imitation. A fraud.

If this stranger could see through her facade, then who else could see? Who else knew? What else was she giving away?

"Your Grace–"

"To think I was beginning to think you were a reasonable Frey, but you're as bad as the rest of them," she raged so loud as to prompt Mika to rush in.

"I already do enough for my people. I should not have to sit and suffer this insult for them as well. Keep your hushin nectar for all I care."

Arafrey rose from her chair as she scowled.

"Goodnight Mr Chadwin. If you wish to trade with the crown, I suggest you do as everyone else and contact Captain Valren."

Arafrey then stormed from the building and returned to the palace.

She held her mask in place until entering her bedroom,

where upon entering she finally released it with a gasp. Tears rolled down her cheeks as she closed the door, her chest tight and shaking with every breath as she returned to her duvet.

As she wept, Arafrey's pain only grew. Her temples pulsated, sending black spots through her sight, but it was nothing compared to the ice splintering her heart. At that moment, Arafrey would have done anything to live her life as an ordinary Frey, but she settled instead on numbing the pain of her pitiful existence.

Arafrey reached for her tonic, pouring what little was left into her mouth. She didn't care. She didn't want to feel anything anymore.

The panic in her chest subsided as her body grew warm and the tonic took hold.

She dropped to her pillows and allowed it to engulf her.

The empty vial still clutched in her hand, she faded into nothingness.

* * *

CHAPTER FOUR

Under the cover of darkness, three cloaked figures convened to discuss their plans most foul. A forgotten alleyway of a sand-beaten town played host, as the three sisters huddled close, their voices fuelled with fire.

"It's been months and still no orders," hissed the brazen one, her arms flapping as she spoke. "Stay put. Wait it out. All the while these Frey grow stronger."

"And you were right to send me to Ruglor," added the second quietly. White hair fell from her hood to rest over a navy cloak as she bobbed her head in agreement. "I arrived just in time to catch them leaving the Stronghold. No doubt they will reach the Agrana shrine before too long."

"This is beyond ridiculous! If we hold out any longer, they'll be too strong for even Mother to face," fumed the brazen one, her fists clenched. "And once again, she chooses not to come here herself. As if anything is more important than our cause."

There was no need for the third to respond as the pair turned their hoods to her. With Mother too busy to attend, all she had to do was say nothing and watch as her sisters grew frustrated and restless. Months of waiting had built up to this moment, the moment her sisters would finally see their Mother as she did. Now was her time. Now was her moment to rise above the ranks of her fellow sisters and lead them to greatness.

It was coming. Her lips quivered as they threatened a smile. *It was time.*

"I have to agree, but what can we do?"

"We should forsake our Mother, as she has forsaken us," announced the first, much to the third's satisfaction. "We can't wait around forever."

There was a gasp from the second as her hands rushed to her face, but the third could hardly contain her excitement. After years of loyal servitude and service to their cause, she would finally be the one calling the shots. It was almost too perfect.

"It brings me such pain to agree with you, Dear Sisters," she lied, dropping her head in supposed shame. "But, even if she has lost her way, she is still our Mother. We cannot merely cast her aside. Who would lead us if not her?"

She raised her head, looking at them each in turn. Her movements slowed, each breath deliberate as she gave them time to consider her words. Their silent surroundings suddenly thick with tension, her sisters reached a most amicable conclusion.

"It should be you," declared the brazen one, looking to

her sister for confirmation. "Our Mother has hardly been the one leading us of late as it is."

"That is true," the soft-spoken one agreed all too readily. "It was you who told us to mark the Duran also."

It was too easy.

"Very well," she conceded with little argument. "Then we shall gather our sisters and prepare to meet the two Frey in Puwhar."

"But the temple there is surrounded by empire soldiers," said the first. "How're we supposed to get in?"

"Don't worry, my Dear Sisters, you leave that to me…"

* * *

CHAPTER FIVE

Reyla's eyelids fluttered as she slipped between consciousness.

There was a time when she was neither fully awake nor unconscious, lying in a state closer to meditation, where she seemed to look down upon herself. In a rare moment of peace and quiet, Reyla thought of nothing. She felt nothing. Thought nothing. It was nice.

Reyla became aware of the damp air around her and the solid floor, but her senses were dulled beyond the recognition of much else. Her muscles trembled and her fingers twitched as they once again became her own, but she lacked the power to move them to her will. Everything ached, and her head throbbed with a strange burning sensation that rushed through her senses and brought her into the present.

Reyla gasped for air, her chest straining as her lungs filled. Pain shot through her shoulder as if to contest the motion, forcing her to recoil as she spluttered and coughed.

"Whoa. Take it easy," came a male voice not far from her.

Reyla's eyes flung open, her heart thumping as she found herself in a small dark room with no windows. Her blurred vision rolled over the space, able to make out the shape of a door to her left and a dim glow hanging above her. Reyla's attention then flicked to the source of the voice, to where a Sudran figure sat with his back to the wall.

"You've been out a while, I wouldn't move if I were you." His voice was kind but gravelly, confirming the dehydration suggested by the puckering of his ebony lips.

"'Kay," was all she could say.

The Sudra hunched over his knees, the skin sagging off his large frame where the muscles had deteriorated away.

What sat beside Reyla was more ghoul than man. A tangled mass of brown hair covered the points of his horns and his features sunk into his narrow face. Shackles wrapped around his ankles and wrists, covering deep red scars which were made all the more obvious by his unnaturally pale complexion. Everything about him, from his listless pink eyes to his tail laying limp on the floor, read as the incarcerated dead, as a man waiting for death. She could only imagine what had caused him to become like this.

Reyla's gut curdled, certain she had determined the true cause of missing persons in Agrana. But to what end?

Reyla shuffled as the feeling returned to her body. Shackles weighed upon her limbs and unfamiliar clothes scratched her skin. She craned her neck to a greyed gown with buttons up the middle; shivers causing goose-flesh to rise as she wondered how it got there.

"Where are we?" Reyla rasped, adrenaline suddenly waking her limbs. Everything cracked as she moved. *How long had she been out?*

"My best guess – we're under an Agrana city somewhere," he replied, his tone cheery despite their predicament. "We're basically *under* the underground people."

"What is this place?" Reyla tried to focus on the facts as anxiety fluttered through her chest. If she died here, then what of her quest? This was no time to be sitting down. She had to find a way out.

"Some sort of facility where they do experiments," the Sudra explained, although that only gave her more questions. Questions she had no energy to ask.

Still lying on the floor, Reyla closed her eyes, drawing as deep a breath as she dared, and sighed. The pain in her head grew, it throbbed at the base of her skull and radiated to her temples. The nerves in her back pinched, causing her muscles to spasm and her shoulder to twitch, but she ignored it, too tired to do anything about it.

"So then, what makes you so special?" he asked, causing her eyes to open toward him.

"There's nothing special about me," Reyla replied. She thought as much as her thumb brushed over her ring reflexively.

Reyla started and clenched her fingers as if to hug the silver ring still wrapped around her finger. It was dumb luck and an oversight on her captors' part, but her stomach tightened as her thoughts turned to Tharin. Did he meet a similar fate? Static wrapped around her finger as she hoped Tharin made it to the shrine without her. Could he carry on their quest alone?

"If you're in here then there must be something special about you, even if you don't know it," the Sudra insisted as he gestured. "This… This is where he keeps his prized experiments."

"So, what makes you so special?" Reyla returned, her speech slurring with the sibilance.

The Sudra smirked, seemingly impressed.

"Killic," he offered, lifting his chin with his shackled hands.

"Reyla." Her lips cracked as she pushed a smile. "Have there been many others in here?"

"Passing through mostly, I don't ever know what happens to them. I always figured the doc was experimenting on them the same way he did me."

Reyla made an internal note but didn't react. Capturing travellers to experiment on wasn't something she had expected to discover, but neither would she put it past the Agrana.

"I guess, I always just assumed their experiments didn't go so well…"

Reyla pursed her lips.

Well… that was encouraging.

* * *

Lying on the cell floor, Reyla lost all sense of time.

She eventually pushed against a wall, her head lulling as she summoned the energy to check herself over.

The drain on her mana reserves pinched from her core and through her chest like heartburn, but a glance showed no clear external injuries beneath her gown. She strained to reach her ankles, rubbing slowly as she ran her hands up. Her hands moved clumsily, hindered by the bindings, but everything seemed in order – if a little bruised. That was until she felt over her neck and into her hair.

Thick, dry blood caked the base of her skull. It was everywhere. Her fingers hovered over the tender wound tangled beneath her hair, trying to gauge its size.

Reyla spread her fingers and curled them over the wound. She pushed on her mana core, awaiting the sweet release of her healing artes to spread from her hands as she activated her artes over the gaping hole in her skull. Only it didn't come.

Reyla tried again, and again, but nothing happened. The mana in her core refused to activate and clenched even tighter around her chest. Her body grew cold, her heartbeat threatening to burst against the pressure. In a futile attempt, Reyla quickly cycled through her artes. Pudra. Shey. Rugla. But nothing worked.

Her heart stopped. No sword. No knife. No artes. She was defenceless. She may as well have been naked for all the security her gown gave her.

"What's up?" asked Killic, their close quarters offering little privacy.

"My artes aren't working," she stressed, each breath suddenly thick as honey. What use was she to anyone now?

"Nor will they. They–"

Killic stopped as the door rattled. It flung open and two Agrana pushed into their cell.

The Agrana were a fearsome race with wide skulls, flat boar-like snouts and hooded ears, but that wasn't the thing that struck Reyla with fear. Reyla's stomach dropped, the empty vessel rattling about her insides as she recognised their armour. *They worked for the crown.* The mustard yellow stripes across their chests and shoulders were unmistakable. *Did that mean the crown was behind the disappearances?*

The guard's arms swung from their broad shoulders like primates as they lumbered into the cell. They towered over Reyla, their oily complexions marbled with dark veins where their skin stretched over hulking muscles.

"You," barked one, pointing to Reyla with a chunky finger. "On your feet."

Reyla struggled to rise, her back and palms fell flat against the wall as she slid up. Her head grew heavy and dipped, her body following as she staggered forward. Blood rushed past her ears as Reyla's eyes rolled back and her body dropped.

The wind was knocked out of her as one of the guards caught Reyla's limp body. He smelt like damp soil, and his skin was cold against hers as he dragged her from the cell. The *shhh, shhh, shhh* of her shackles against the ground trailed behind her. She was powerless to stop it.

Reyla's ears pricked as the cell door closed and a heavy latch dropped. Footsteps came closer as the other guard hooked their arm under Reyla's shoulder, the two passing her between them like a ragdoll.

Reyla's eyelids wavered as she clung to consciousness. Her breathing shallowed as she counted the steps of her captors.

One, two, three, turn right.

The air was stale here too.

Six, seven, left.

The *shh, shh, shh,* of her shackles echoed off nearby walls. *More tunnels?*

Three, four.

The Agrana came to a stop.

A loud knock followed as one of the guards rapped upon thick wood. Reyla forced her eyes open as hinges creaked, squinting to focus.

Sandwiched between the guards, her sight was restricted and her vision clouded as it threatened to go dark. The room was well-lit, an office of some kind given the desk in the middle, but no windows. A door lay open across from her, a trove of presumably confiscated weapons and clothes within, but Reyla was unable to see if her own were among them.

"Not in here," fumed an unseen man. "In the lab, you fools. What use have I for her in here?"

The guards grunted, garbled their apologies and pulled Reyla back into the corridor. She tried to remember how many steps they had taken before stopping, but the numbers faded with her strength.

The planet spun as the guards began walking.

The *shh, shh, shh* of her shackles was the last thing she remembered as everything went dark.

* * *

Reyla jolted awake, unable to move as restraints pinned

her down. A bright light from above stung her eyes forcing them closed. She strained against the thick straps running across her body, around her limbs and over her forehead, but lacked any real strength.

She sighed, defeated as she dropped onto a cold hard slab.

"Ah, you're awake," came a voice, causing her eyes to turn.

The Agrana Reyla laid her eyes upon was much smaller than the guards who had collected her and his skin was clean and tan-coloured. His head seemed too big for his body, a halo of wild grey and white hair running around his head and over his hooded ears. A white coat hung off his narrow frame, continuing past her line of sight as if it were oversized.

Reyla swallowed the lump appearing in her throat, but she was unable to look away as her heart raced. Unlike the guards, everything about this man was clean, clinical and callous. The mere sight of him struck fear into her core.

Unable to move, Reyla followed as he placed a pad on her wrist. It had a strange string coming from it, but she couldn't see where it went or what it connected to.

"I am Doctor Gronk," he told her, the plainness of his voice all the more sinister as he placed another pad on each of her temples. "I'm going to ask you a series of questions and, in the interests of science, I require you to tell me the truth."

Gronk placed another pad on the opposite wrist and pulled a rust-coloured box into her sight.

"This device allows me to see if you are telling the truth." He flicked a switch on the front of the box causing it to light up.

It was unlike anything Reyla had ever seen before, the technology far beyond that of anyone else in Alamantra. Small windows of light flashed on the face, accompanied by regular beeping, once high, once low, as if the machine had a heart.

"Answer truthfully and we'll move on. Lie and well…" Gronk flexed his fingers as bolts of lightning shot between his palms, the implication clear. "Understood?"

"Understood," she repeated, catching her tone as she threatened a growl.

Every fibre of Reyla's being jutted between fight and flight in the face of this calm, measured little monster. One thing was for certain, she needed to get as far away from him as possible.

"Now," he began, moving from her line of sight as he spoke. "Let's start with something basic. What is your name?"

"Reyla Fenwilt."

Reyla imagined all the different ways she could escape if only she had the power and regretted ever taking her artes for granted. There had to be a way to get them back.

What had Killic been going to say when the guards interrupted anyway? Some type of mana blocking like they had in Old Wood perhaps, although that would be difficult for her to counter…

"And where are you from?" he asked, returning with a silver scalpel to make an incision on her arm.

Reyla winced. "Freya."

"More specific," Gronk barked, swabbing the wound before sewing it back up with a needle. "Which town?"

"The capital. Ceynas."

Reyla breathed through the pain as Doctor Gronk moved around the table to make another incision. Each slice radiated fire, but it was a welcome distraction to the pains in her head and shoulder.

"And what did you do there?" asked Gronk, no longer close enough for her to see.

Reyla paused, considering the possibility that he was lying to her and could not tell if she were telling the truth or not. Even if he could tell if she were lying, maybe she could defeat his machine if she chose the correct words; a tactic Reyla was well-practised in.

"I'll remind you that not answering is as bad as lying," Gronk warned, appearing above her to show the severity of his countenance.

"I worked in the palace," she told him, returning his amber stare with a hazel-clad flame to gauge his reaction.

"The palace, eh?" He smirked, seemingly undeterred by her efforts. "What did you do there? Handmaid was you?"

"I was an aide," she corrected. It was true, Reyla was, at one point, an aide within the palace. She hoped it would be enough.

"An aide? Hmmm..." Gronk mused aloud, the rhythmic thumping of the machines causing time to slow and her heart to tremble.

Would his machine see through her deception? Or could she make it through on half-truths and misdirection?

"Your chi levels are off the chart," Gronk continued, appearing to accept her answer as he changed the subject.

"My what?" She frowned.

"Your chi, your artes, your mana. Whatever you Frey like to call it."

"Oh." Reyla had never heard it called that before.

"Nearly broke my machine when they brought you in too." The Doctor produced Reyla's necklace from Wilona and rammed it into her face. "Is this how you do it?"

"That's mine," she hissed through gritted teeth.

"But what does it do?"

"Finds water. It was a gift. I don't know how."

"Hmmm... Interesting... Interesting..." He retreated from her periphery and returned with a small box which beeped and whizzed as he held it over her. "Your body's capacity to regenerate chi is incredible. How do you do it?"

Reyla caught her breath, holding herself still so as not to draw attention to the ring on her finger. It was a question so direct that Reyla could no longer hide behind half-truths. She had no other option.

"I have been blessed by the Gods," Reyla replied with as much a fanatical air as she could muster. It was a risk, but she wagered upon a lighter punishment should he think she was delusional rather than lying.

Reyla knew little of the Agrana, but she knew why the two kingdoms were not as close as they could be, despite a joined interest in science. The Agrana had no religion and celebrated no Gods. Many Frey considered them abominations and cursed their technology, although Reyla was beginning to understand why.

"The Gods deemed me worthy to wield their power," she professed. "It is the highest honour."

Gronk threw his head back and cackled. He disappeared again, returning with his most intimidating device yet. It was bigger than the other and shaped like a small crossbow, only the arrow was connected to a small dull crystal and the head was coned like a suction cup.

"Blessings from God indeed." Gronk scoffed. "Well, whatever it is, we're going to find out. Let us meet and confront this god together, and dissect the source of his power."

Reyla's stomach churned as the strange device hovered

over her.

"You know, it's a common misconception that chi is stored in the heart or the lungs, when in fact it all centres around your belly," he explained, unbuttoning her gown to expose her midriff. "Let's see just how much chi these *blessings* give you!"

Gronk placed the suction cup over Reyla's navel, the rubber pressing firmly against her skin. There was a click as the device came to life and the suction cup pulled.

Reyla was helpless as the device ripped the mana from her body and out through her stomach. She lifted off the slab, her teeth clenched as black and white spots filled her vision.

She just had to survive long enough to regain her artes, she told herself. *She was strong enough to survive this.*

She had managed worse.

She–

She...

She passed out.

* * *

Subject 236 – Log Entry No.2

The subject has now produced not one but three chi-crystals.

Each is white and more powerful than normal chi-crystals, and strong enough to overpower some of my least powerful devices.

This is indeed one of my most interesting cases yet. The power held in this one Frey is insurmountable and beyond anything we're currently able to produce under sanctioned methods. I cannot contain my excitement at all the things I could do should I uncover the secrets of her power.

Samples taken show no serious irregularities however her ability to heal seems increased compared to other Frey subjects.

Curiously, she made no attempts to heal her head wound, despite her power. Does she lack the ability? Or did we drain her reserves last time?

I hope to learn more from the Frey herself, but she has yet to tell me anything useful. Perhaps this will change after more study.

I decided to run down the generator in the meantime. I plan to insert one of her white crystals into the system to get a clear measurement of their power — my current tools are not equipped to handle such high readings. Although I expect some kind of Frey trickery, it would do us well to continue to harvest the chi while I can.

* * *

Reyla was relieved to see Killic when she awoke.

"So that's what they're doing down here," Reyla

accused, her voice hoarse. "Draining the mana from unsuspecting citizens?"

"And then some." Killic sighed. "They keep us drained so we can't fight back. My core aches so much, I couldn't transform even if I wanted to."

"We have to get out of here," Reyla asserted with as much urgency as her weakened state allowed. "There's a small arsenal of weapons in the Doctor's office and–"

"You say that like I haven't tried." Killic shook his head. "At least he patched you up this time."

Reyla's hands were still bound as she reached to check her head, finding tightly wrapped bandages.

"I– I can't just do nothing." Reyla fought against the depression rippling her tone.

What would happen if she were to fail now? What would come of her quest, her people, her princess? She couldn't just sit around and do nothing.

"You said we're under the city, right? So, you managed to reach it? The exit?"

"Yeah, me and one of my first cellmates." Killic bowed his head in their memory. "We found the stairs up, but they soon caught us. We put up a good fight though."

Reyla's body dropped with her disappointment. She was in no condition for battle and with her mana depleted she had little energy to give. There was no way she could fight her way out. Even if she had her artes or a sword, the

Agrana were mostly enormous and the halls small, she doubted she would fare well against even one of the guards. It was hopeless.

"Big fella he was. Pudra," Killic continued without prompting, his tail flicking with quiet amusement beside him. "No matter how much they drained him, he still had his artes. He was smart too, and played up how tired he was. It took 'em a while to catch on, which is when they made their mana-counter."

"We've been introduced." Reyla grumbled, remembering the small whizzing box.

"Another, Shey lass," Killic added with an ebony grin. "She used her own piss as a projectile to take out the guards."

Reyla smirked, her eyes turning to the bucket in the corner. She hadn't considered using her new artes to control other liquids. Would it work on oil – or perhaps even blood?

She pursed her lips and quietly hoped she would get the chance to try it out for herself someday. All she needed was a little bit of mana.

* * *

CHAPTER SIX

Alone in the darkness of the Agrana marshes, Tharin turned to his ring for guidance. The silver tingled around his finger, the gentle pull calling him north.

He came to a stop as he happened upon an overhanging verge big enough to offer him shelter. His eyes cast over the clear night sky as he dropped his gear to the ground. The Manastream waved through the atmosphere above like ribbons connecting the stars, only, they were no longer a beautiful mystic blue but more of a yellowing teal.

Tharin collected sticks and branches before setting them down beside his backpack. He activated his artes over the ground and raised a bowl to place his kindling. After drawing water from the branches, he set them alight, the action as natural as breathing after months of practice.

As the fire burned, Tharin reached into his gear to retrieve some biscuit-bread. He was fortunate not to lose too many supplies in the ambush, but his backpack now sported a few holes where it had caught several arrows. Even so, it was the biscuit-bread he chose. It reminded him of home.

Tharin shifted with the wind, clutching his biscuit in both hands like a squirrel as he ate. The twisted trees swayed in the moonlight, their long, pointed shadows clawing over the marshes toward him. A shiver ran down his spine causing the hair on the nape of his neck to stand on end with the uncertain feeling that someone was watching him. They weren't watching, however. Tharin stretched his senses in every direction. There was no one. He was completely alone.

Tharin sighed, unable to remember a time he had ever been alone and silent for so long. Not that he minded the quiet, he was just accustomed to having someone around.

The youngest of three sons, his family home was always busy. Tharin had moved into the barracks for a time while training but returned after joining the Princess' Guard. His brothers had moved out long before, but they made sure to visit daily, to flaunt their respective successes in his face.

His family may not have approved, but Tharin had found his place among the military ranks. No longer confined to the role of noble or son, he excelled and for the first time, he didn't feel lesser to his peers. He became part of a team and that unity gave him strength, which is why he would always regret not being able to follow his brothers into the war.

Tharin pulled out his bedroll and wrapped it around him as he hugged his knees. He thought of the shrine and Reyla, the silver ring tingling against his skin. The shrine was close, and the ring pull was strong and consistent, maybe a day or two between them.

Not long now and all would be well.

Reyla would be there waiting for him, *he just knew it.*

* * *

As the moon rose, so too did the inhabitants of the marsh stir.

Ready for action, the mother called her children close, her *long-arm* wrapping around them each in turn. They huddled in the undergrowth and watched in wonderment as the *tall-skinny* huffed and puffed over his fire and sulked under his sheet.

She found him curious. He looked so sad and defeated as he drifted into a deep sleep beneath the verge – not the smartest thing to do in the marshes. Lots of danger around.

The mother noticed one. One of the *slinky-slitherrers* coiled itself around a tree and slowly drooped its body down over the verge.

It started raining causing the *tall-skinny's* fire to calm. Not good. The *slitherrer* didn't like the fire and was likely waiting for it to go out before making its move.

Slowly, they tiptoed closer to the *tall-skinny*. The fire lulled as the *slitherrer* tightened around the roots above the *tall-skinny* and dropped its head down for closer inspection.

Her two little ones used their *long-arms* to reach under the bush roots and pull up lumps of the *dry-moss*. They held it tight as they shuffled over to the fire. Their bellies low to the ground, the little ones reached out their *long-arms* to the fire and dropped the *dry-moss*.

The little ones snatched back their *long-arms* as the *dry-moss* burst into life. The *slitherrer* retreated and the *tall-skinny* snorted, but he continued to sleep.

The mother neighed her appreciation. The little ones had done well, and their tails shook furiously behind them. She motioned with her *long-arm* for them to come back, but, as they so often would, they chose to ignore her. She shuffled forward, moving each of her *short-arms* slowly and carefully towards the *tall-skinny*.

One, two, three, four. One, two, three, four.

The mother gained on the little ones and scolded them silently. She studied the *tall-skinny*. He was helpless, childlike. Although she didn't know much, the mother still understood the role of a parent. She understood the *tall-skinny*, like her, was another's child and if her children were lost and alone, she would hope others would understand that too. So, she did the thing she hoped any mother would if they found a child lost and alone.

She used her *long-arm* to stroke his hair and fix the sheet wrapped around him. It was warm now and the *slitherrer* was gone. Basking in the safety of the fire, she shuffled in beside him and welcomed the two little ones with her *long-arm*.

The *tall-skinny* was so much smaller up close. He snuggled against the side of her belly and his head rolled over to rest on her back. Her eyes closed but her ears turned and twitched as the little ones settled around them and drifted to sleep.

She would protect the children.

That was her role, after all.

* * *

Tharin relaxed against the warm furry wall and pulled his arms in to rub his neck. He had slept well, but was stiff and his legs were heavy. Unusually heavy.

His eyes opened.

"What the–?" He gasped, unable to move as a small creature lay over his lap.

Tharin frowned as the creature jumped up to meet him, waving a hairy trunk in his face. It was a little over a foot tall and resembled the elephants of Sudra only smaller with dark, chocolate fur and a big shaggy dog-tail.

He scrambled, turning to find a bigger version behind him and a second smaller one rushing to greet them. His panic subsided as the trio surrounded him, patting his body with their trunks and tussling his hair.

"Well, good morning to you too." Tharin snorted, unsure what was happening as the little ones broke off and ran circles around his fire. Mounds of peat-like moss still fed the hearty flame. "Did you do that?"

The creatures neighed in response, seemingly pleased with themselves, and he laughed. It was the perfect way to start the day.

Tharin had breakfast and gathered his gear as the creatures played. It seemed like the bigger creature was in charge, their mother perhaps. Although he wasn't sure what the creatures were, let alone how to tell which gender they were.

'*Reyla would know,*' he thought, pouting sadly. She wasn't there, but he was no longer alone, which he supposed was something.

They played a little while Tharin used his artes to fold his campfire into the ground, extinguishing the embers and removing all trace of his being there.

"I need to get going," Tharin explained, shouldering his gear. "I have a long way to go."

The mother neighed, her trunk rearing as the little ones pressed against his legs. Tharin smiled, rubbing his hand over one of the smaller ones.

"Oh, okay then. You can come too," he conceded

readily, waving his hands towards them. "But only until we get to the shrine."

The family brayed with glee, following as he turned north.

"Just wait 'til you meet Reyla." He grinned, eager to see her himself. "She's probably already at the shrine waiting for us."

* * *

CHAPTER SEVEN

Amynus entered the Duran barracks to a sea of Sudra filling the tables, each clad in shining bronze armour and leather lappets. He strode down the aisle, his crimson cape gaining air behind him.

"Amynus," called Sabutok, rising to his feet as he waved. Amynus' insides clenched — he would never grow accustomed to seeing Sabutok in red and gold. "Over here."

He took a seat across from Sabutok, the long wooden table between them piled with empty plates and jars of mead. Amynus recognised a few of the Sudra around them as men he had sparred with over the years.

Among so many Sudra, it was easy to forget they had ever left Halda. The hall buzzed with idle chatter and the air ran heavy with meat and mead. Although Duran banners hung on the grey walls and the men were all clad in bronze, his countrymen dined without care, as if nothing had changed.

"Men, raise your drinks," Sabutok declared, sliding one to Amynus. "Today we welcome another into our ranks. To Amynus, a prince among his men."

"Hear, hear," cheered the men.

"Thanks," Amynus breathed, his cheeks warm.

"It may not be the Sudran army, but your father would be proud." Sabutok grinned, the scar over his eye creasing.

Amynus forced a smile and lifted the drink to his lips. Sabutok was the only one still willing to speak of his father of late. Not even his mother mentioned him anymore. He knew life would eventually move on, but had never expected it to be so soon.

"Where've they got you posted?" asked Sabutok, replenishing his mead.

"Guard patrol."

"That's not too bad. At least you get to walk around a bit," Sabutok replied. "You could be stationed somewhere all day like this lot."

"Swear I've been staring at the same building so long I'm seeing it in my sleep," complained the Sudra to his right. "Al' bet staying in the palace isn't too shabby though."

"It has its perks." Amynus smirked and knocked back mead, the flavour much sweeter than the ale in Sudra.

"And he has access to his mother's staff," chimed one to his left. "Wouldn't mind a go myself. These Duran women don't compare."

"And you would know?" Sabutok's eyes slanted toward the man.

"Erm. I…"

"Tamun," called a voice over the commotion, the table suddenly still as Commander Raltz marched over. "Ah, glad you've not left yet."

Amynus jumped to his feet and saluted. "Sir?"

"I need you to deliver this to the emperor's office," he said, producing a wax-sealed scroll. Raltz turned to the table. "Celebrating your induction, are we?"

"Yes, Sir."

"Well then, just make sure it gets there by morning," Raltz instructed, handing over the scroll with a lopsided smile that caused his wrinkles to deepen. "And do make sure you don't leave any mess behind. I'll hold you personally responsible."

"Of course, Sir. You can count on me."

Amynus returned to the table and retrieved his drink.

"You can count on me," the men mocked as Raltz left earshot, their table erupting with laughter.

* * *

The skies were dark as Amynus returned to the palace later that evening. His stomach sloshed as he swayed through the garden, the moon lighting his way through the honeysuckle and roses.

Amynus smiled with a sense of serenity as he remembered the difficult hike up to the palace plateau in Halda. He hummed an old army song beneath his breath, his thoughts cleared of vengeance and lust for the first time in months.

The palace lay quiet as he entered, the torches had been extinguished except for those strewn through the corridor. He pushed on the door to the emperor's office with his shoulder, allowing it to swing closed behind him as he crossed to the grandiose desk.

Amynus lifted his hand to his mouth to stifle a belch. Alcohol reeked from his lips as he placed the scroll before the emperor's chair and returned to the door. He reached for the handle but snatched his hand away as the door to the council room opened.

Amynus held still, peering through the crack in the door as candlelight flooded the corridor. Wobbling, he squinted his eyes, following tall shadows as they stretched over the wall.

"It's been lovely," cooed a voice that was certainly Aeryn's, her tail casting shadows as it flicked. "I'll see you soon, Mr Emperor."

A shiver ran over his skin, his face souring as he imagined what could have transpired behind closed doors. His instincts told him to act, but curiosity held him, his breath caught as his heart sounded battle drums.

"Always a pleasure," replied a voice – but not the

emperor's.

Amynus stepped back, frowning as the door closed, leaving Aeryn alone in the dark corridor.

Still holding his breath, Amynus observed through the crack in the door. His pulse gained strides as Aeryn beamed with satisfaction and admired a sealed scroll she pulled from her smock. The emperor's coat of arms was pressed into the wax seal as Aeryn cast a watchful glance over each shoulder.

She activated her artes over the paper as she whispered: "Apperiner."

Amynus jolted as the scroll vanished. Sickness grew in his stomach. He had never seen such artes before, nor did he recognise the words Aeryn spoke, but he knew it beyond a shadow of a doubt. *Dark artes.*

Witches had once been a plague on Sudra. They had terrorised the people with their dark artes and sinister practices for decades, until finally meeting their match. They were thought to have been destroyed entirely, their numbers scattered or burnt in example, but Amynus could find no other explanation for it.

Amynus blinked on the off-chance his mind was playing tricks on him. He was man enough to admit he had overindulged, but the look on Aeryn's face was enough to sober any man. Bloodlust filled her stony eyes. Her ebony lips curled into a vicious snarl to expose her fangs. His blood ran cold.

The air around her hung thick, her overwhelming power reaching him even through the door. He placed a hand to his mouth and pressed his mana core to hide his strength. It riled his stomach and the alcohol in his belly threatened a hasty return.

The witches were his parents' greatest adversary, and to think that one of their kind lived among them so brazenly left him revolted and violated. How many more of their staff had pledged themselves to dark artes? Who could he trust in their loyalty when his mother's most trusted aide was set to betray them?

Amynus finally released his breath as Aeryn removed from his sight, and her footsteps disappeared down the corridor. His hands shook as he remained rooted to the spot, his hazy thoughts leaping from one extreme to the next.

What did he just see?

What did he just hear?

Amynus shook his head with the dim hope that he was mistaken and went to find his bed. He would have to figure out the rest when he was sober.

* * *

CHAPTER EIGHT

For the first time since his daughter's coronation, King Galafrey left the Frey palace.

Exactly eighty-seven days after burying his queen, Galafrey crossed the courtyard without a word. The skies were greyed and the air cold as he left the palace grounds and turned toward the market, the clink of his knights' armour close behind.

It was early morning still, but many Frey timed their days by the local wildlife and were awake with the first calls of sunlight. The Frey he passed bowed with tight smiles, their skin streaked with the black lines of the sickness. Galafrey bowed his head in response, but his face remained as expressionless as always, his stone mask disguising the suffocating remorse besetting his tired and miserable existence.

Locked away in his office, it had been easy to forget there was a pandemic tearing through his kingdom at all, but here it was apparent. His people were wasting away before his very eyes. Their faces were sunk from exhaustion, and their skin greyed and backs bowed. If not for the trees surrounding them, he would have mistaken his citizens for Sudra toiling in the face of starvation. It shook his aching heart to see them suffer so.

The market was strangely quiet as he entered. No music played from the pavilion, nor did the vendors call for sales. The stalls held little produce and stunk of decay. Those few who waited for service swayed like dandelions, threatening to fall should the wind blow even a little.

Galafrey stopped as he came to the flower stall, his eyes running over the holly and roses as he searched for the perfect bouquet.

"How may I serve you today, Your Majesty?" asked the Frey serving with a bow, her golden hair pulled into a tight ponytail.

"A bouquet. Turana Lilies if you have them."

"Afraid most are out of season at the moment, Your Majesty," she apologised, averting her eyes as if it would be rude of her to face him. "I have some lovely Winter Lilies if that would suffice?"

The florist turned, collecting a bucket to show him. The lilies inside had white petals that were sprinkled with blue crystalline pollen and the stems glittered with a sapphire blue.

"They'll do," he said, his monotone voice covering his disappointment. Elsafrey had acquired a fondness for all lilies while tending the palace gardens, but Turana Lilies were her favourite.

Galafrey watched on in stern silence as the florist bundled the lilies and wrapped their stems with woven vines. She tied the vines into a delicate bow before presenting it to the king.

"Keep the change," he said, accepting the bouquet as he handed over a silver coin. He cared little for the cost or change but assumed one silver would be enough.

"Thank you." The florist bowed, her wide eyes suggesting he had overpaid by some degree more than he had expected. "May the Gods be with you."

Galafrey inclined his head and continued walking. He clutched the bouquet close as he turned south, the tension in his shoulders growing with each step as he grew closer to the cemetery gates.

"Wait here," Galafrey instructed, prompting his knights to take positions before the stone bears twinning the entrance. "I will not be long."

Galafrey entered the cemetery, his breath catching as he beheld the tombstone carved in the likeness of his beloved. He had commissioned the piece for their thirtieth wedding anniversary, but since that day was never to come, he chose to have it placed upon her grave instead.

The artist had done an incredible job. It was perfect. Perhaps too perfect. Even though stone, it looked as if it could wake up at any moment, which was all Galafrey wished for.

"Happy birthday," he said, his voice low so only

Elsafrey could hear as he placed the lilies by her feet.

Galafrey slunk onto his knees with teary eyes upon the statue.

"I'm sorry. I was unable to make it here sooner. I… I didn't have the strength." He sighed, looking away as his heart grew heavy.

Over the months since Elsafrey's passing, he had found little strength for many things. It took all of his being to get dressed and eat each day. Unable to face his loss, Galafrey buried his head in paperwork and hid in his office, the only room that held no memories of her.

Galafrey considered himself hopeless and wretched. He had always thought Elsafrey was the stronger of them, but never did he imagine he would become so lost without her. If not for Arafrey and Valren, his kingdom would have fallen into ruin.

"Dominic should arrive by week's end, they've come to see the leaves fall," he continued, imagining her response as if she sat down beside him. "It seems Prince Logan has been exchanging letters with Valren, they have something they wish to share with us."

Valren had also recruited volunteers, but even with help from the Pudra, they were going to have to get creative to have any hope of surviving an invasion from the empire. Galafrey suspected the emperor's looming nuptials were the only reason the Freya borders remained intact. However, with any luck, Nymati would keep him occupied for a few months more.

"You certainly called that one," he added, recalling a conversation the pair had after hearing news of Drazah's demise with a weak smirk.

Elsafrey always appreciated the Sudra's primal nature and adored their history and culture, but often scrutinised Nymati's leadership and indifference — which was saying something given Elsafrey's unlimited patience with her own citizens. Galafrey supposed she and Nymati were never destined to become friends, but Elsafrey's suspicions were often proven correct in the case of the Demon Queen, making relations with Sudra particularly difficult.

Galafrey rubbed a cold hand over his face, his fingers meeting the golden halo of his crown.

"Ara wears your crown well. She truly is your daughter. We have much to be proud of." He bared his remorse, ashamed of his lack of involvement in that respect. "Although I suppose you would know better than I..."

Galafrey drew a deep breath, his eyes on the statue. He had avoided visiting before, imagining it would be too painful for him to visit Elsafrey's grave, but now he was finding it too painful to leave.

"Just a few more minutes," he promised, his heart a little lighter.

"I have much to make up for."

* * *

It was nearing noon when Galafrey returned to the palace to find the foyer filled with boxes and busy Frey.

"Your Majesty," said Valren. He passed the boxes to the staff coming from the dining room.

"What's all this?"

"A Mr Chadwin just delivered it." Valren hurried to give Galafrey his full attention. "Said he found a Frey outside of Grendin who breeds hushin flowers. Our good fellow has him churning out nectar at an extraordinary rate."

"How generous," Galafrey stated, scanning the bounty before him. "I wonder what brought this on."

"Well actually–" Valren paused as Arafrey appeared on the stairs, a guard in green and leaf-leather behind her. "Ah, Princess, just the person."

Arafrey scowled as she returned his attention, her hand reaching weakly for the banister. Her skin was dove white but dark circles ringed her emerald eyes. She looked more ghastly than Galafrey considered himself.

"Are you just waking up?" scolded Galafrey, unable to catch his tone as he noticed her unbrushed hair. "It's almost lunchtime."

"I had a busy evening and slept in," Arafrey replied, her eyes dull and her voice disinterested. "What was it you wanted?"

"We've just had a shipment of hushin nectar from the Chadwins. I thought perhaps you had something to do with it." Valren indicated the delivery, his tone strangely accusing.

"Why would I have anything to do with that? Producing the soothing balm is your department, Captain," Arafrey snapped, her back straightening.

Galafrey considered Arafrey's attitude another failing on his part. She was still bitter that he had tasked Valren to run the operation. It was likely a mistake to give Valren her project without speaking to his daughter first, as the pair had fallen into bickering like siblings, but Arafrey had enough responsibilities to worry about and he didn't want to trouble her.

"Then perhaps you could explain these?" Valren produced a large bouquet of vibrant red roses and offered them to Arafrey.

"Do I look like a florist, Captain?" Arafrey descended the stairs with a degree of urgency as she aimed for the door.

Galafrey watched on in quiet amusement as Valren took a note from between the stems. He unfolded it and cleared his throat.

"Priestess. Thank you for dinner," Valren read so loud that those moving the boxes in the dining room may hear. "Inform me when you require more hushin nec-"

Arafrey huffed and snatched the note from his hands before he could finish reading. Her cheeks burned redder than the roses she rushed past. "Now if you'll excuse me."

Galafrey's brow creased as Arafrey stormed from the palace without another word. He turned to Valren, finding an unusually wide smile across his long face.

"Seems your daughter has an admirer," Valren teased, a twinkle in his eyes.

"Chadwin…" Galafrey was terrible with names. "Remind me. Why does that sound familiar?"

"The Chadwins were general merchant traders, but recently acquired half the ateliers and apothecaries from here to Pudron. Their son, Miles, has a real zest for business."

"Miles Chadwin," Galafrey repeated, his voice deepening. "It seems I shall have to keep my eye on that one."

He snorted, the corner of his lips peaking as he imagined his daughter finally dating and finding her way.

Perhaps there was hope for her yet.

* * *

CHAPTER NINE

Reyla's body convulsed, her back arching over the slab as electricity shot between her nerves. Foam pushed through her clenched teeth, seeping down her cheeks, the shock burning through her veins.

Reyla's body dropped as Gronk released his artes. Her eyes rolled in her head, following as the room spun around her. Steam rose from her olivine skin as she twitched uncontrollably, the smell of burnt hair filling her nostrils.

"That would have killed most Frey," Gronk offered, his voice manic, as if he was no longer able to hold back his excitement. He enjoyed the challenge Reyla set him.

She didn't answer, her breathing laboured. Sweat leaked from every pore. It was like no pain she had ever felt before, but she was unwilling to give up. She would never tell him. Not now. *Not ever.*

He revelled in her pain and she could only begin to imagine the many horrors he had unleashed upon those who came before her. He was a *monster*.

"Are you ready to tell me yet? I have all day, and it seems you have the energy to spare. You may as well tell me the secret to your power now. The pain will stop once you do."

Perhaps it would have been easier to give up and tell him of her quest, but she could not bear the idea of the Agrana using her power for any reason. She would rather die than allow someone so dreadful to gain the power of her blessings. She would tell no one of their quest, those were Elsafrey's last orders to her, after all.

"Fine, don't answer." Gronk snorted, instruments clattering as he discarded them. "Once the empire invades Freya, I'll have access to a whole kingdom of you to test and experiment on. Then I'll not need you."

Reyla's eyes flicked toward Gronk, her vision focused upon a contented smirk.

"Oh, that got your attention, did it?" he mocked. "Reckon they'll be ready once Gabris is done playing house with Nymati. And then, I'll have all the Frey I could wish for!"

Gronk released a cackle so shrill it vibrated her eardrums. Reyla tried to ignore him, certain his words were chosen to torment her. They were surely lies. But what if they weren't?

Reyla swallowed, but it stuck in her throat. She couldn't deny the easy target Freya gave the empire and their artes would make an excellent addition to empire ranks in their quest for domination.

"So you see, one way or another, I will find my answers," Gronk boasted. "Once I figure out what makes you tick, we'll no longer have to drain the Manastream. The possibilities are endless!"

Reyla turned her eyes back to the ceiling, bracing as Gronk reached for the harvesting device.

"You and me girl." Gronk grinned, holding the device over her. "We're going to change Alamantra together."

* * *

Reyla stared at the light of her cell, thankful for the cold floor beneath her.

Her skin still tingled from the shock of Gronk's artes. Even with her shallow breaths, she could smell the singed hair upon her arms and static ran around her head.

"You don't look so good," said Killic, forcing a worried smile in jest.

Reyla returned a weak wheeze. "You don't look so hot yourself."

Killic chuckled. He did his best to lift her spirits between her visits to the slab. The pair kept themselves amused with talks of the outside world, but Reyla quickly lost the energy to hold a conversation and spent much of her time listening. She didn't mind, accustomed to doing so, but Killic's cheerful disposition often reminded her of Tharin, which only brought her more guilt and concern.

"Can't believe Drazah is gone," said Killic. "It was a proud day for Sudra when he and Nymati took the throne. I must've been nine and still remember it clear as day."

Reyla fancied Killic was a decent man. He was careful not to speak of his past too deeply but asked little of her own, which suited Reyla fine.

"The Doc said she's caught herself an emperor."

"Yeah, well, Gronk says a lot of things." Killic huffed, adjusting his position. "I guess it just goes to show how powerful Nymati truly is. It's not often a woman survives her paramour. Gosh, I'll bet Amynus is the spit of Drazah too."

Reyla returned a weak affirmation. She knew little of the Sudra in general. They had bad reputations, but the vast majority of that came from children's tales warning overzealous men away from their women. Sudran men were often depicted as honourable warriors, providing for their paramours and families. Nymati and Drazah, however, were in a league of their own, with tales of their conquests told in the tavern more often than her own.

Reyla winced as a spasm shot through her shoulder. Unable to treat it, she curled in on herself, the usual dull ache now a nagging burn. It was as if the wound were fresh as it diverged to engulf her body. Reyla hugged her knees to her chest, her shackles clinking as she breathed through each wave.

What she would give for the sweet release of her artes

at that moment.

It wasn't fair. After everything, she was back to being helpless. There was nothing she could do.

Reyla released a roar of frustration.

"If only I had my artes," she snarled, smashing her fist into the floor. "I would have us free in no time. I swear by all that is green, I'm going to burn that *bastard* doctor alive for all he has done!"

"So, what if you could regain your artes? What good would healing do us?"

Reyla scoffed. "After all Gronk's drained from me, do you still believe healing is all I am capable of?"

Killic tilted his head as he considered her words, his hair so stiff it held in place. "What if there was a way to regain your mana?" he asked, his tone too flat to decipher his intent.

"What d'you mean?"

"Well, in Sudra our women burn through their mana too fast, so they feed on others to regain their energy. Sudran men, however, we just regain it naturally over time."

"I suppose we're like that too, except we..." Reyla righted herself as something occurred to her.

"Except what?"

"Except, through meditation, we can connect with the

Life Tree and siphon off its energy."

"I think the Life Tree's a bit far away."

"Yeah, but it's only a conduit," Reyla returned. "Something to filter the Manastream through."

The pair turned their eyes to the light above them.

"The Agrana make mana-crystals from harvesting the Manastream, right?" Reyla questioned herself as she spoke. The idea was almost absurd, but it roused her spirits against the hopelessness of their situation.

"You think you can drain the lights? Surely, they thought of that or they wouldn't have put them in here."

"It's worth a shot," Reyla insisted. "And better than jus' waiting around to die."

Killic pursed his lips in agreement, his matted hair bobbing as he nodded his head. "So, how'd you do this?"

"Quietly," she warned, closing her eyes.

Reyla relaxed against the floor. It was customary for Frey to sit when meditating but Reyla didn't have the strength to remain upright. She placed her shackled hands over her stomach and exhaled, clearing her thoughts as she controlled her breathing.

By the good graces of her mental fortitude, Reyla managed to block out her pains and return her woes to the depths of her consciousness to reside with the rest of her demons. Unburdened, her mind slipped deeper into a meditative state and left her body behind as her mind's eye opened.

Reyla sensed Killic beside her as her sights expanded. His body appeared as a swirling mass of electric blue mana in the darkness – and a great amount of mana at that. Reyla hesitated at the clarity of her vision.

When she had connected to the Life Tree before, she had been unable to isolate individual mana sources as she could then. Reyla suspected it was another change brought on by her blessings, but the flow of mana painted the landscape of her vision in a blinding array of swirling lights.

Aware of others on the edge of her consciousness, Reyla cast her sights further. Their signals were weak and huddled together. They appeared to be clustered in threes and fours on the same level as their cell, leaving Reyla to the grim assumption that these were the other unfortunate souls trapped by Gronk and his dark machinations.

Above them, a vast web of shimmering light spread over the landscape. Thin tendrils connected brighter pools of mana that criss-crossed into the distance, linking back to the light of their cell.

"I think I can see it," she told Killic, her voice echoing back to her as if she were in a cave.

Reyla reached out with her mind. An invisible hand stretched from her body towards the light, grasping at the mana inside. Reyla snatched at the source, pulling it back to her body, but it slipped from her grasp. Each time she tried, the light faded, and the mana evaporated. She tried again, and again.

"Hey! It's working," cheered Killic, his voice a distant echo from the real world. "The light's flickering."

Reyla didn't respond, her spirits crushed. She grasped at any light she found, but each time, her efforts were proven futile.

Still deep within a meditative state, Reyla cast her sights further, towards the bright pools of light. She hoped to draw from their source but soon became overwhelmed by the maze of interconnecting lights and glistening webs of the Agrana city above. She was lost.

Where was her body?

Which way to the power?

There was no way for her to tell through the whirling storm of mana held within the city above. Which way should she go? It was then something tugged at her.

Static ran through Reyla's finger as the ring activated, pulling her away from the mess of the city. She clenched her fist as if to hold onto the ring tighter. It carried her further away from her core, stretching her consciousness to its very limit.

Flashes of blue lights sped by, streaking past her sights like showering meteors across the Agrana marshes. Then, in the distance, a tall pillar of light beamed over the horizon. It started deep within the planet's core and rose way up into the atmosphere creating a raw beacon of unfiltered mana.

The Manastream.

The pull on Reyla's finger grew stronger and faster as she drew closer to the bright pillar. Thick streams of mana emerged from its shape like thousands of mystical blue snakes combining as they fought to reach the stars. It blazed with the might and glory of a thousand suns and Reyla basked within its warmth. But there was something else hidden among the chaos.

A powerful presence lurked before the pillar, it's form hidden by the light of the Manastream. Reyla wavered as the presence stifled her dwindling existence. It smothered her spirit but still, Reyla persevered with the draw of her ring.

The rings had never steered them wrong before. *'If I can just reach the Manastream and syphon even a small amount of mana,'* she pleaded as if to encourage herself. *'Enough to break from the cell and reach Gronk's office. That's all I need.'*

Reyla's heart stopped as the presence wrapped around her, holding her still. She strained against it, hoping, praying, as she tried to draw a sliver of mana from the pillar, but the invisible grip only grew tighter.

"Reyla?" Killic's voice was barely a whisper now. "What's happening? What should I do?"

The Manastream was so close. Reyla called out for it as a sliver of mana waved towards her – when the pull of her ring betrayed her.

Everything flashed by Reyla in reverse, the presence still wrapped around her as she returned to her body. The landscape of glittering lights became a bright blur, her entire being shaking as she crossed the marshes and closed in on their cell. She was almost there and her body in sight, when the presence pulled back.

Reyla jolted as her sights opened to a view of their cell – except not from her eyes.

She saw herself lying on the ground with Killic beside her, his matted hair no more flattering from above. Reyla hardly recognised herself. Half-healed sutures polka-dotted her skin and her hair was half-shaved beneath the bandage around her head.

Killic was right, she looked terrible.

"I'm listening."

Reyla started. Hazel eyes flung open as she returned to their cell, aiming her sights at the light above.

"What happened?"

"Shush," Reyla hissed, tense as she fixed her gaze upon the light. "Someone is watching us."

"What? Who?"

Reyla had an idea, but she had to be certain.

"Can you hear me?" she asked, her voice low as she looked up from the floor.

The light flashed, plunging them into darkness for a second before returning. Reyla sighed, the tension about her body releasing.

"Okay. Flash once for yes, twice for no," she instructed, her empty stomach tingling. "Do you understand?"

The light flashed again and Reyla dared to believe she could be saved from this nightmare.

"Are you the one we came to Agrana in search of?" Reyla asked, aware of Killic beside her as she chose her words.

The light flashed in the affirmative causing Reyla's heart rate to quicken. She had long suspected the spirits of their ancestors were hiding their true power, but now she finally had proof. Her mind raced through everything she needed to know, but there was only one question she wanted to ask.

"And Tharin? Is he safe?" she asked in quick succession, holding her breath as she awaited an answer.

Another flash. Reyla breathed easy, a smile across her face.

"Who's Tharin."

"I'll tell you later." Reyla shushed him and spoke to the light. "Has he reached you yet?"

Two flashes. *No.*

"Is he close?" Reyla's tone rose with her spirits.

Only one. Reyla cheered. This was their way to salvation. She could feel it.

"I need you to tell him where we are. We need your help," Reyla begged. "Can you do that?"

The light held still.

"Please, you have to–"

Reyla stopped, as footsteps approached their cell door and the lock lifted. She lay limp as the guards entered and grabbed her by the shoulders.

Reyla closed her eyes as they dragged her from their cell, praying to any God willing to listen that Tharin would receive her message.

He was their only hope.

* * *

Subject 236 – Log Entry No.8

The Frey has now produced eight chi-crystals, each pure white and incredibly powerful. When placed into the generator the first crystal increased power by 32% compared to the 5% of chi-crystals and 1% of regular mana-crystals harvested from the Manastream. This is beyond incredible.

I intend to run the generator down again before proceeding with the next phase of experimentation and harvest what I can in the meantime. It is becoming ever more apparent that she will not willingly give me the answers I seek, however, I expect to find more once I conduct a more thorough investigation.

* * *

CHAPTER TEN

Tharin followed the pull of his ring north, accompanied by the woolie family.

The woolies, as he had named them, huffed and neighed with glee as they proudly escorted him. The mother was graceful, despite her size. She walked by his side, her head reaching waist height and her trunk so long she carried it slightly coiled at all times. Mother was loving, but stern; her dark, chocolate-coloured eyes never straying far from her children.

The two little ones ran between the trees, chasing bugs and playing as children do. One was the instigator of mischief and had flecks of ginger fur running through its back. Tharin called this one Bark. The other followed its sibling into trouble with ease, it was cast with the familial markings of Mother but lacking her grace. He named this one Mini.

Tharin didn't expect them to follow him far, but he was thankful they did, glad for the company.

He wondered if Reyla would let him keep the woolies. Mother could help carry their supplies on her back; he would lead with that. Bark and Mini were more of a liability but they had their use, he just needed to discover it before reuniting with Reyla.

The skies were bleak as Tharin followed the woolies into a clearing between the twisted trees. The air was thick and heavy as the natural flow of the Manastream grew close. Large grey funnels appeared on the horizon, spewing smoke into the air and clogging the clouds, but Tharin had no intentions of investigating them further. He'd already experienced his fill of the Agrana's hospitality and planned to avoid them at all costs going forward.

Tall grass lay underfoot, and a crumbled stone wall circled them, the stones ancient and moss-covered. Bark ran ahead, following the wall around to a fallen arch. The remains of a long-forgotten structure held the arch in place and, beyond, steps led deep down into darkness.

Tharin checked his ring and craned his head back to the skies. The Manastream pooled above him before breaking across the atmosphere in all directions. His finger pulsed as if he were pinching it, the pull drawing him to the ground below.

"Wait here," Tharin instructed, motioning his hands for the woolies to see.

The woolie family settled as Tharin removed his pack. He rubbed his shoulders to regain some feeling, before climbing through the fallen arch and descending the stairs beyond. The air grew cold and stale as the stone passage continued deep underground. The light from the sun soon faded, but Tharin continued, guided by violet light escaping from the chamber below.

"Reyla?" Tharin called, his heart skipping beats as he finished the stairs. He was excited, hopeful, and a million other things as he scanned the degraded chamber, but they soon faded away. Reyla was not there.

What was there, however, was far more troublesome.

A dark crystal hovered in an upturned vase. Dark purple mana oozed from the crystal, filling the vase and seeping into the floor, poisoning the Manastream. For how long Tharin didn't want to consider.

Tharin drew his sword and swung the blade through the vase, shattering the glass. He retrieved the crystal, activating his artes as he collected mana into his palm. Rather than calling upon any arte in particular, Tharin held the activated mana in place, the power within his grasp strengthening his muscles as he tightened his fingers around the crystal. His knuckles grew white. The chamber glowed by the power emanating from his artes as the pressure grew until, *poof*, the crystal crumbled into sand.

Everything went dark as Tharin released his artes and brushed the grains of crystal against his cloak. He smirked, looking forward to showing Reyla his new trick. She was naturally skilled in so many things, it was rare he ever beat her at anything, but this time, he was hopeful he had finally found something to impress her with.

Tharin's stomach dropped as he remembered she

wasn't there. He hoped she was okay.

Disheartened, Tharin used his artes to guide his way to an old chair leg among the rubble. He summoned fire and set it alight, holding the makeshift torch high above his head to light the chamber.

One side of the chamber had caved in, leaving stone and soil to fall inside, but the other was still intact. The walls were not soil, but something closer to stone Tharin had not seen before. Its surface was cold as he ran his hands over the multitude of runic markings that were carved onto the surface.

Tharin checked each symbol he found. They were familiar to him only from the ones present in Roshia's shrine, but there was only one symbol he cared for. The flame of his chair leg cast flickering shadows as he searched.

"Gotcha."

Tharin studied the emblem. It was similar to the other emblems, except that this one had five feathers that fanned out more like a cape than the wings they had seen before.

Was this it? Had he found it?

Tharin placed his hand over the emblem, concentrating as he activated his artes. He prayed. He willed. He begged. And still, nothing happened.

"It won't open for just you," came a soft voice. "But it seems your friend won't be joining us."

Tharin turned, his frustration hampering his surprise as his eyes slid to meet those of another.

A spirit hovered before him, one dressed in a jumpsuit and flaring lab coat. She was the lankiest Agrana Tharin had ever seen. Her arms hung from her stretched frame like a sloth and her hair was stacked in knots above her like some kind of tree.

The spirit tilted her head as she placed her hands on her waist expectantly.

"You're–?"

"I am Rendun Artemis, first of the Agrana," she said before he could finish his thought. "We must make haste. Your friend is in danger, as are many others."

"Reyla? You know where she is?"

"I know all that transpires within my lands, all of their sins." Rendun's eyes narrowed and wrinkled her snout. "I think perhaps we have an opportunity to help one another. You need your friend and me… I have a problem only you can solve."

"Without Reyla, I'm not sure how helpful I can be," Tharin mumbled. He wasn't being modest, he truly believed as much.

"This is one of those, 'two machines, one crystal' kind of situations," Rendun explained, electricity sparking from her fingertips as they clicked. "You see, your friend is in a facility under one of the capital buildings. It seems our faithful ruler has been allowing one of his followers to develop new technology by using any means necessary, including using his constituents as the basis of his experimental techniques."

Rendun paused, allowing Tharin to consider her meaning, but she had used too many big words leaving him dumbstruck. He pressed his brow.

"Your friend is in a laboratory; she hasn't much time," Rendun stressed. "The Agrana who hurt her is hurting many of my kin. Their mana tech harnesses the energy of the Manastream, but it is not enough for the king. He wants more, always more.

"Please," Rendun begged, the translucent figure levelling her eyes with his. "In place of a trial, I ask that you save your friend and liberate my people from the laboratory. Put an end to the experiments and expose the wretched king. Then return to me, and you shall have your blessing."

"But how?" asked Tharin, his stomach tight in knots. "How do I do any of that?"

"Think of Reyla and follow your ring." The spirit cupped his cheek and smiled. "Once inside the city, I will guide your way, young Frey. Look to the lights. I will ensure your safe passage.

"It will be up to you to do the rest."

* * *

CHAPTER ELEVEN

Emperor Gabris savoured the mouth-watering vapours of the vast platter of roasted meat and vegetables lying before him as if it were his first meal and last.

His once quiet hall was filled with the familial warmth of idle chatter as Nymati and her sons joined him. Not even Amynus' brooding soured the mood as the ghosts of his past remained firmly locked away with their portraits.

"Done," Malaki declared, the young Sudra releasing his cutlery to the plate before him.

"Very good." Nymati smiled and passed Malaki a napkin. "Have Saffia take you to bed."

"I'll do it," Amynus offered, wiping his mouth and rising to his feet. "I have to be up early for drills anyway."

While Amynus held no love for him, Callius was fast gaining respect for the boy. He was set to become a fine soldier with his battle prowess gaining him a reputation among the higher-ups as they argued his posting. It was only a shame that his foul mood appeared to be more of a personality trait than grief.

The hall fell quiet as the children left, but the

uncomfortable silence was long gone as Callius and Nymati remained at the table.

"You've hardly touched your food again," Callius worried, noting Nymati's filled plate and stagnating wine. She had even refrained from smoking recently and he found it unsettling. "Not feeling well?"

"I've felt better." Nymati pushed her plate away. "I'm sure it's just pre-wedding jitters."

"Speaking of which." Callius tried to distract from his warming cheeks by motioning for the staff to clear the table. "Preparations for the ceremony are almost finished. The minister asked if there are any Sudran traditions you would like to incorporate into the wedding?"

"Actually, there is one," Nymati replied, a gloved hand reaching habitually for her necklace. "In Sudra, the bride and groom send a gift to each other the morning of their wedding. It's a silly tradition aimed to calm any nerves, but I have always been fond of it."

Nymati smiled, her eyes glazing over as she stroked the ruby necklace – just as she always did when thinking of Drazah.

It had taken a while for Callius to catch on, but once he had noticed it, it was impossible to stop. His heart nearly broke every time Nymati's smile faded, and her fingers brushed over the glimmering gem.

The way Nymati cherished it, Callius had long suspected the necklace was a gift from Drazah. Now, through this latest deduction, he knew when the necklace was gifted and, at the behest of his ego, what he had to beat when choosing his own gift.

"What a wonderful idea." He grinned, mentally choosing the perfect gift from the palace treasury. "Once we're wed, we can return to Halda and gather our men before continuing with our conquest. Tidus has already begun recruiting Sudran volunteers."

"I–" Nymati stopped herself and eyed the waiting staff as they cleared the table. "Take what you have and clear the room," Nymati ordered, Callius' blood turning cold as her voice boomed.

"What's wrong?" His heart galloped towards hasty conclusions as the staff hurried from the hall.

Nymati did not respond. Her features maintained a strange frigid ire as she waited for the doors to close.

Callius found Nymati difficult to read at the best of times, but he had no idea what to expect. Lately, Nymati had been cautious, perhaps even paranoid. The betrayal of the incident in the tent was still raw, but this was something else. His stomach rolled.

Nymati drew a deep breath, her fingers curling into a tight fist that lay on the table.

"Nymati? What's wrong?"

"There's something I must tell you," Nymati confessed, a tremor in her voice. "I was hoping to wait until we were wed, but I suppose it's no matter since we are already bonded–"

"Bonded?" Callius nearly swallowed his tongue. "What do you mean bonded?"

"I- I thought you knew. That night in the tent?" Nymati's slender brows pressed. She eyed him with dumbstruck accusation. "How else did you think we survived such bloodshed?"

Callius gaped. He knew little of Sudran parabonds and what he knew gave him little confidence at all. Was this why his spirits were so high? Why he woke each morning invigorated? What else had this bond done to him?

"I thought only Sudra could create a parabond," he said, his mouth dry as he considered the implications.

"As did I. Although, I don't see the issue if we're to marry."

Callius rubbed his chin, her nonchalance prickling his temper. "And what more do you hide from me?"

Nymati looked away in shame.

"I never meant to deceive you," she replied in a mournful whisper. "It's not custom for we Sudra to discuss our artes with outsiders. Not even with our kin do we discuss these things, but it is time you knew the truth."

"The truth?"

"What I tell you now must never leave this room," Nymati warned. "Swear by our bond that you will keep my words safe. That you will not share them with any other until the day we pass them on to our children."

Callius hesitated, his heart doing backflips at the mention of children. *Plural!* He shook his head clear. "Of course."

"Then it is time I told you the secret of my people."

"The secret?" he repeated, feeling like a parrot as his body tensed.

"A truth we have kept hidden for hundreds of years. Not even my people know the full extent of what I am about to tell you." Nymati kept her eyes on him, her face set, serious. "When I became queen, it became my job to protect this secret and I have not once uttered the words, not even in passing. Not even to my sons. As the leader of my people, it is now your job to protect it as well."

"I... I understand."

Nymati drew a deep breath, her chest lurching as if fighting down vomit. Callius fought his nerves alongside her. What could the Sudra possibly be hiding that was so terrible that it struck her so?

"Did you know that Sudra was once as vibrant and green as Freya and Puwhar?" she asked, although he didn't see the connection. "That was until a terrible earthquake tore the continent in three, creating the rivers Ballish and Leste."

Callius squinted his eyes, desperate to determine her

point. He remembered a story of how the Ballish was born, but it came from the scriptures and was said to be the work of a Rugla God.

"It struck the planet so deep that the Manastream split in two, causing it to leave Sudra almost entirely. Lakes dried and the sands rose until there was nought left but desert. However, this was only the start of our problems."

Callius' jaw tightened as he prepared for the worst.

"Soon, our ancestors noticed a decline in the strength of their warriors. It was negligible at first, but the effects spread rapidly until eventually, we had those of us who could not transform at all." Nymati wet her lips, venom slipping onto her tongue. "The affliction consumed my people, stripping them of everything we were.

"To protect these... *citizens*... my ancestors implemented a code of silence, allowing those without artes to live perfectly normal lives. While this began to protect the unfortunate few, only a small percentage of Sudra currently possess the ability to reach their true potential."

"How is that even possible?" His mouth hung from disbelief as he imagined trying to accomplish such a feat with his people. "For a whole kingdom to keep such a secret. It's spectacular."

"Not really, when you think about it." Nymati shrugged, again surprising him with her nature as her scorn made way for satisfaction. "Self-preservation is a strong motivator. We have little need for our artes other than battle or our women feeding, so it was pretty easy to hide. Not even our own families know the true abilities of the other."

"Incredible."

"With no hopes of a cure, my ancestors closed our borders to outsiders and perpetuated the legends left by those who came before. We teach our children that there's honour in fighting without transforming. We parade our fighters in the coliseum and position our very best on the front lines." Nymati flushed with further pride, speaking as if it were her idea. "This way our legacy lives on and my people are happy, oblivious to the decline around them."

Callius ran his tongue over the back of his teeth as he processed her words. Even if only a small percentage of Sudra could transform, they were still an incredible force. A meagre handful of Sudra scattered among his ranks would bolster his army's strength tenfold.

"So, the soldiers in Caracus that day?"

"The vast majority of them were hardly even trained," Nymati replied. "Of the thousand men who marched to Caracus, six hundred of them were military. Of those six, maybe fifty could fully transform. The numbers are no better among our women."

Callius snorted. "And this show for my benefit, it was your idea?" Nymati smiled, causing him to laugh even harder. "Now that is impressive."

It was indeed, but it brought up so many questions his mind was struggling to decide which to ponder first. He needed to change his battle strategies and see if there was a way to return the Sudra to power. That brought its own issues, granted, however, there was one thing that struck him as important to their current discussions.

"So, when Drazah faced me that day, you already knew he was going to challenge me, didn't you?"

Nymati's smile faded and her eyes dropped.

"Yes," she whispered, her voice cracking.

"I suppose that's why you agreed to marry me also? To protect your secret?"

"At first," Nymati replied, turning glittering ruby eyes to meet his. "But then you told me of your dream that night. A united Alamantra. A land of peace and prosperity. You and I ushering our people into a new age. Such a wondrous notion, I admit I thought you mad, but now, I see it too."

"You don't think me a fool?"

"I do." She returned a sideways smile. "But if wishing for a better life for your people makes you a fool, then I am the biggest fool of all." Nymati sighed. "I only hope they appreciate all we do for them."

Callius reached for Nymati's hand before it could touch her necklace. His large fingers wrapped around her dainty digits; they were warm against his as he squeezed.

"We will make them proud," he assured her, adrenaline puffing his chest. "There's not a force capable of stopping us now."

Nymati curled her fingers around his own, her thumb brushing over his knuckle. "We will rule Alamantra together, you and I."

"Together," he repeated.

He liked the sound of that.

* * *

CHAPTER TWELVE

Arafrey lay atop her duvet. She watched dust particles as they floated in the sun beaming through the crack in her curtain.

Ceal had woken her with a plate of strawberries that morning. Arafrey ignored the plate, sending Ceal away with orders to inform Bodair that she was unwell. However, Arafrey had no headache. She felt little at all. Yet still, she returned to her bed and reached for her tonic.

When faced with the prospect of spending the day alone with her thoughts, Arafrey sipped greedily. Tired of grieving. Sick from worry and stress. Arafrey embraced the numb thoughtlessness. With all that she had to suffer, did she not deserve just one day of mindless self-indulgence?

Arafrey stared unblinking as the sunbeam crept over her bedroom floor. Her vision clouded, the dust particles shone through her darkness as she allowed it to consume her. She could face her despondence no longer.

She was done.

* * *

CHAPTER THIRTEEN

Reyla's head lulled forward as Killic pulled her up against his knee.

"Here, drink this," he whispered, raising a dirty cup to her cracked lips. "You need to keep your strength."

Reyla turned her head away. Killic needed the water more than her, she would last little longer.

Gronk hadn't bothered replacing her shackles. There was no need. She could barely move. Her whole body lay numb, each heartbeat causing an impossible drain as her vision grew dark.

This was it. This is where her journey ended.

Reyla accepted her failure bitterly and yet, somehow, it made sense. A weight lifted from her chest as she resigned herself to her fate, unashamed by her relief to no longer bear the mantle of Alamantra's saviour.

Reyla had never thought herself worthy of such a status or quest. She had never wished to be anything more than a palace guard, content to live her life in the shadow of her princess. Youthful ignorance allowed her to dream of becoming a knight, but experience told her it was never to be. It had been foolish of her to think that she, a lowly commoner, could save Alamantra, but perhaps that was never her destiny.

"Killic, I need you to do something for me." Her voice was raspy and her hands shook as she reached feebly for her fingers. "I– I'm not getting out of this one."

"No, Reyla, you can't–"

"Please," she insisted, her breathing growing more laboured as she pulled the ring from her finger and fumbled against his palm. "Take this."

"I don't–"

"Listen," she forced out, the effort of talking draining what little energy remained. "Just wait... wait 'til you know I'm done... Then put it on. Find Tharin. Find the shrines. P–P-P-Promise me. Promise."

Killic frowned but nodded his head, curling his fingers around the ring. "I promise."

Reyla smiled and breathed easy, overcome with an unfamiliar sense of serenity. She had done her part. The rest was up to them.

Reyla closed her eyes. She was ready.

It's better this way.

* * *

Subject 236 – Log Entry No.12

The subject has now produced 11 white chi-crystals. 10 remain.

The generator is finally below 30% and the adaptor is complete. Moving forward with plans and exploratory surgery—dependant on survival.

No further data.

* * *

CHAPTER FOURTEEN

Tharin ran through day and night. Driven by desperation, he pushed on through bog and rain, following the pull of his ring until his legs cramped and his lungs burned.

He dropped to his knees, gasping for breath. Sweat dripped from his brow as he sunk to the ground, the dew-covered grass cooling his limbs. The weight of his gear bore down on his spine, his body shaking.

Tharin stared at the ground as if it were his rival. He wasn't sure how much longer he could maintain his pace. A furry snout snuffed at his pointed ear and sucked at his face.

"Bark! What're you doing here? I told you to stay. It's far too dangerous." Tharin scolded the creature, then hugged it close. "You're going to be in a lot of trouble when we get back."

Bark neighed, lifting his fuzzy trunk. Tharin sighed, rubbing a shaky hand over Bark's head, the fur sticking to his damp gloves.

"Not far now," Tharin said, looking to his ring. "Guess now's as good a time as any to rest. I'll need my strength when I get there."

Tharin's chest tightened at the prospect of entering an enemy base. While his artes would prove invaluable and give him the advantage in most situations, he was hardly skilled in tactics or infiltration. His blessings gave him strength and agility, but what use were they when he had little experience to speak of?

"We'll figure something out," Tharin said, digging his face into Bark's fur as he hugged him close. "That's what Reyla would say. And she always would, y' know."

Bark neighed in agreement.

"Except it'll be me they tell stories of this time."

Tharin righted himself and wiped his brow.

'Hold on Reyla.

I'll be there soon.'

* * *

CHAPTER FIFTEEN

Killic couldn't sleep that night.

They had come to take Reyla from their cell sometime before breakfast and had not returned since. It didn't sit right with Killic. Reyla had never been gone so long before. Gronk would often work late but never overnight. However, that alone was not proof of Reyla's demise.

And so, he waited.

It was as if time had slowed down as he watched the cell door, praying it would open. He drummed his knees and tapped his toes on the floor. He adjusted his shoulders, then rubbed his chin. The minutes crept by as he imagined the horrors unleashed in Gronk's laboratory.

Killic rolled Reyla's ring around his fingers.

It was so small and simple. There was hardly anything to it at all, yet Reyla said it could help him.

A quest? Shrines? Tharin?

What did it all mean?

It was all so confusing. How was a ring supposed to help him? How was he to believe that anything could help him now?

Killic was once a man of great faith. He once had hopes of a loving paramour and a large family, a simple life and a military career. He had celebrated the Gods and prayed as much as any Sudra, but they had forsaken him to years of captivity and unspeakable experiments. His incarceration had extinguished his hopes and crushed what little will he claimed, leaving him with nothing but the heartache and regret he had left Sudra to escape in the first place.

He wanted to have faith in Reyla. He wanted her to be as powerful as she claimed and to reap vengeance on the devil that would keep them there.

She had to come back.

The hatch within the cell door opened and a tray pushed through, announcing breakfast. Goopy rice and a chunk of stale bread. Disgusting. On any other day, he would give his arm just to taste meat again, but he would have no appetite while Reyla remained absent.

Killic ignored the tray, the unnatural glow of the silver ring drawing his attention. Static tickled his fingers as the ring glowed with a soft undulating light. It called to him as if it had a will of its own. As if it were urging him to put it on.

He hesitated, his finger hovering before the silver band. It didn't seem big enough to fit his finger but, as it slipped towards his knuckle, the silver expanded, warping around his finger and setting in place. The metal warmed against his skin. Static tingled through his hand, adrenaline coursing through his veins, as he waited for the ring to activate. But nothing happened.

Killic sighed, embarrassed for allowing himself to believe Reyla's story. Still, it was nice to feel hopeful again, however briefly.

He sunk back against the wall, his eyes closing as he held a silent prayer. Then, as darkness filled his vision, the ring on his finger tugged.

Killic caught his breath as the tug drew his mind from his body. The invisible force carried him away from himself, the velocity pressing his stomach against his spine. Then it stopped, suddenly releasing him.

Killic arrived in an endless darkness. The void held nothing, no light, air or sound. Nothing but a single ghostly figure in a buttoned, grey nightgown.

"Reyla!" He gasped, rushing to her aide. "I thought you were dead."

"Not quite, but it doesn't look good, I'm afraid."

Reyla turned her head, prompting a window to appear in the nothingness. It looked into Gronk's laboratory where she lay on a table, her body open and mutilated. The doctor flew around her like a sadistic hummingbird as he cut, pushed, chopped and pulled at Reyla's insides. The mechanical chirping of his machines buzzed between slice and squelch.

Reyla averted her gaze, her eyes on Killic. "I never thought the ring could do this. Interesting..."

"Reyla?"

"I'm afraid we'll have to skip the pleasantries. We don't have much time and there's much you need to know."

Reyla placed her hands on Killic's cheeks and brought his forehead to meet her own. Light shone through the darkness as their skins touched and everything that Reyla ever was flowed into his being.

Reyla's memories flooded Killic's brain. They flashed before his eyes as she guided him, a lifetime of experience and knowledge passing on to him within seconds. She recalled the cloaked figure, Auldafrey, Princess Arafrey and the trials. The Hand of Miera, the blessings and the spirits. *Arafrey.* Tharin, Chloris, the empire and Queen Elsafrey. *Ara- No, not her.*

And then it was done.

Killic gaped at Reyla in amazement.

It didn't take long, but he now knew everything Reyla had ever done, ever felt and, looking at her soon-to-be lifeless body, it pained him as it did her. He couldn't believe the journey she had made just to end up there, on a slab, the victim of a crazed scientist.

It wasn't fair.

Reyla's image flickered, her strength slipping. Her eyes grew sad, unable to hold on any longer.

"Please, take care of my friend," she whispered, before her image faded away, leaving Killic alone in the nothingness.

Warm tears rolled down his cheeks as Killic opened his eyes to their cell.

He held on to Reyla's memories as if keeping them alive would help her somehow. He remembered her victories, her battles, her loves and her losses. He mourned for the hopes and dreams she had never managed to fulfil and wept for the romance that was never meant to be.

Killic closed his eyes tight.

"Reyla," he called, waiting for an answer.

But it never came.

* * *

CONFESSION

* * *

*Heartbroken, I cast my sights over Reyla as Gronk's machines
ceased beeping and released a deafening drone.*

Bile gargled in my stomachs.

That was it. Alamantra was doomed.

My body shook from inaction,

as Reyla's spirit crossed into the veil.

I had to do something.

It couldn't end like that. It couldn't.

Without thought or care,

I opened my void to the veil and

drew Reyla's spirit into my presence,

thus breaking my first oath...

* * *

THE LIGHT OF MIERA

A Guard's Request

To Be Continued …

ACKNOWLEDGEMENTS

To everyone who has made it this far, thank you and sorry for the cliff-hanger! But we will be back soon with the next book in the series, A Soldier's Return.

I would like to thank everyone who has reviewed and read The Light of Miera, your feedback and support drive me to continue writing and develop my style in any way possible. I'm currently drafting the final book of the series and can't wait to share it all with you!

A massive thank you to my editor Amy Wilson, artist Art Womble and proofreaders DC Bradshaw and Tan00ks, who helped me in pulling this story together for consumption. I couldn't do this without your support.

Those of you ingrained into the Treat Your Geek community have helped to keep me sane through these last few years of trauma and I would not have achieved anywhere near as much as I have without you. I love every moment of chaos we spend together and look forward to all the things we will create in the future.

This book is dedicated to Papa Mash. He was my favourite person and supported each and every single one of my creative endeavours. It royally sucks that he won't be around to see all that I will accomplish, but I know that he would be proud of me regardless.

Thank you

Ash Hester

ABOUT THE AUTHOR

Ash Hester started her career in comics and animation, but always had a love for storytelling and fantasy. Contributing to several indie press projects, she later founded Niche: Treat Your Geek to showcase news and reviews featuring the many talented people within her reach. Fuelled by Anime, Television and Video Games, her imagination showed no bounds, leading her to begin writing her first epic fantasy novel in 2019.

Yorkshire born and Scottish grown, Ash always gravitated towards geeky circles. Raised on a healthy diet of Star Trek and Pokemon, she found herself on the anime, cosplay and sci-fi convention circuits in her university years. With many years in and around the industry, she continued to encourage the passions of others and inspired others in their creative endeavours.

If you have enjoyed this book, please consider leaving a review for Ash Hester on Amazon or Goodreads to let her know what you thought of her work.

Website: www.authorahester.uk

www.ingramcontent.com/pod-product-compliance
Lightning Source LLC
Chambersburg PA
CBHW070349170726
48291CB00001B/243